A Warrior's Reward

"Will you grant me something I've wanted all the long years of soldiering, something I could obtain only in England?"

"What might this be, Lord Edmund?" Olivia asked, lifting her eyebrows disingenuously, for she had a good idea what it was he wanted.

"To hold a lovely English miss in my arms and give her just . . . one . . ." He lowered his head slowly, giving her time to evade him if she wished. When she held still, he pressed his mouth to hers, breathing out the word *kiss* on a long sigh as he buried his lips in the soft pillows of her own. Their lips clung for a moment as he pulled away.

"Magic," he proclaimed. "Everything I yearned for as I fought." He pulled her close once again. . . .

A
Lord for Olivia

June Calvin

A SIGNET BOOK

SIGNET
Published by New American Library, a division of
Penguin Putnam Inc., 375 Hudson Street,
New York, New York 10014, U.S.A.
Penguin Books Ltd, 80 Strand,
London WC2R 0RL, England
Penguin Books Australia Ltd, Ringwood,
Victoria, Australia
Penguin Books Canada Ltd, 10 Alcorn Avenue,
Toronto, Ontario, Canada M4V 3B2
Penguin Books (N.Z.) Ltd, 182–190 Wairau Road,
Auckland 10, New Zealand

Penguin Books Ltd, Registered Offices:
Harmondsworth, Middlesex, England

First published by Signet, an imprint of New American Library,
a division of Penguin Putnam Inc.

First Printing, April 2002
10 9 8 7 6 5 4 3 2 1

This book is dedicated to all the reluctant warriors,
past, present, and future, who fight not from
a love of war, but to protect those people
and values they hold dear.

Chapter One

Lord Edmund Debham allowed his weary mount to stop in front of an unprepossessing hedge tavern under an ancient sign depicting a black lion. The ivy dripping from the walls nearly obscured the light that glowed through smoke-grimed windows, indicating the presence of life inside.

Eyeing the structure cynically, Edmund dismounted, muttering, "As good a place as any to get my throat cut, old friend. I'll try to see you get your hay and oats before passing to my reward." He gave Storm a comforting pat.

Once inside the dark, smoky hall, Edmund felt no surprise at all that no one came to attend him. The shabby old building had held no false promises of bustling landlords and smiling, buxom maids. He moved toward the sounds of voices and faint light that emanated from the north side of the small dark entryway. Pushing through a rough-timbered door, he paused to survey the room out of habit rather than any pronounced desire for self-preservation.

A branch of candles on a small table gave the room what little light it possessed. Around the table sat four men, their attention totally absorbed by the cards in their hands.

Edmund's scrutiny did not reveal anyone else in the room, though he would not have given long odds that the farthest, darkest corners might not hold villains enough. He walked toward the table, wondering when he would be noticed. He wasn't. So he pulled out a nearby chair and sat down heavily, weariness pulling against him more strongly than his promise to Storm. The card game, which Edmund recognized as Brag, held the locals' attention with all the intensity of gentlemen in the priciest gaming hell in London. He studied the group, hoping to discover who might be the innkeeper.

Quickly identifying him by the stained apron he wore, Edmund scanned the others while awaiting the end of the hand. There was only one among them who might be called a gentleman. A youth with disheveled dark locks and a wild look in his blue eyes, his clothes set him apart from the innkeeper and the others, who looked to be farmers or laborers.

Suddenly the table exploded in exclamations as the innkeeper exposed three aces to take the small pile of change in the center of the table.

"Neat as a pin," the young gentleman declared. "Well done, Dutton, old friend." He clapped the innkeeper on the back. "Well, who's for another hand? Come along, I've plenty of blunt left!" He gestured to a pile of pence and shillings beside him, but the others at the table began to mumble and shake their heads.

" 'Tis easy enough for you, young master," a tall, red-haired man grumbled. "You've just had yer quarter's allowance, and no chores to do come morning!"

"Just so," the oldest of the group agreed, knocking out the pipe he had been nursing. "Time I sought my bed."

"I've not had my quarter allowance," the young gentleman groused. "Dutton here has had it. Most of it, at any rate."

"Nay, lad, I've barely touched 'ee." The innkeeper's north country accent seemed out of place in the middle of Buckinghamshire. He motioned to a roll of gold coins spilling from a leather purse by the young man's right hand. "Happen I'd take a good deal more nor yer blunt, but Miss Ormhill would grab me by the ear tomorrow, think on!" He scooped up his winnings and stood. At that moment he spotted Edmund at last. His surprise at seeing the silent stranger caused him to drop the handful of coins, which rolled and tumbled across the table and onto the stone floor.

"Be thee an apparition?" He stared hard, then shook his head. The others seated at the table, equally as startled, muttered among themselves and shifted backward uneasily, so

that Edmund had the sensation that the room had suddenly
tilted away from him.

"Not at all," he reassured them. "Only a tired, lost traveler
hoping to find a warm meal and perhaps a friendly hand of
cards before seeking his bed." Edmund looked hungrily at the
golden pile by the young gentleman's hand. "Allow me to introduce myself. Edmund Debham." He held out his hand.

Standing hastily and leaning across the table to grasp Edmund's hand, the youth stammered, "You're . . . You're . . .
No, don't tell me, I know. Ah, yes! Capt. Lord Edmund Debham. Daring Debham, you were known as after Badajoz. It
is an honor to meet you, Lord Edmund. I'm Jason Ormhill."

"Not captain anymore. I've sold out," Edmund replied,
shaking the eager hand held out to him.

The boy frowned a little. "Ah, yes. Once Boney was beat,
the fun went out of it, I suppose. I'll bet you were glad to be
in for the final kill, eh?"

Edmund winced at the memory of Waterloo. He had
never loved soldiering, though he knew some who had. *The
boy would be much more pleased with Harry Smith than
with me,* he thought. "I would have been as satisfied if
Napoléon had stayed put, I thank you!"

Jason looked puzzled, sure that any soldier must have
loved every minute of glory in the recent battle. "What
brings you to these dull environs?"

"Dull! Well, young varmint, I'd give you what for, for
that one, if I weren't so filled with ennui myself." The
gnarled old man winked at the room at large and stood,
startling Edmund by revealing what he had not noticed before, a clerical collar. "Perhaps you'd best not play him,
Jason. Looks like one of those London Cap'n Sharps, come
to fleece you."

Edmund winced, but the youngster rushed to his defense.
"Never say so, Uncle. Lord Edmund is an honorable man.
Quoted in the dispatches more than once."

"That's a high honor, given how stingy Wellington is
with praise. I'm Milton Ormhill, vicar of Saint Stephens
here in Flintridge." The older man held out his hand.

A twinge of guilt smote Edmund. He had kept himself in

funds during the long years with Wellington by his skill at cards and his hard head for liquor. He was, indeed, an honest player, but an extremely able one. *Am I really contemplating taking this youngster's blunt?* But the thought of some coins for a bed rather than joining Storm in the stable tempted him too much. *Won't clean him out, though. Just a few hands.*

Dutton, the innkeeper, grinned. "Aye, well, whatever ye do, no drinking, young squire. No telling what might happen, else." General laughter greeted this admonishment which Edmund thought very good advice for the youth. Dutton scooped up what remained of his coins. The red-haired man had been gathering up what lay on the floor while this exchange was going on, and distributed them to their rightful owner before leaving.

"I hope your prohibition of drink does not extend to me." Edmund reached into his vest pocket, prepared to withdraw one of his last three coins. "I could use a good dose of the heavy wet. And my horse could use some attention, too, if you have a stable lad."

"Aye, no fear, m'lord. My boy'll see to him right well. And the first drink is on me, m'lord, for one as has served us so well against them Frenchies. I've naught to lay before you but soup and a joint of mutton, though."

Under the warm regard of the landlord and the youth, Edmund felt the ice that encased his heart melt a little. He took the offered brandy and saluted them both, then downed it. "Join us at cards," he invited the innkeeper.

"Mayhap I will." Mr. Dutton nodded. "Just let me roust out my son to look after tha steed." He went to the door and set up a shout that produced a sleepy lad of perhaps fourteen to care for Storm.

Their first few hands showed the innkeeper to be an intelligent but cautious player. Young Ormhill's playing was adequate but uninspired. Edmund experienced luck along with his skill, and won. *Enough,* he decided. *I've blunt now to last me a few days.* Though his winnings would perhaps only stave off the inevitable, something about starving to death repelled him. He even allowed himself a tiny bit of optimism: Perhaps he could find some honest way to earn a living before this money ran out.

"Well, gentlemen, it is late. I am sure you have had enough cards for the evening." He started to gather the small pile of coins.

But both men loudly protested. The evening was young, and he had to give them a chance to get even. Edmund's conscience submitted. *If they insist, after all* . . . He swiftly parted both landlord and youth from some more of their blunt.

The landlord looked at him shrewdly as he dropped his cards at last. "Ye're a fine hand, m'lord. Cannily done, think on." Something of malice flashed in his eyes. "I'm no match for 'ee, in skill nor pocket, so I'll bid 'ee good night."

"Cannily done indeed!" Young Ormhill scowled sulkily. "Luck, that's what it was. I can beat him. You know, Dutton."

"Aye, happen you could." Dutton nodded. "Play on, then. I'll have a pipe and watch 'ee for a while." He went to his cabinet and brought out several full bottles of brandy. "Doubtless ye'll be wanting some refreshments." He poured Ormhill a drink and watched with satisfaction as the lad tossed it back.

Puzzled at this change in behavior from his previous protective admonition that the boy shouldn't drink, Edmund stood. "Better quit now. I've a wish for my bed."

"Come, Lord Edmund," Ormhill protested. "Think I can't see you're trying to protect me? Very much obliged to you! I'm not the green 'un you think me, though."

Edmund frowned. "Bantling, you need a lesson. But I've a kindness for you and would not teach it."

"Pah! Arrogance, not kindness, m'lord." Ormhill stood up, anger flushing his features. "High and mighty Lord Edmund, famous war hero, and now you fancy yourself a London beau, too proud to play deep with the provincials." He dropped a second heavy leather purse onto the table. "I've plenty of blunt, and the skill to take yours, too, if you're man enough to accept my challenge."

Teaching the young cub that lesson suddenly seemed more attractive to Edmund. His nerves still raw from his

brother's last tongue-lashing as he had expelled him forever
from the family, he had no stomach for insult from another
quarter.

"Very well, then." He sat back down and poured himself
a generous dose of brandy, a nod to keeping the contest even
against the young man. "Dutton, you are witness to his willingness—nay, eagerness—to play me."

"Oh, aye, m'lord, and of yers to play him. And may the
best man win." So saying, he gave young Ormhill another
wink and poured a second helping of brandy into his glass.

Odd, Edmund thought. *He warns the boy against drinking, then fills his glass. Have to keep my eye on that one.
Could be some mischief afoot.* He started to protest further
drinking by his opponent, but saw from Ormhill's outthrust
jaw that no advice of his would be welcome.

*A lamb for the fleecing. Such a disagreeable lamb,
though.* Edmund smiled grimly, gathered in the cards, and
began shuffling them.

At first Edmund steadily raked in the winnings. He did
not offer to quit again, though. Young Ormhill had a determined set to his jaw and an apparently bottomless pocket.
As he watched the coins pile up beside his elbow, Edmund
recalled how, when he had quit his brother's house for the
last time, his old nurse had run out to hug him once more,
weeping. She had taken his hands in hers, kissed them, and
said, "The Lord will provide." He wondered if that strict
Scots presbyter would consider a game of chance eligible to
be counted as the Lord's provision for him. Perhaps it was,
for neither He nor anyone else had made another.

Ormhill partook several times of the brandy bottle, each
time urging the same on his opponent. Edmund shrugged
and accepted, warning him, "If you think to get me drunk
and have the advantage of me, think again. I am notorious
for my head for liquor."

"No such thing," Ormhill protested indignantly. "Improve your game. Improves mine. More I drink, better I
play. True, ain't it, Dutton?"

The tavern owner pointed the pipe at Edmund. " 'S God's
truth, my lord, and an honest boy for warning you."

Edmund only smiled at the ludicrous thought that this stripling, who grew drunker by the minute, could manage to both outdrink and outplay him. "I'm much obliged, Mr. Ormhill, for your confession in the interest of fair play." The sarcasm in his voice made no impression, though.

Ormhill's temper had improved after winning the last round. He waved his hand expansively. "Fair play, that's right. Gotta have fair play." He splashed another measure of brandy in both their glasses.

Ormhill won the next hand, too, clearly a fluke, as he looked bleary-eyed and his hands were unsteady as he shuffled the cards. Brag required concentration and the ability to calculate the odds of various card combinations. It also required control of facial expressions so the opponent would not guess the strength of one's hand. Edmund decided that one reason he had misjudged the last few times had been that the boy's drunkenness gave him a vacuous countenance in which it was impossible to read anything. *I'll play more cautiously,* he thought, *for the lad does have the devil's own luck. But it can't last, nor can he concentrate as he needs to do.*

Edmund confidently made his bet, and watched with surprise as the youngster played a brilliant hand and swept up another goodly portion of what he had previously lost. He pushed the brandy glass aside when Ormhill filled it once again, and concentrated hard on his play. Still, Ormhill trounced him and again had recourse to the brandy.

"I think we are about even now," Edmund suggested.

"Nonshense. You only wish to quit because *I* am w-winning."

"A while ago you said I only wanted to quit because *I* was winning."

"Tell you what." Ormhill turned in his chair, nearly falling out of it in the process. "We'll play 'til one o'clock. Tha's 'nuther hour. Finish the hand we're on then, and stop, no matter who's ahead."

Another hour. If he continues to win at this rate I'll be cleaned out by then. But how can he, with such massive amounts of brandy in him? Reluctantly, Edmund nodded. "One o'clock. Not one second after."

Ormhill leaned over and offered his hand on the deal, nearly oversetting the sturdy, battered old table in the process.

Long before one, Edmund pushed the last of his pile of coins over to Ormhill's side of the table. "That's it," he said. "Except for a coin for our host to cover my horse's stabling, I'm out of blunt. 'Fraid our game must end."

"N-n-no," Ormhill said, waving an unsteady hand in front of Edmund's nose. "One o'clock. 'S-what we said. Shook on it. Didn't we, Dutton?"

Dutton nodded silently from his chair.

"But I have naught to wager," Edmund insisted.

"Take your vowels. Look, your luck must change soon. Don' give up now."

Edmund put his head between his hands. "My vowels are worthless, Ormhill. I'm cleaned out."

"Be glad to wait until your next quarter's—"

"I have no allowance," Edmund could not help but shout, and his sense of desperation, renewed by this reversal at cards, made his voice crack. "No income. Nothing. You see before you a prodigal son who came home and was told he wasn't good enough to sup with his brother's hogs."

He lifted his head and looked into Ormhill's uncomprehending eyes. "I've naught but my horse and tack and the clothes on my back."

After a thoughtful silence: "Rather fancy that vest," Ormhill offered. He picked up the brandy bottle in front of him and drained it. "Stake it 'gainst a guinea?"

Insanity, desperation, exhaustion, all overwhelmed Edmund. *Why not? Lose the clothes off my back, then my horse and tack, and I can walk naked until I am taken up by the law and fulfill my destiny as predicted by my brother.*

To his brandy-befuddled, exhausted mind this seemed suddenly a very good idea. He opened the last bottle and poured each of them a generous measure. Even his hard head felt muzzy. The cards swam before his eyes. But young Ormhill actually swayed in his chair. *Surely, surely, he can't play a decent hand now,* Edmund thought desperately.

He soon knew better. As the clock ticked inexorably nearer to one o'clock, his young opponent piled up vowels for his shirt, coat, and riding breeches. Much merriment accompanied the loss of his undergarments, though the joke was less appreciated by Edmund than by Jason and the landlord.

Eager to bring the evening to its disastrous conclusion, Edmund then wagered his tack. He lost his saddle and bridle, and his beloved Storm soon followed.

"You . . . you'll treat him well," Edmund demanded. "Carried me from one end of the peninsula to the other. Saved my life more than once, too."

"I'll re-rev . . . worship him." Ormhill nodded. His head rested on one hand; his cards almost dangled in the other. But he played brilliantly. At 12:45 A.M. Edmund had nothing more to wager.

"And that's an end to it," he groaned, as Ormhill prepared to play another hand. "I'll strip and be off."

Ormhill stared. "Wha'zat mean?"

"Just what I said." He stood and started to take off his coat.

"Wait a minute." Ormhill seemed to focus clearly on him for the first time in an hour. "You don' mean ye're really and truly done in?"

"Rolled up, horse and foot."

"What . . . what will you do?"

"Take a long, refreshing walk toward London."

"Can't do that! Scandalize the county!"

"Aye, it would and all," Dutton chimed in, yawning. "Get taken up by the bailiffs."

" 'Sides," Ormhill drawled, "catch cold."

"In late July?" Edmund laughed as he started on the buttons of his vest.

Horrified, Jason urged him, "Come on. Mus' have sompthin' . . ."

"I've nothing left but myself."

Ormhill stared at him hard, then slid back in his chair. "Dutton?"

"Sir?"

"Wh-wha's a man worth?"

Dutton rubbed at his stubbly chin. "Well, now, that depends, young sir. If'n he's a common laborer, sixpence a day. If'n he's a shepherd, or . . ."

"But what if he's a lord?"

"Shouldna think he'd be worth a thing, begging yer pardon, m'lord, if he has neither land nor blunt nor prospects."

"Bah! Lord Edmund on the marriage mart'd be worth a fortune."

Edmund shook his head. "Penniless and without prospects? Nonsense."

"Hmmm. Still, a cit looking to hook up to a noble family?"

"Rich cits didn't get that way by being stupid. My family has completely cast me aside, so marriage to me would not pave the way into the *ton*. I'm broke. I haven't the least notion of how to earn an honest dollar except with a sword, and I've done with war. Price me at common labor, if you will, and we'll play one more hand."

"Couldn' do that. Wouldn't seem right."

"If I lose, you'll have to employ me, right? Better than dying of starvation, as I would if taken up by the law for indecent exposure, for there's none to pay for my keep in jail." Hope reentered Edmund's fuddled brain. If the young chub took this bet, he would win a way of sustaining life even if he lost. Of course, he had friends who would help him, but charity appealed to him even less than the other alternatives.

Stumped, Ormhill sat, chin in hands, considering Edmund as if he hadn't really seen him before. Finally he leaned back in his chair and snapped his fingers, or attempted to. Lack of coordination deprived the gesture of its sound.

"No. Not as a laborer. If I win, you'll marry m'sister."

"What? You can't seriously want someone like me to marry your sister!"

"Do! I' fact, you're perfect."

In spite of himself, Edmund felt a jolt of hope. *Doubtless some property comes with her. Something wrong with her, of course, but I'm in no position to be choosy.*

"Wan' anyone to marry her. Can't marry 'less she's wed to a lord. Right, Dutton?"

" 'S truth, young sir."

"Mine is only a courtesy title, you know." Edmund's brief hope began to fade.

"Don' matter. Jus' so she marries a lord. Tha's all it says."

"It?"

"M'father's will. Says Livvy must marry a lord."

"She must be an antidote, if you think I am a perfect candidate for her husband."

A crack of laughter from the landlord seemed to confirm this thought.

"Well, wouldn' say that." Ormhill rubbed his mouth, seemingly at a loss for words.

Edmund ruminated. "Never mind. I'm in no position to be choosy. If she has a decent dowry, I'll take her. Couldn't support her otherwise."

Jason scratched his nose. "Mus' be honest. She has, and then she hasn't. Has a tidy little farm of her own. But her husband can't sell it, and if I decide he's mistreating her, I get it. M'father's will tied it up right and tight. Husband can use th'income to feed and clothe the family. Can't nalannate . . . nailienate . . ."

"Alienate. As in sell it, or wager it away?"

"Tha's it. Not even the income."

A tidy little farm! Warmth crept into Edmund's voice. "I don't care about that. Or about her being an antidote. A place to live. Land! You've offered me a glimpse of heaven. I don't even want to win this hand." He started to sit down.

Ormhill stared. "Gotta wanna win," he wailed. "Notta real bet, otherwise."

"That's true." Hopes dashed once again, Edmund recommenced removing his clothes. His hands seemed all thumbs, and he knew he had seldom been this foxed before.

Ormhill studied the by-now tall stack of coins sitting by his elbow, with the pile of hastily scrawled vowels on top of them. Abruptly, with the loose-limbed gesture of inebriation, he swept the whole into the center of the table.

"M'stake, Lord Edmund. 'S at enough?"

"I have to be honest, Ormhill. I've always dreamt of being a country gentleman. Land to manage—heaven! Even though I'd have an antidote for a wife. Don't know but what

I'd prefer the farm to the money." He managed to peel off the vest.

Desperately, Ormhill tried to invigorate his opponent. "Did I say she's a managing female?"

"But not a shrew," Dutton interjected. "Can't say Miss Livvy is a shrew."

"No, not a shrew, but she likes to get her own way, you see. Wouldn't want you to manage her land—manages it herself. And, uh . . ." Ormhill looked desperate. "And . . . and . . ." His face lit up. "She's a bluestocking," he announced triumphantly.

Edmund eyed the pile, calculating. He had little wish to marry a learned female, and even less a managing one, if any other option were open to him.

"I'll make it worth your while," Ormhill declared. "I'll give you my vowel for another thousand. Plus your clothes 'n' horse'n' all."

Over a thousand pounds. It seemed a fortune set against his bleak future. It would be an honest bet, then, for he would certainly rather have that sum than Ormhill's sister.

"Done!" Edmund sat down, pulling his jacket loosely around his shoulders, and took up the cards to shuffle. "One hand. Winner takes all."

Ormhill offered him a drink, and when he shook it off, tipped up the brandy bottle and drank deeply. He dealt the cards just as the clock struck one. Edmund examined his hand through bleary eyes. He had two kings and a jack, but no brags to use as wild cards. Everything depended upon what cards the boy had received.

Dutton watched avidly as Ormhill studied his cards. Edmund knew the innkeeper could tell this story over many a bottle in years to come. When the two men laid down their hands, it was bleary-eyed, loose-jointed, half-unconscious Ormhill who emerged the victor.

"Tha's it, then!" Grinning hugely, he stood up, swaying dangerously before finding his balance. "At last, I've got a lord for Livvy!"

Chapter Two

After a celebratory glass of brandy, Ormhill insisted on taking his winnings, including Edmund, home with him. Storm was turfed out of his meager stall, and Edmund struggled to mount the bay stallion, very much the worse for all the brandy he had drunk.

Ormhill, even more well-to-go, had difficulty controlling his showy, restive black gelding, whose white stockings flashed as he half reared and jibbed against the ill-balanced load and inept handling of the reins. "Whoa, Moonstar. Hold still, won't you," Ormhill beseeched the beast as he struggled against gravity. It took a strong push by the hostler to get him firmly in the saddle. Once seated, the young man gave his animal its head. Home was sufficient enticement for the black to set a spanking pace down a dusty country lane. Under the light of a nearly full moon Edmund had no difficulty keeping his new owner in sight. His head ached too much to ponder his status as "winnings." He had one thought and one only—to find a warm bed and sleep for at least a year.

The road widened out into a well-kept boulevard, which in turn became a carriage roundabout in front of a handsomely proportioned Georgian mansion. Every window was dark, and no one came on Ormhill's hail to take their horses, so he rode Moonstar right up the short flight of stairs to the front door, which he slammed vigorously with his fist, roaring out, "Livvy, Livvy! Wake up. I've brought you a lord."

Edmond dismounted at the foot of the stairs and stumbled

up them to catch at the gelding's bridle. "For God's sake, man, get down. You'll be in the hall with this animal next."

Unfortunate prophet! Edmund was thrown back as the door opened and Ormhill pressed his mount through it. The servant, an elderly man, jumped aside with surprising agility to avoid being run down. Ormhill halted at the foot of an elegant stairway in the center of the hall.

Once again he called, "Livvy, Livvy. Wake up."

Edmund followed him in and joined the elderly servant in trying to calm the prancing animal and entice its rider to dismount, when a woman appeared at the top of the stairs.

"Jason, for heaven's sake. What are you about?" The female figure at the top of the stairs was ominously substantial, and her voice just as ominously shrill. Edmond flinched. Even in his inebriated state he realized that a snug little farm might not be adequate compensation for having to marry a woman with such a carrying voice and nasty tone.

As soon as she saw Moonstar, she yelped, "Get that creature out of the hall!"

"Not till you see what I've brought. Look. I've brought a lord."

"What? Here? Who?" Though no less shrill, the tone of the woman's voice shifted to one of interest, and she began to descend the stairs with a heavy tread.

Edmund, one hand at Moonstar's bridle, the other soothingly stroking his muzzle, looked up, shame and embarrassment warring with curiosity to see just how distasteful Miss Ormhill might be.

As she came into view Edmund flinched. The woman was not only stout and shrill of voice, she was plain and by no means young. *Can this really be my bride-to-be?* he thought, becoming unpleasantly sober. *I can't say he didn't warn me, though I think he and the innkeeper erred in saying she wasn't shrewish.* Still, he acknowledged that Miss Ormhill might have some justification for her loud protests, with a horse stomping and snorting in the hall, while Ormhill yelled like a wild man.

Edmund briefly contemplated mounting Storm and fleeing the scene. He went so far as to cease trying to calm

Ormhill's animal, turning instead to seek his own horse. He had not far to search.

Storm, whose warhorse disposition had served Edmund so well in battle, had followed his master up the stairs and into the hall, apparently concluding that if the other horse could enter this house, he could, too. When Miss Ormhill charged toward them, arms waving in shooing motions, screaming at the top of her lungs, it must have seemed to Storm that they were once again in battle, for his head snaked forward, his formidable teeth bared, and Edmund barely managed to grab the reins in time to save the woman from a nasty bite.

As might have been expected, this did not exactly soothe the stocky dame's temper. She began to scream, "Murder, murder, help!" She backed away so swiftly she tripped over her own feet and fell to the floor with a crash, which undid all the efforts of Jason, the elderly doorman, and three other servants to calm and control Moonstar. He reared onto his hind feet and began thrashing and pawing at the air, unseating Ormhill and completing Miss Ormhill's rout. She turned, clambered up the first few steps on her hands and knees, and then ascended them with astonishing rapidity given her bulk, yelling all the way.

Moonstar took two or three turns around the great hall, evading all attempts at capture. Storm gave a victory snort and allowed himself to be led outside. Edmund stood at the bottom of the steps, looking up at the handsome mansion, now alight and buzzing with activity, and spoke soothingly to his mount while his brain churned. Perhaps it would be easy to escape his fate. That woman, no matter how desperate she was for a husband, might reject him after this contretemps. He suspected he was grasping at straws, though.

Finally Moonstar emerged, a servant on each side of his head and one in the saddle. Trembling and prancing nervously, he allowed himself to be led away. Edmund followed, leading Storm. Flight would be dishonorable. A little too sober to believe he would escape Miss Ormhill's clutches, he turned his mind to practical matters such as bedding down his horse and then, upon returning to the house, inquiring about the well-being of Jason Ormhill, whom he had last seen hurtling backward through the air.

The hall was filled with servants, and they were gossiping loudly among themselves. When Edmund crossed the threshold, he heard hoarse whispers of "That's him. The one as is to marry our Miss Livvy." Comments, mostly favorable, on his face and figure ceased when he loudly addressed the room at large.

"Where is Mr. Ormhill? Is he injured?"

A tall, dignified older man stepped forward. "Just had the breath knocked out of him, my lord. Miss Ormhill says I am to take you to your room and valet you for the night. Will your servants and baggage be arriving tomorrow?"

Edmund considered confessing the truth: that he had neither servant nor baggage, except what occupied the carpet-bag he had detached from behind Storm's saddle and now held in his hand. But the servants would know soon enough that he was penniless; he preferred for what remained of this one night to receive their respect and solicitous attention. So he ignored the questions, merely inclining his head.

"Lead on," he ordered. "I place myself in your competent hands."

Edmund fell asleep almost instantly, but as usual when he had imbibed too deeply, awoke two hours later and could only toss and turn, worrying about his situation. He had little hope that Miss Ormhill would reject him. She must surely be eager to wed, or young Ormhill would not have set up their wager in the first place. Edmund had always known he would have to marry late in life, when he had made enough of his estate to support a wife and family. He had hoped for a marriage based on the kind of love his parents had shared. His mother's bad choice in a second husband had deprived him of the estate, and he now had gambled away any chance of marrying for love and must face the consequences.

When the sky began to lighten, Edmund arose, dressed himself, and slipped quietly down the servants' stairs and through the kitchen. He begged a roll and some cheese of the surprised cook, who was already ordering about a small army of helpers busy at breakfast preparations. He consumed the roll on the way to the stable, where Storm greeted him eagerly. No grooms being about, Edmund fed him a measure of oats and some hay, filled his water bucket, and curried him as the animal ate.

The noise Edmund made in the process brought a sleepy stable boy to investigate. The lad stared at him in awe. "You be the lord wot our master won at cards!"

"The same," Edmund said, smiling grimly. A sudden thought gave him a glimmer of hope. "Tell me: the heavyset woman my horse almost bit. Is that Miss Ormhill?"

The boy nodded. "That be Miss Lavinia Ormhill."

Hope died. Jason had called his sister "Livvy," clearly a pet name for Lavinia.

"I am told she possesses a farm. Do you know where her land lies?"

The boy scratched his head. "Miss Ormhill's farm?" He looked about him unsurely.

"Surely *this* isn't Miss Ormhill's property." He had assumed that this fine Georgian mansion, with its sturdy stable and surrounding park, belonged to Jason Ormhill.

"Beaumont? No, 'tis the young squire's."

"Do you know where Miss Ormhill's land lies?"

Still looking puzzled, the boy gave sketchy directions, which, however, proved adequate. Edmund quickly found the public road again, turned left as directed, and proceeded up rising ground to the tiny village of Flintridge. At the end of its one street he turned down a country lane that led to a dilapidated cottage surrounded by over-grazed pastures and neglected fields which obviously were set to deliver a minuscule crop.

This might have been thought to cast Edmund into the doldrums, but in fact it lifted his spirits. He could bring little enough to a marriage, but one thing he had to offer was a love of the land and an eagerness to learn all he could about managing it. Young Ormhill's estate manager clearly might be relied upon for good advice in that regard, for in the morning light the land belonging to his host had impressed him for its well-tended fields, fine livestock, and variety of woods. The boundary between it and Miss Ormhill's land was easy enough to spot. It was, quite simply, the difference between good husbandry and bad.

As he rode back to Beaumont, he remembered Ormhill saying his sister managed her farm herself. He'd have to have an understanding with her on that score before their marriage. There was no way he could sit on his hands and watch such potentially fine land go to rack and ruin.

The subject of his musings sat at the breakfast table when he returned. He checked at the door, and hardly knew whether to feel relief or further dismay, for she had a friendly, even eager look on her face, and in the morning light he could see that she was older than he had supposed, being well on the shady side of forty. *She must be young Ormhill's half sister,* he thought, *to be so much older.*

"Miss Ormhill," he said, bowing to her from the doorway.

"Lord Edmund. Come in, come in. Don't look as if I might eat you. I know last night's folly was Jason's doing. A naughty brat, to be sure, and apt to get up to anything when he is in his cups. Perhaps you may bring him into line, sir, if this marriage goes forward."

Edmund smiled vaguely and, after a moment's hesitation, went to the sideboard to fill his plate. When he approached the table, he took a place across from his prospective bride.

"You are in favor of the marriage, then? For I assure you, I would not be a party to anything that smacks of force."

"As if Jason would, or could, do that! Indeed, yes, I am in favor. I have heard of your reputation as a soldier, sir, and knew your father and mother. Good people. 'Tis a shame you could not have inherited instead of that stiff-rumped half brother of yours."

Edmund choked on his ham. "That would require displacing a good deal more than merely my brother, Miss Ormhill. I am—"

"I know. Fifth in line, after Heslington, his three sons, and your other brother. Doesn't matter, though, whether you succeed to the title. A courtesy title will be sufficient. Just so your wife can be addressed as 'my lady,' all will be right and tight. Lady Edmund will do nicely." She smiled at him before addressing herself once again to her breakfast.

Miss Ormhill's acceptance of her father's unreasonable requirement for her marriage astounded Edmund. It was as if she were speaking of someone else.

"There is one matter that we must discuss," he said.

"What is that, Lord Edmund?"

"The question of the management of your land."

"Of my land? What business is that of yours?"

Edmund grimaced. "Ormhill told me that you had been made quite independent, and I can live with that, but I must have the management of your land."

"Management?" Miss Ormhill sputtered indignantly. "Management of *my* land? Why, the nerve!"

"If you were managing it properly, I would say nothing. But the condition of that farm is a disgrace. To be sure, I am no expert, though I would like to be. I will consult young Ormhill's estate agent, for he clearly knows what is what. You would have been better served to have allowed him to manage your farm. I could not stand by and watch your fields deteriorate further. Nor should you want me to. After all, your prosperity will only be enhanced by better management."

"But—"

"It is all very well for a female to manage her household, and even to hold the purse strings, if need be, but I feel strongly that the management of your farm belongs in masculine hands. Specifically, in my hands. I must insist upon this point."

"As a condition of the marriage?" Miss Ormhill asked, her face wrinkled most unbecomingly with an irritated frown.

"Yes. You may well say I am not in a position to lay down conditions, but—"

"Well, you certainly are not in a position to lay down conditions to me, nor why you should wish to do so, I cannot tell. In point of fact, a man *is* managing my farm, but as you have observed, he makes very poor work of it. So if you require that as a condition of the marriage, I will agree."

"I do beg your pardon. I thought Jason said that you managed your farm."

"One, the other, or both of us is indeed confused, young man. But I wish to cooperate in any way necessary to further this marriage."

Edmund did not really know whether to be pleased or horrified by her acquiescence, but having received it, he had no further choice but to proceed. A man must, after all, pay his gaming debts.

"Well, then, Miss Ormhill, you may consider this an offer in form. Shall we publish the bans or obtain a license? I must warn you, I am quite penniless, so you must decide, as the fee for the license would have to come from your pocket."

Miss Ormhill half rose from her seat, her expression ominous. "What can you mean?"

"I expect Jason had little chance of explaining matters to you—none at all, I now recall, as he was too far gone to be coherent. You may wish to withdraw once you know I am quite penniless. I lost all I had to him, and then—"

"Don't, for God's sake, tell her that tale!" Jason Ormhill's alarmed voice rang out from the doorway to the dining room. "We must ease into this thing."

"I'm afraid it is too late. I have explained—"

"You've explained nothing." Miss Ormhill stamped her foot, making the table jump. "Will you please be so kind as to tell me why this . . . this . . . rake has just offered for me? For *me*! Demanded control of my land, which I thought sufficiently peculiar, and then offered marriage to me!"

"To you?" Jason turned on Edmund. "Now that is a cork-brained thing to do, Lord Edmund." Jason's expression became as thunderous as Miss Ormhill's. "Don't tell me you have been overcome with passion, for that won't fadge. As for getting control of her land, well, you shan't have it! As one of her trustees, I would never give it to a man who reneged on a bet."

"Reneged? Not I. But she is not competent to manage her land, nor to choose who will, if what I saw this morning is an example. Her trustees must acknowledge that."

"Explain instantly what is meant by this bet," Miss Ormhill demanded. "None of your roundaboutation, either, Nephew."

"Nephew? Thought you said she was your sister." Edmund began to feel he had landed in Bedlam. The way they were looking at him, the Ormhills thought him a candidate for the same place.

"Is this not Miss Ormhill?" he demanded.

Ignoring him, Jason continued trying to calm his aunt. "Listen to me." He launched into an abbreviated explanation of the events of the evening before. Edmund listened as closely as Miss Ormhill, hoping to find a clue to his own puzzlement. Jason got no further than Edmund's financial situation when he was interrupted.

Miss Ormhill looked ever more ominous. "Penniless, a gamester, cast off by his family? You think to bring such as that in here, just like that, and have him accepted?"

"No, that is why I didn't want him to tell you. Odds are ten to one you'll go straight to Olivia with it."

"Better odds than that!" the stout damsel declared, quitting her place and marching toward the door.

Chapter Three

"Olivia?" Edmund mused aloud, beginning to discern the answer to the puzzle. "Who is Olivia?"

Ignoring him, Jason moved to intercept Miss Ormhill, holding her back with difficulty. "Wait, Aunt Lavinia. Just listen, will you? Lord Edmund will suit Livvy very well, you'll see. But he needs some time to work on her, to court her. She needn't know about the wager until—"

"Oh, yes, she does, and I will tell her." Miss Ormhill pushed past Jason and stormed into the hall. "Buckman, has Miss Olivia returned?"

"Yes. She went straight through to her office, though. She asked not to be disturbed."

"There, you see, Aunt. This will disturb her a great deal."

"It certainly will. Imagine her brother losing her in a game of cards. Though you have no authority over her, you know."

Once again the heavyset woman tried to run Jason down. He pushed against her shoulders, and she walked him backward as she progressed down a hallway under the stairs. Edmund was strongly reminded of a bullfighter impaled upon the horns of a stout, angry bull.

"Aunt, listen to me. You want Livvy married, don't you? You want me to be able to travel; you've always said you thought I should. You don't want her to be an old maid, and me to be tethered in the country the rest of my life, do you?"

His aunt stopped abruptly, almost causing Edmund to run into her from behind. "Well . . ."

"There. You see. Now, it's not like you think. I didn't *lose* her; I *won* him. So Lord Edmund won't shab off as Corbright did, even though her fortune is tied up so tight, 'cause he's honor-bound to marry her. Part of our wager. He's got no money, so he can't hope for a better marriage elsewhere. It beats the Dutch out of starving, don't it, Lord Edmund?"

Edmund nodded. Humiliated to be so situated, he nevertheless believed in looking facts straight in the eye. "So you are not the Miss Ormhill I am to marry?"

Miss Lavinia Ormhill turned around to address herself to Edmund. "No. How can you possibly have thought . . . Oh, I see. It *can* be confusing. Livvy is also Miss Ormhill. Olivia Ormhill." She eyed him calculatingly. "You must indeed be desperate to offer for *me,* young man."

Edmund stammered, trying to say something polite. She stopped him with an imperious lift of her right hand.

"Speak me no nonsense, young man. I cut my eyeteeth many years ago. A plain female of a certain age cannot be your idea of an ideal bride. Don't feel sorry for me, either. I have no inclination to marry, and not being encumbered by an unhappy brother as my poor Livvy is, I do not need to do so. Now. Let us go back to the dining room and discuss this thing rationally."

When the events of the evening before had been fully explained, Miss Ormhill came over to her nephew's side. Indeed, she spoke with some awe in her voice. "Very ingenious, Jason. Astonishing what you can accomplish when you are cast away! I do pity you, Lord Edmund, to be so utterly destitute. Did your father make no provision at all for you?"

"My mother's estate was to come to me. That and my father's recommendation that I should be trained and employed as my brother's estate agent were my only patrimony. Unfortunately, what was to have been my inheritance had to be sold to pay my mother's debts after she and her second husband died in a carriage accident."

"Yes, I recall that. Her second marriage was something of a disaster, I think. Beau Gregham was a rake and a gamester." Lavinia Ormhill continued to regard him suspiciously. "But can you not appeal to your brother?"

Edmond gritted his teeth. "He has disowned me."

"But why? Just because you gamble? But what gentle-man doesn't?" Miss Ormhill responded. "Ought to be proud of you. Your bravery is well known, and you've not been the subject of any notable *on dits,* that I am aware of."

"Not because of my gaming. Let us say we agreed to dis-agree, both as to his manner of handling my mother's af-fairs, and as to my choice of a profession. Our parting was quite, quite final, on both sides. I would not ask anything of him even if I had any hope that he would assist me."

"Ah, yes, I see. Managing estates seemed entirely too tame to you. You *would* go off soldiering, thus causing your brother to cast you off. Harsh."

"It wasn't like that at all." Edmund shook his head. "I never wanted a military career. I loved the land and meant to make my life in the country from the time I could begin to plan my future. In spite of which, when my father died, Carl bought my colors, outfitted me, and thrust me on a ship bound for Portugal."

Miss Ormhill protested. "You cannot have been much above twelve then!"

"I was sixteen and utterly his to command. He obtained a commission and packed me off, against my mother's pleas. I had no recourse."

"How odd. It would have been an expensive investment for him. To pay out so much blunt to set a boy up in a pro-fession he did not desire seems quite unaccountable to me."

Edmund turned away, looking blankly out the window. How hard it was to admit the truth even to himself, much less to others. "My brother always hated me. I will not bore you with my family history, but he wished me out of the way. If I had died in combat, he would have been well sat-isfied with his investment."

Jason swore softly; Miss Ormhill gasped. "Such perfidy! Did it have something to do with the irregular nature of your parents' marriage?"

"It had everything to do with that. The scandal of my fa-ther marrying his sister-in-law deeply embarrassed Carl."

"Thought that was illegal," Jason said, looking alarmed.

"You aren't a bastard, are you? Can't be called Lord Edmund if you are, even if you *are* a marquess's son."

"Your uncle can explain it all, I daresay. Something of a legal anomaly, I always thought. Marriage to a deceased wife's sister is not illegal, precisely, but the church frowns upon it, and such a marriage can be voided easily."

"But it wasn't voided?"

"No, Carl spared me that. He never let me forget the possibility, though, or how much such an action would devastate my mother. So even after I reached my majority, I stayed in the army as he wished. Doubtless to his chagrin, I didn't die, as you can see. Came back to England for the premature victory celebrations," Edmund replied wryly. "Mother had remarried by then, and her husband and I had an instant, mutual antipathy for one another. I had no home or prospects, so I shipped out for America, then returned just in time for Waterloo. That was when I learned my mother had died deeply in debt and my estate had been sold. My brother was her trustee, you see, in accordance with my father's will."

Jason groaned. "Feeling as he did about you, he probably did not try to avoid the sale."

"Indeed, he lost no time doing so. I suspect he was delighted. He knew how much the property meant to me. In fact, the sale did not cover all of the debts: Beau Gregham was an expensive husband. What prize money and other resources I had went to settle them. Still, I resigned my commission, knowing I simply could not soldier anymore. I yearned for the English countryside, for the fresh air, the rural way of life. I went to my brother one last time, calling on him to train me and employ me as father had asked him to do. When he learned I had defied him and left the army, Carl disowned me. As I said, the final interview held animosity enough on both sides to make the rupture quite, quite final."

Surprised to find he had told these new acquaintances so much about his personal affairs, Edmund apologized for burdening them with his troubles. But both Jason and Lavinia assured him of their sympathy.

Miss Ormhill, in spite of her unfortunate appearance, clearly did not lack sensibility, for her eyes teared over as she contemplated Edmund's situation. "So cruel! I feel for you, young man. But take heart. You might indeed be the man for our Olivia. You do have a title, after all, even if it is a courtesy title. And you are no fortune hunter." She paused and frowned, then continued in a musing tone, "Not in the usual way, at least."

Edmund wondered just how plain the younger Miss Ormhill must be, for both her brother and her aunt to consider him a suitable *parti* for her.

"I was pretty well-to-go when you explained matters last night, Ormhill. Why are you in such a pelter to marry your sister off, especially to an indigent stranger of whose character you know very little?"

"I know you, sir, by reputation," Jason protested indignantly. "And every woman needs a husband."

"Try another," Edmund demanded, folding his hands across his chest.

"Oh, very well. The matter stands thusly. Just before my father's death three years ago, he revised his will, including saying, 'Olivia shall marry a lord. I have ever felt she ought to be called "my lady."' It may have been a jest he made, which our humorless solicitor misunderstood. Or possibly a reference to her titled fiancé, Lord Corbright. Nevertheless, it was signed in front of witnesses. Signed in haste, I might add, without Father's reading the finished document, because he was dying. He knew I had the wanderlust even then, and asked me remain with her until she was safely wed. Of course, he expected that to be as soon as the mourning period was over."

Jason stared out at the horizon, blinking away suspicious moisture at these memories.

"Unfortunately, when her husband-to-be saw the will, he cried off. Not that he is a fortune hunter. Rich as the Golden Ball! He felt that he had been insulted, that the will implied he could not be trusted with Livvy's property. Also, he could not like the thought of a wife being so independent of her husband. By the will, any marriage settlement must give Olivia the right to live on and manage her own land and receive its income in the case of estrangement."

"It *is* an unusual arrangement," Edmund said.

"Yes, well, my father had a sister who made a disastrous marriage. Her husband treated her terribly, and wasted her fortune while he did it. Father swore such would never happen to his daughter. At any rate, the broken engagement hurt Livvy deeply. She withdrew from society and now declares herself a spinster. She manages my land as well as her own, and fills her days with schemes of drainage and crop rotation, while I am left kicking my heels here in Buckinghamshire." As he spoke, Ormhill became progressively more agitated. He banged his fist upon the dining table, making the dishes rattle. "I'm bloody well tired of it! So it is up to you, Lord Edmund, to free me."

"An appalling situation for you, I agree. But it seems to me that your father never intended this outcome."

"No, but a man cannot break his word to his father, given on his deathbed."

To this point Edmund had seen Jason as a spoiled, self-centered creature. This response raised the boy in his estimation. He gnawed at his lower lip. "I shall do what I can, of course, to win her over, but it sounds a difficult task. When I agreed to the wager, I assumed she was eager to be wed."

"As you thought I was your intended, one look at me must have confirmed you in that opinion," Miss Ormhill said, amusement glinting in her eyes. "But she must be told of the wager, Jason. She will smoke it out soon enough, and then you'll find her fighting shyer than ever."

"Once she gets wind of it, the game will be up," Jason groused. "I thought to present him as a friend, and—"

Edmund responded firmly. "I agree with your aunt. I won't be a party to force or trickery. Your sister must be told of the wager. Get over the heavy ground lightly, then we shall see."

Jason wrinkled his nose as if at a bad smell. "She has this cork-brained notion she'd rather be a spinster."

"Which is not such a terrible fate as you men seem to think," Miss Ormhill growled. "Still, though right for me, it won't do for Livvy, no matter what she may believe. And I dislike seeing Jason so discontent. I'll give you what help I

can on the project, gentlemen. But as for your managing her
land, Lord Edmund, I know she won't allow it. She's made
quite a study of the thing, and done well by herself and
Jason, I must admit."

"She manages Jason's land?" Edmund whistled softly.
"Then I take it the dilapidated farm I viewed earlier this
morning is yours, Miss Ormhill?"

"Yes, to my sorrow." Lavinia Ormhill began to chuckle.
"I've rented it to a shiftless rascal, and can't seem to get a
better tenant. I suppose I should have turned it over to Livvy
long before now, but I felt she had enough on her plate."

"Far from wishing to wrest the management of her land
from her, I am filled with admiration. Her knowledge vastly
surpasses mine." Edmund frowned. "It means I have just
that much less to offer as a husband, alas, since she needs no
assistance. What would I do with myself, I wonder?"

"Now, you aren't going to shab off, are you?" Jason
cried.

"No, of course not. It was a wager, and I am bound to
marry her if I can."

"Don't look so downpin, Lord Edmund," Miss Ormhill
soothed him. "You may be just the man for our Livvy: A
man who recognizes her ability, and won't try to take over
from her, yet one who loves the country life, might be perfect for her, if she will but give up her decision never to
marry. Surely you can find a role to play in our family's extensive holdings. Manage mine, at the very least." Having
reached her decision, Lavinia Ormhill clapped her hands on
her knees. "Well, shall we approach the lioness in her den,
Nephew?" She leaned forward expectantly.

"You insist she be told the truth?"

"I do." Miss Ormhill folded her arms across her broad
bosom. "I'll not be moved on that score."

"Ah, well. Come along, then, Lord Edmund. We shall try
our fate, eh?"

Chapter Four

Once again the trio traveled the narrow hall that led to the offices. This time Jason led, followed by Edmund, while Miss Ormhill brought up the rear.

At the end of the hall, Jason carefully opened the final door and peered in. Satisfied, he quietly pushed it open, motioning his comrades-in-arms to remain behind. From his vantage point in the hall Edmund could see a young woman, her back to them, sitting at a wide, cluttered desk. It was positioned to face a French window that revealed through diamond-shaped panes of glass a panoramic view of the valley below the manor.

Edmund steeled himself for the meeting. In spite of the Ormhills' tale that she had chosen not to marry, he realized that the younger Miss Ormhill must be of a similar stamp as her aunt. After all, Jason and Lavinia closely resembled one another. The swarthy complexion, heavy brow, long Roman nose, and strong chin of the nephew found their counterparts in Miss Lavinia Ormhill. These features, pleasing enough in a man, served a woman poorly. Edmund pitied the other Miss Ormhill if she shared them, and himself for having to look at such over his meals for the rest of his life.

But a gaming debt must be paid if at all possible. *At least she is young,* he comforted himself.

Gazing at the bent head of the young woman in front of him, Edmund noted immediately that unlike those of her relatives, her neck was long, slender, and graceful. Delicate curling tendrils of brunette hair escaped a high, loosely arranged upsweep of curls, giving the neck a tender appeal. He caught his breath, barely daring to hope, as Jason proceeded to his sister's side and kissed her cheek.

She lifted her head to look up at him affectionately, presenting Edmund with a delightful profile that might have served the most exacting of cameo makers. Dark curls kissed a high forehead above a patrician nose and sweetly curving lips.

"Hullo, love," she said in a throaty voice. "You're up and about early for a man whose allowance was burning a hole in his pocket the night before. Did you have luck?"

Jason stepped to her side and took her hands in his, laying down the quill pen she had held. "The best of luck, Livvy. I've found you a husband."

"How thoughtful of you, dear," she murmured vaguely. "But I don't want a husband, you know." She reached up and patted his cheek. "A pity you could not have got me someone to bring in the hay."

She tried to return to her work, but Jason tugged on her hands impatiently, pulling her from her chair. "No, no, you don't understand, Livvy. He's a good man, and a lord, you see. I've brought you a lord. Come, let me introduce you."

Miss Ormhill allowed herself to be turned to face Edmund, whom Jason urged into the room, closely followed by his aunt. Jason hastened to make the introductions, grandly announcing his guest as "Lord Edmund Debham, youngest brother of the fourth Marquess of Heslington."

Edmund's breath caught in his throat as Miss Ormhill turned toward him. She was exquisite. Her eyes were as blue as the summer sky, and her complexion smooth and creamy. She had a perfect oval face with a tiny cleft in her chin. Her only resemblance to her brother and aunt lay in the color of her eyes and her full lower lip. He was as astonished as he was relieved to find that this was the woman he had agreed to marry. But it made her unwed state even that much more amazing. He had felt skeptical of the Ormhills' story of love betrayed as a reason for her being single, but now he had to give it credence.

Olivia Ormhill curtsied, then offered Edmund her hand.

Her firm grip brought her hand against his own in a contact that affected him like a shock from a Leyden jar. To his vast relief she gave him a shy but welcoming smile instead of the contempt or aloofness he might well have received. *Perfection,* he thought, taking in her tall, slender form and elegant dress.

"Aunt," she said, nodding in acknowledgment of Lavinia Ormhill. "So you are here to lend countenance to this match?" Her lips curved again in a smile that was almost mischievous.

"I hope you will not be hasty in your decision, dearest. Lord Edmund has much to recommend him."

Miss Ormhill's eyes briefly swept Edmund head to foot. He knew he did not show to great advantage at this moment, having been forced to dress himself in the clothes he had been wearing the night before. That his garments were neither new nor in the highest kick of fashion he suddenly felt keenly. Miss Olivia Ormhill looked to be a young woman of refined taste.

He swept his hand through his unruly brown hair and felt himself licking his lips like a frightened lad from the nursery. *This won't do,* he admonished himself. *If you could lead the forlorn hope in an assault on a Spanish fortress, you can face this lovely creature.* He set himself to charm her, straightening to his full and rather imposing height and smiling down at her, the lazy, caressing smile that had won so much feminine admiration in the past.

"I, too, hope you will not be hasty, though at the moment I am afraid your aunt is too sanguine. I do not have so very much to recommend me, Miss Ormhill, other than my own person and an ardent desire to wed you."

"So sudden a wooing, Lord Edmund," she murmured. But her expression remained pleasant. She cocked her head to one side curiously as he hastened to explain, for he would not have her humbugged.

"I'll be brutally honest with you. As a result of a dispute with my eldest brother, I am quite cast off by my family. Thanks to your brother's skill at cards, I am also virtually penniless. But——"

"But he is a hero, sister," Jason hastened to add. "Wellington mentioned him in his dispatches, and you know how stingy the duke is with such praise."

"And he yearns for the country life, Olivia. No Bond Street lounger, this," Lavinia added in a challenging tone.

"I see." Miss Ormhill's delicate eyebrows began to draw down in a frown. "Is this proposed marriage the result of a wager?"

When Jason hesitated, Edmund answered for him. "It is, Miss Ormhill."

"Really, Jason!" She half turned away, then rounded on her brother. "Penniless, did he say? You won a great deal from him last night?"

"Well . . ." Jason looked acutely uncomfortable.

"All that I had," Edmund stated baldly. "Your brother is a formidable opponent."

"And were you drinking at the time, Jason?"

"Now see here, Livvy. It is just as Lord Edmund says. I played well and—"

"Drinking heavily?" She tapped her right foot on the ground in the manner of impatient, determined females from time immemorial.

"He drank as much," Jason growled, not meeting his sister's gaze. "Tell her, Lord Edmund."

Not quite sure of the relevance of this part of their tale, Edmund nevertheless asserted, "I did, indeed, drink heavily."

"I don't doubt it." Miss Ormhill turned those clear blue eyes on him, all traces of humor gone. "You aren't the first to attempt to fleece my brother in such circumstances. But in fact, he fleeced you. You see, the more my brother drinks, the better he plays. No one understands it, but it is true. We've discussed the unfairness of playing others thus, Jason."

"It is because I learned to play while dead drunk," Jason explained, looking proud of himself. "Anything I learn while drunk, I have difficulty remembering when sober, but remember soon enough with a few drinks in me. And I can do sums foxed I could never tackle sober."

At her use of the term *fleeced,* Edmund had winced. But
what right had he to pride? It was a bit too true to his intentions, at least at one point last night, for him to protest. He
did not want her to doubt the validity of the wager. He ardently hoped she would choose to honor it, as her concern
for the fairness of the game suggested she might. Never had
he wanted anything as much as to convince this lovely creature to marry him.

"I was warned, Miss Ormhill, by both your brother and
the innkeeper. You need not scold your brother, for I played
with that understanding in mind."

"But did you believe them?"

He hesitated, then shook his head.

"As I thought. He took advantage of you, while you tried
to take advantage of him. A pretty pair, to be sure! I don't
precisely see how you managed to lose your money but win
me from my brother while he was in his cups, my lord. In
these parts, at least, he is reckoned unbeatable in such circumstances. However, that is neither here nor there. The
choice of my husband lies with me. Jason wagered a stake
he could not pay. He has no power to compel me to marry,
my lord. And I will not do so. Most particularly not a penniless gamester who does not shy away from taking advantage of his opponent. Moreover, one who has nothing to
recommend him but a courtesy title, a name for foolhardy
bravery, and a pleasing appearance." Those bright blue eyes
scanned Edmund coldly and contemptuously before turning
back to her brother, who was spluttering out a protest.

"You must make matters right with Lord Edmund yourself, Jason. I am not a chit to be wagered away in a card
game."

"You mistake the matter, Miss Ormhill," Edmund
snapped, caught on the raw by her harsh words. "I do not
come to you as a winner claiming his prize, but as a loser,
bound to marry you by the terms of our wager. Your brother
warned me that your circumstances were such as to make
you independent and that your disposition was far from
pleasant. I see he did not exaggerate. Yet however little I

might wish to take such as you to wife, I am bound by my word."

Edmund had the satisfaction of seeing her face color with embarrassment and anger. She needed taking down a peg. Nor did he misstate his feelings. His sudden desire to marry this self-possessed, beautiful, wealthy young woman had just as suddenly been blasted to nothingness by the heat of her scornful diatribe. To do so would be utter misery. Better she had been plain and dowdy. Better she had been Miss Lavinia Ormhill, who at least had a heart, and needed his help with her land.

"How dare you speak so of my niece," her aunt protested.

"Of all the rag-mannered, ill-advised things to say," Jason shouted at him.

"Take your 'winnings' with you, Jason! I hope I may never set eyes on him again." Miss Ormhill turned her back on them. Closing the ledger she had been working on with a bang, she swept around the edge of the desk and toward the window.

"But . . . but . . . Olivia, this isn't fair. I have at last found you a husband in no position to object to the terms of your settlement under Father's will, and can make you 'my lady,' as Father wished."

"I do not believe in slavery, Jason. If he were the most desirable of husbands I would not have him under such circumstances." Miss Ormhill jerked open the French doors. "I suggest that the two of you work out some other way of satisfying the wager. And be sure it does not involve me!" She stepped out onto the stone veranda and briskly walked away.

"Now you have done it! You've forfeited," Jason snarled wrathfully at Edmund.

"I have not. I won't be abused in that way by any woman. But I will keep my word, however reluctantly, if she can be persuaded to change her mind. Though how you ever expected such a creature to fall in with this scheme, I cannot imagine."

"You've made mice feet of this whole thing, both of you," the elder Miss Ormhill declared before following her niece out of the room.

*   *   *

Olivia stormed down the path that led from her office to the stables. Nothing would ease her feelings but a hard, fast ride. Anger at her brother's scheme was the least of it. The disdain she felt for Lord Edmund did not surprise her. The pain his stinging words of rejection had caused her did. What was he, after all, that she should wish his regard? She had spoken nothing but the truth about him.

That everything about him appealed to her, from his wavy brown hair and warm brown eyes to his handsome face and tall, vibrantly masculine form, should have nothing to say to the matter!

When she heard her aunt calling her, she had to fight the desire to break into a run and gain the stable and her mount before Lavinia could catch up to her. But ingrained habits of respect caused her to turn reluctantly.

"Don't put on that mulish face to me, my girl. What you just did was appalling."

"What I just did? Aunt, how can you? Surely you don't wish me to marry such a . . . a . . ."

"Handsome, well-mannered, well-bred, and willing man? Yes, I do. Or at least, I wish you to give yourself time to see if you would like to do so. But even if I did not, I would deplore your hateful words. Equivalent to kicking a man when he is down, Livvy, and not at all in your usual style."

Olivia turned and began walking away. She could not, would not admit to her aunt what she hardly admitted to herself: her heart had fluttered, then raced, at her first sight of Edmund Debham. The touch of his hand on hers had sent a thrill straight to her toes. The attraction she felt to him had astonished but not displeased her at first, for she had never thought to feel thus again for any man.

Then she had discovered the truth: he was nothing but a rum-soaked gamester, a shabby one at that, and a Captain Sharp, attempting to best her brother under unfair circumstances. And then to learn that he had lost. That he sought her hand only because he had no alternative. *Oh!* The taste of ashes was in her mouth. She barely heard her aunt scolding her.

"If you must refuse them, carry it off with humor; that is what you have always said, and what you have done in the past. What maggot got into your head? Now you've got Jason horribly upset, and he has already been far too unhappy lately for me to be comfortable as it is."

This caught Olivia's attention. "What . . . what do you mean, Aunt?"

"You know how moped he has been. He is an active young man, ripe for adventure. At eighteen, no wonder! It is his birthright to discover the world. To remain shut up here in Buckinghamshire with his older sister and his ancient aunt is torture to him."

"If he would only interest himself in the management of his estates . . ."

"Well, he won't. Not until he has had a bit of fun."

"I have said many times that he may go, that he should go. I am no longer the young girl my father begged him to protect. As if he could have protected me at fifteen anyway."

"You know he would never break his promise. Nor would you have him be the kind of young man who would do so."

Olivia shook her head impatiently. "We have been over this a hundred times. But what did you mean to imply? You do not suppose he will do himself an injury?"

"Yes, my dear, I do. Oh, I don't mean that he'd take his life, not on purpose. But there are other ways. Drinking and gambling in taverns . . ."

"With Uncle Milton to keep him company! Coming it too strong, Aunt." Olivia strove for jocularity.

"May I point out that my brother had retired to his bed long before the mischief was done last night? Nor was this the first time Jason has gambled into the night with strangers. And then there is the riding."

Olivia shuddered. Jason had always been a bruising rider. Lately he had become a reckless one. Not two weeks ago he had come a cropper at a wall he never should have attempted, injuring his favorite hunting hack in the process.

"Yes, you understand me. Somehow this situation has got

to be resolved. And that poor young man may just hold the key."

"But not the key to my heart. Not that you care for that!"

"The man who had the key to your heart threw it away. The heart can be a very false guide, my love. You pride yourself on being a rational female. At least consider the advantages of wedding Lord Edmund."

Olivia shook her head. "You heard him. He doesn't want to marry me. But even if he did, and even if I gave up my determination to be a spinster, I simply can't—won't—give myself to such a man. Now, if you will excuse me, Aunt, I have some . . . some fields to inspect."

"At the least, apologize to him for your harsh treatment. You don't know his full situation." Not to be denied, Lavinia took Olivia's arm and steered her back toward the house as she explained what she knew about Lord Edmund.

"And I don't doubt his brother disowned him," Lavinia added at the end of the recitation, "for he is a hard man. Your father disliked him intensely."

"Yes, I remember now," Olivia murmured. She had met the marquess a few times in company with her former fiancé. "The question is, just how much like him is Lord Edmund?"

As Lavinia tried to calm Livvy and convince her to at least consider marrying Lord Edmund, stressing his love for the land and admiration of her abilities to manage it, her nephew was loudly quarreling with him, convinced he had deliberately provoked his sister into her resounding refusal.

"Not fair," Edmund protested. "Nor was the wager itself fair. You led me to think you had a homely, plain sister, eager to wed. Knowing her as you do, you must have been foxed beyond reason to propose the wager in the first place."

"I hoped you'd take your time with her, court her. Thought you might win her over, at least enough that she would marry to please me. But I think she refuses to marry to displease me! And then you go and insult her and end all hope!"

Jason seemed to grow angrier and more agitated the longer they talked, so Edmund turned and walked away.

"Where the devil do you think you are going?"

"It doesn't matter. It will come to fisticuffs or worse, if you go on any longer."

"Oh, ho! A duel. Well, I hope you may challenge me, you card cheat."

Edmund whirled on him. "Take care, bantling."

"Why? Why should I? You have just forged the last chain in my shackles. At least a duel would relieve the tedium."

It was at this point that Olivia and Lavinia arrived back at the door to her office. "A duel? No, no!" Olivia raced into the room. "You can't! I won't allow it."

Jason snarled. "Don't pretend that you care a whit for me, Livvy, for it won't fadge. I'm leg-shackled to you for life, and I've no taste for a long one, on such a tether!"

Olivia shrank from the bitter ferocity of his expression. All her aunt's fears seemed confirmed by Jason's shouted words and livid face. Truly frightened for him, she turned an imploring face to his opponent.

"Lord Edmund . . ."

"You needn't fear, Miss Ormhill. I won't act as your brother's executioner. I am not quite that low, in spite of your assessment of me."

Olivia studied his tense, almost haggard expression. *He must have truly been devastated by his brother's rejection, and my words were so harsh.* Not for the first time in her life, she regretted her hasty tongue.

"I must apologize for my remarks, Lord Edmund. They would have been rude in any event, but after hearing the story from my aunt, I realize I have wronged you."

His face softened marginally. "Not so completely as I wish I could claim. I was desperate and drunk last night, a good combination for causing a man's sense of right and wrong to slip."

"As my brother's did, with less excuse. Now, Jason, I want you to release Lord Edmund from his obligation to us, and to restore his property."

"No, I can't accept that," Edmund protested. "He won all

from me, fair and square. The marriage idea was ridiculous. I should never have entered into such a bargain in the first place. What we can do, Jason, is go back to the stake I proposed first: a year of my labor in exchange for its worth."

Olivia and Lavinia both objected to such an idea, while Jason said with a sneer, "Which is exactly nothing, as Mr. Dutton so accurately observed."

"Not true. Did I not understand you to say, Miss Ormhill, that you needed help with your haying?"

Olivia Ormhill once more looked disdainfully at him. "I hardly think you could be of much help."

"Why not? I am strong and willing. I will work alongside your crew from sunup to sundown—you'll see. And once the haying is done, I will find other ways to make myself useful through the year."

She shook her head, amusement lightening her expression. "You are a gentleman, Lord Edmund. What I need is someone who knows how to load a hay wain."

"Why?" Jason demanded. "What is wrong with old Bleck and the Joneses?"

"They have found employment elsewhere, at double their wages."

"Double? Now who would pay that?"

Olivia looked away briefly. "Everyone around Flintridge has an abundant harvest this year. Laborers may name their price."

"Then pay them more."

"Most of them prefer to work for a man when they can."

Jason shook his head, baffled. "Then we shall simply purchase hay."

"If you had attended more to estate matters, you would understand how dearly that would cost us. The estate must be self-sufficient insofar as possible, if there is to be any profit in what we sell. Without our hay, we will have to sell off much of our livestock, thus ruining my breeding program, not to mention your stud."

"Then all the more reason you need me, Miss Ormhill," Edmund insisted.

Olivia laughed softly at his naiveté. "You might master a

scythe, Lord Edmund, if you did not cut off your leg first, and to pitch hay up to a wagon . . ."

"Unconscionable," Lavinia objected. "One cannot allow a gentleman to work in such a way."

Olivia continued without responding to her, "But one man's labor will not solve my problem. I have many fields left to cut, and hay lying on the ground. I need an experienced crew to load and unload the hay wains as quickly as possible and make up the hay cocks, for such a harvest as this year's will spill over our barns, I am sure."

"Anyone could load a hay wain," Jason yelped. "What a piece of work you are making of this. It is just a matter of stacking it up as high as possible, after all!"

Olivia turned back to him, a challenging light in her eyes. "Then you accept Lord Edmund's proposition to substitute a year of his labor instead of this marriage scheme?"

Jason frowned. "No, I do not! I only meant you can hire any strong man to bring in the hay. It would be unseemly to put Lord Edmund to work in our fields. He is a gentleman." Jason almost shouted, "And your future bridegroom."

Olivia shook her head. "You'll vex me about this scheme forever, won't you." Her aunt's warning, combined with her brother's attempt to force Lord Edmund into a duel, made ending the impasse between her and Jason imperative. She put one finger to her lips and tapped them, thinking. "I know. You are so fond of wagers, perhaps you will enter one with me?"

"What sort of wager?" Jason asked suspiciously.

"Very simple. As you seem to believe anyone can load a hay wain, I propose that the two of you each load one. If you both, working separately, can load your wagon to the usual height, and have the hay remain on it until it reaches the storage barn, I will marry Lord Edmund. If you cannot, you consider yourself released from your pledge to my father. Also you will restore Lord Edmund's property to him, plus what he had won from you before you began to drink heavily, and let him go on his way."

Jason's eyes lit with triumph. "Done! By Jove, you shall have a husband by this time tomorrow!" Jason grabbed her in his arms and swung her about exuberantly. "Did you hear, Aunt Lavinia? Olivia has at last been caught!"

"I suppose," Lavinia said doubtfully.

"You agree to these terms?" Olivia asked Edmund as soon as she could free herself from her brother's embrace. "Understand, I do not refer to merely loading the wagons up to the top of the sideboards. We would be forever at the job, and be overtaken by the rains, if we transported our hay at that pace. A properly loaded hay wain is almost a full story high."

"I understand, and accept most gladly, Miss Ormhill. I have only one question: what if one of us succeeds in loading the hay wain and the other does not?"

Her brows arrowed together. "I hadn't thought—"

"Then allow me to propose a slight modification to the wager."

"Such as?" She looked as wary as her brother had a few minutes ago.

"If only one of us can load the hay wain and have the load survive intact to the storage barn, the wager between your brother and myself is at an end, but you will agree to allow me to remain here for one year. I will work for you in various capacities on the farm, while you teach me as much as possible of what you know about estate management." Edmund's voice rang with enthusiasm.

"You surprise me, Lord Edmund. One would almost think you wish for that outcome."

Lavinia interrupted. "Indeed, when we talked earlier, and he was demanding the right to manage my land—"

"He *what?*" Olivia drew back, astonished.

"Never mind; I will explain later. At any rate, at that time he told me he would seek to learn how to manage my land from Jason's estate agent."

"Exactly so," Edmund said. "And now I know that agent is you, Miss Ormhill."

Olivia felt her cheeks warm at this compliment, so rare from a man. "You do not scruple to apprentice yourself to a female? There are many around here who think it quite impossible, indeed, almost blasphemous, for a woman to manage an estate."

"I am a pragmatist, Miss Ormhill. I believe what my eyes tell me. As I rode about this morning I could see evidence of advanced agricultural practices, and have been told that you are the one who is responsible. I therefore conclude that I have much to learn from you."

Olivia's mouth opened slightly and her eyes widened, showing a softness he had not seen in them since she had learned of the wager. "You are an unusual man, Lord Edmund." Again she tapped her finger to her lips. "Very well, I will agree to that, on one condition: that Jason agrees to learn right alongside you."

"Oh, no! If I win, you wed. If I lose, you don't. That was our stake," Jason responded.

"I wish to modify it," Olivia said. "If you lose, you learn." Her expression became stern. "Accept that part of the bet or I'll have none of it."

Chapter Five

"Now see here, Olivia," Jason began, obviously intent on arguing over the stakes his sister proposed.

"A word in private, Ormhill?" Edmund's tone of voice reflected his several years as an officer in His Majesty's service. He gestured Jason to follow him out onto the veranda.

"You've clearly decided to lose this bet and wiggle out of your obligation to me," Jason groused as he followed Edmund.

"No such thing. How could I know she'd propose this wager, much less these terms? At least it gives you a chance to achieve your aims. Otherwise I may as well leave today."

"And if we lose the main wager, this side bet you have proposed will give you an excuse to remain here and become better acquainted with Olivia. Perhaps you will discover that you like one another very well!" Jason brightened at this thought.

"It seems unlikely," Edmund said, "but possible." In truth, he thought it impossible. Miss Ormhill's raking him over the coals had made him disinclined to even attempt to win her over. Still, he didn't like to upset the youngster further. "And even if that is not the outcome, you will be capable of managing your own lands."

"Don't want to manage them," Jason snarled. "Told you. Want to travel."

"In that case I shall manage them for you, once I am able. Remember, if you lose, you will be free to travel."

Jason shook his head. "A wager can't erase what I

promised my father, whatever Livvy may think of the matter. I agreed only because it gave you a chance of marrying her."

"Then I wonder if it is a valid wager." Edmund felt troubled about the situation. On the one hand he sympathized with Jason's devotion to duty. On the other, he saw that Olivia was trying to free him from an unnatural restriction.

"As long as we understand between ourselves—Oh, hang it all! We can load two hay wains, can't we?"

"I'm not sure. But consider this: If I take over management of your estate, Olivia may find that time sits heavy on her hands, and will look about her for a husband. And it will be far better for you to spend the next year learning than roving aimlessly about the countryside seeking oblivion in card games and wine bottles."

"Will it?" Jason scowled. "You can't know what it is like, Lord Edmund. You've had the opportunity to travel, to see the world. I can't so much as leave Buckinghamshire without my sister. It's not only boring, it's humiliating."

Edmund laughed mirthlessly. " 'Tis true I've seen a large part of Europe, but through a haze of dust and blood. Never did I pass a day in Spain, Portugal, or France without yearning to return to English soil. In the heat of New Orleans and the muddy, blood-soaked fields of Quatre Bras, I dreamed of just such a peaceful valley, of just such calm summer days. Even the thought of cold, rainy winter days on English soil filled me with longing! This is where I yearned to be, and whether I be here as husband or agent, or even a mere farmhand, here is where I'd like to remain while you travel to your heart's content. If that is impossible, I can gain credentials here that will allow me to find employment elsewhere."

"Indeed, you win either way," Jason groused. "Oh, very well. This bet is the best I can do, it seems. But we doubtless will lose. If I know my sister, and I do, it is not as easy as I thought when I mocked her, else she never would have agreed to the terms."

"No, it isn't." Edmund chuckled. "Ormhills are certainly dangerous to wager with."

"Oh, I say!" Jason's gloomy countenance brightened. "I'll bet you know how. You must teach me!"

Olivia and Lavinia had followed the men out and stood nearby, fearing another confrontation. "*Do* you know, Lord Edmund?" Olivia demanded, hurrying toward him.

Edmund smiled reminiscently. "When I was a boy, I was fascinated by all the activities on our home farm. Never one for the books, I'd escape my tutor to help with the planting and harvesting as often as possible. Though it was a long time ago, I did stand atop a hay wain more than once, helping to load it. Not that I was much help. There is a technique to it, as you well know, Miss Ormhill." He lifted his eyebrows in amused accusation.

Olivia's cheeks pinkened a little. "Of course. Otherwise I'd be a fool to make this bet. And you may *not* teach Jason what you know. He made the wager thinking there was nothing to it, and that is how he must fulfill its terms. I'll have your word of honor on that, gentlemen!"

"You have it, Miss Ormhill," Edmund said, extending his hand to her.

"Devil take it! Well, know this, Livvy: If we lose, I cannot agree to break my word to my father. I will drop trying to get you to marry Lord Edmund, and I will work on the estate, but that is all."

"Oh, Jason." Olivia sighed. "Please reconsider."

"Absolutely not! Nothing will ever make me do anything so base." Jason stormed from the room.

"Oh, dear." Lavinia hurried after him.

"I am sorry you have been forced to witness our family turmoil, Lord Edmund," Olivia said, mortification plain in her flushed cheeks.

"Do not consider it, Miss Ormhill. I assure you, my family's disagreements were legendary, and have recently become so parlous as to end all sense of kinship."

"I owe you another apology, for an offense less easily dismissed, sir. I spoke hastily—and cruelly—to you earlier, when I learned of the wager. Now that I know something of your situation, I—"

Edmund interrupted her by holding up his hand for silence. "We both spoke more sharply than we should have. I must confess there was a great deal of truth in what you said. I have done quite a bit of gaming in my life, and I did, at one point, hope to separate Jason from his purse. And I cannot deny the mercenary nature of my matrimonial aspirations, can I? In fact, only one of your charges was patently untrue."

Olivia cocked her head to one side. "What was that? I am sorry to say I do not remember everything I said in the heat of the moment."

"You accused me of foolhardy bravery, Miss Ormhill."

"Oh, that was truly inexcusable of me," Olivia wailed, wringing her hands in chagrin. "I have heard what carnage Waterloo was. You have risked your life in battle in the service of your country. I had no right to trivialize it in such a way."

"I meant to deny my bravery, not my foolhardiness."

"What . . . what do you mean? My brother says Wellington himself praised you."

"I performed only one act of true bravery in all my years of service, Miss Ormhill." Edmund's expression turned somber. "That was the first time I went into battle, as a raw sixteen-year-old. That in my terror I did not turn and run when the enemy began to fire upon us, I will allow to be called brave. After that, I went into each battle as to an unpleasant job. I learned, you see, that death on the battlefield is utterly random. Good men die, bad ones live. The brave perish, the cowardly survive, and vice versa. It seemed pointless to worry about my fate."

"But you were mentioned in the dispatches. . . ."

"If I fought hard, it was not out of bravery, but out of anger at the waste of it all, the ugliness of it. When the men under my command and my fellow officers began to fall, wounded or dead, a kind of fury rose up in me, a desire to protect those I cared for by killing as many of our enemies as possible."

Olivia watched in fascination as Edmund's expression took on the ferocity of a man in mortal combat. A little shudder went through her. *He would be a formidable opponent,* she thought.

Edmund saw Olivia's eyes grow round, her expression almost fearful, and swore softly. "I beg your pardon. I had no intention of speaking of such dreadful experiences to you—a gently bred female should not have to think of such things."

"I am not so weak a creature as to be unable to bear hearing unpleasant truths," Olivia snapped. "And I think you would be called brave by any definition, so my apology stands."

He smiled. "I most definitely do not think you a weak creature, Miss Ormhill. But I prefer not to speak of the war if I can help it. I want to forget it!"

"I can understand that," she murmured.

"But tell me: Do you really mean to keep your brother kicking his heels in Buckinghamshire forever? I'd say his bad temper now is only a mild foreshadowing of what is to come if he is denied the right to pursue his own way for very much longer. A young man of his temperament, full of juice, must be given a long lead."

"It is not I who keep him here! You do not understand."

"I think I do. He will not be freed by anything less than your marriage."

Olivia turned her head away. "I do not intend to marry."

Edmund watched her expression grow stormy. "Why do you hate the idea so?"

She bristled. "That is none of your business, Lord Edmund."

"No, of course it isn't. But I seem to have landed in the midst of your business. I could deal with the situation better if I understood more. Most women are eager to marry. You act as if it is a fate worse than death. Was your parents' marriage terrible? Have you always disliked the idea of marrying, and dared refuse it only after your father's death?"

"No, Lord Edmund. I just do not wish to put my fate in the hands of a man."

Edmund spoke softly, gently. "Your fiancé's rejection broke your heart. You still love him, don't you?"

Olivia shook her head. "No, I was well rid of him. His character has become better known to me in the intervening years."

He studied her face thoughtfully. "Perhaps you no longer trust yourself. Having chosen so badly once, you fear to trust your judgment again."

Olivia felt as if she had been taken into strong, capable arms for a comforting hug. Not only was Lord Edmund sincerely trying to understand her point of view, but he had succeeded in discovering what she had never been quite able to put into words. She could only nod, her eyes brimming with tears. Determined not to cry in front of him, she said, "If you'll excuse me, I have work to do." She withdrew to her office and busied herself with adding some columns of figures. It was all pretense, of course, for she sat there and fought against the tears that threatened to engulf her. Experience had taught her that once tears had begun, they were almost impossible to shut off. Odd how the understanding and tenderness Lord Edmund had just displayed loosened the spigot in a way that no amount of hurtful comments from her brother could do.

Edmund watched her for a few moments, then turned to survey the vista spread out before him. Beaumont Manor overlooked Norvale, the fertile valley he had surveyed from the road that morning. A variety of grain crops grew there, and along the banks of the small river that meandered through it, rich grass waved in the summer wind.

"Time and past to cut that grass," he muttered, understanding Miss Ormhill's anxiety to get on with the harvest. He remembered enough about farming from his childhood to know that grass must be cut while it was still green if it was to retain its nourishment when dried. And once cut, it must be dried in the fields before being stored, which meant the task must be completed before rainy weather brought on mildew. These pleasant late July days were haying time, and the farmer delayed at his—or in this case her—peril.

Edmund vowed silently to see that the tart-tongued but appealing Miss Olivia Ormhill succeeded in bringing in the harvest. *My life is in a muddle, and I have no idea how I may come about, but this at least I can do.*

That evening Jason seemed to have conquered his bad mood. After dinner he and Edmund had an excellent game of billiards over brandy and cigars. When Edmund had won the third game in a row, and was richer by the possession of Storm and his own waistcoat and riding breeches, Olivia stuck her head in the door. "Six of the clock comes early, gentlemen," she advised. "You might wish to turn in soon."

"Six of the . . . !" Jason stared at her, openmouthed. "You cannot be serious."

"Indeed!"

In spite of her advice to Jason and Lord Edmund, Olivia did not go directly to bed, but returned to her study to go over her accounts. *If I sold those three colts Jason wanted to keep, I could afford to offer higher wages to get back some of my workers.*

The thought of the howl her brother would set up over that made Olivia shudder. She stood, stretched her back, and walked to the French doors to stare out over the valley. The river blazed with orange fire, giving back the light of the newly risen full moon.

Harvest moon, she thought wryly. *If only we actually have a harvest!* Her glum mood lifted, though, as she took in the beauty of the scene. The rising moon was hidden by the side of the house. She opened the French doors and stepped quickly along the veranda, determined to drink in the magic of a full moon. As she rounded the corner she crashed into someone. "Unnh," she groaned as she staggered back. Momentary alarm had her struggling to flee even though she had not yet caught her balance. Strong arms caught her as she swayed dangerously near the edge of the porch.

"Miss Ormhill." Lord Edmund pulled her sharply toward him, dragging her against his chest and holding her there to steady her.

"Lord Edmund. You startled me!" She pushed against

him. "What do you mean, sneaking around my office like that?"

"I stepped out to admire the moon. As you did, I don't doubt. But I have found something even more magnificent to admire."

His eyes swept her face with wonder. "Tomorrow will decide my fate, Miss Ormhill. I will become your employee, or be on my way. One way or another, everything will change."

"You don't mention the third possibility," she said, tilting her head and looking up at this handsome man, fascinated against her will by what she saw in his eyes.

"That Jason will also manage to fill his wagon and get it to the barn? I think that as unlikely as you do." He grinned, and she felt her lips turning up in an answering smile.

She had apologized for her insults, soothing his raw pride. Now she stood smiling up at him in a beguiling way. Edmund felt again the attraction that had swept over him upon first catching sight of her.

"Will you grant me something I've wanted all the long years of soldiering, something I could obtain only in England?"

"What might that be, Lord Edmund?" she asked, lifting her eyebrows disingenuously, for she had a good idea what it was he wanted.

"To hold a lovely English miss in my arms and give her just . . . one . . ." He lowered his head slowly, giving her time to evade him if she wished. When she held still, he pressed his mouth to hers, breathing out the word *kiss* on a long sigh as he buried his lips in the soft pillows of her own.

For a long, enchanted moment Olivia let him press his lips to hers in a kiss so gentle and yet so fiery she felt longing spread throughout her body. It was he, in fact, who broke off the kiss. Their lips clung for a moment as he pulled away, and she lifted her hand to touch her mouth with wondering fingers.

"Magic," he proclaimed. "Everything I yearned for as I fought." He pulled her close once again, and bent for another kiss.

She pressed against his chest, though, stopping him. "You said one kiss," she reminded him. The pounding of her heart and the sweet yearning in her body told her she must deny him what she herself wanted far too much.

"But I didn't say I'd not ask for another."

"I, however, think one was entirely too many." She broke away, determination to resist him giving strength to her shove. "You think to take by seduction what you could not accomplish by wager. But I'll not wed you, so you may as well desist."

He drew back as if slapped. "So our bet is off?"

She hesitated a moment. "No, but as you said, that particular outcome is extremely unlikely." She turned her back on him and virtually raced through her study and upstairs to her room, where she forced herself to read a boring treatise on drainage until the urge to return to him for the second kiss was overcome by sleep.

Edmund remained a while, staring out over the countryside, struggling against bitterness over his situation. Never had he yearned so much for a woman, and never had he been less likely to win her over. It wasn't just his lack of fortune that put her out of his reach. He had forfeited hope of her respect last night when he had made that foolish wager.

When Edmund joined Jason at the breakfast table, he laughed at his host's reaction to his clothing. "I asked Morton to bring me some workmen's garments, rather than ruin my own clothes." He modeled the old leather breeches and smock shirt. "These will be more comfortable, too. You'd best do the same."

"Rot! I can't appear dressed like that among my own workers. I would look and feel a right fool. I will anyway, you know. Me, the squire, on a hay wain."

Edmund grinned. "You'll get a nice view of the countryside from up there."

"Yes, and that's another thing. Been thinking about that. Why do they stack the hay so high? Just bound to tumble off, isn't it?" Jason looked a little uneasy.

"Your sister explained yesterday. Unless you have a fleet

of wagons and battalions of workers, it would take too long to carry the hay to the barn if the wagons were not loaded to the skies."

"Well, it seems to me it would be better to make a number of trips than to risk dumping a load of hay on the way."

"And she also explained that a good worker can load a wagon in such a way that that doesn't happen." He studied Jason's expression. "What is it, lad? Don't like heights?" Edmund challenged as he loaded his plate with ham slices and coddled eggs.

"Don't call me lad! And I'm not afraid of anything," Jason snapped.

"Nonsense. Everyone's afraid of something. The bravest man I ever saw in battle was terrified of mice. Jumped up on a chair like a girl whenever one came near."

"Like a girl?" Olivia Ormhill swept into the room, her voice chiding. "I never mind mice, nor snakes, nor bugs. Not all females are so hen-hearted, my lord."

"I daresay they are not." Edmund looked at her appreciatively. Miss Ormhill looked a treat in a green riding habit and a gleaming white habit shirt. She carried the train looped over her wrist with an ease that was obviously second nature to her as she stepped briskly up to the buffet. She filled her plate, then sat next to her brother.

"Well, at any rate, I'm not afraid of heights." Jason returned to his original topic. "I'm afraid of not being able to keep the hay on that wagon. I want to win this bet!"

Olivia grinned wickedly. "You have good reason, brother! Yesterday my newly recruited crew dumped their loads as they climbed the hill to the barn. If it had not been so inconvenient it would have been quite amusing."

Jason did not find this information humorous. But before he could voice his feelings, Edmund interrupted him.

"Where are we going to be working? I did not see any cut fields yesterday."

"On my farm, near the river. When it begins raining, that area will become damp, possibly even flood, so we must get the hay made there first. 'Tis a half hour's ride, no more. We have a lovely day, so we'd best finish our breakfast and be off. Forgive the truism, but we must make hay while the sun shines." She then focused single-mindedly on demolishing the hearty plateful of food in front of her.

When the elder Miss Ormhill entered the room a few minutes later, she looked puffy-eyed and out of sorts. "I don't see why you could not have held this event later in the day," she groused as she took a cup of coffee and a plate of buttered toast from the servant.

"Oh, Aunt, you had no need to get up for this." Olivia stopped eating to look pityingly at Lavinia. "I know how you hate to be up before ten of the clock."

"As if I would not be there to observe what very well could determine the fates of my niece and my nephew." Aunt Lavinia nibbled uneasily at the toast before pushing it away.

Both the Ormhill siblings stiffened at this reminder of the importance of the wager. Jason scowled at his plate; Olivia gnawed at her lower lip.

Edmund made himself look away. He had realized last night how hopeless his situation was. So why was he thinking only of again kissing that full lower lip, of gently nipping with his own teeth where Olivia's white eyetooth indented her pink flesh?

Chapter Six

By the time they left their breakfast, the sun was up and the day already promised to be warm. Edmund mounted Storm and rode alongside Jason and Olivia. They were followed by a gig driven by Lavinia Ormhill, and a farm wagon loaded with provender for the midday meal. When they reached the field where they were to work, Edmund stood in the stirrups and looked around, wondering how extensive Miss Ormhill's holdings were. No fences showed where Jason's lands ended and Olivia's began.

As if in answer to his thoughts, Jason pointed to a large stone marker. "From here to the woods at the head of the valley," he said, sweeping his arm in a wide arc, "is Olivia's property. That is her manor house, Wren Hall. It has a fine view of Norvale." He leaned toward Edmund and whispered hoarsely, "The hall and grounds are rented to some friends of ours, but, coincidentally, they are vacating at Michaelmas. You newlyweds can live at Melmont till then; I plan to be on my way to France as soon as your vows are said." He winked at Edmund, for Olivia had heard every word and was glaring at him.

She wagged her finger at him. "I'm not ready to cancel my search for new tenants just yet." She urged her horse toward the knot of workers ahead.

He was amazed at the small number of people awaiting them, rakes and pitchforks at the ready. *She really* is *hard up for workers! She never will get all of these fine meadows cut and stored if this is all she has to help her.*

Two hay wains stood empty, and a murmur of surprise swept through the workers as they watched the young squire and his friend climb into them. But when Olivia told them to begin loading the wagons, they fell to with a will, and soon a veritable blizzard of fragrant dried meadow grass flew at the men in the wagons.

Edmund had reviewed over and over in his mind the few times he had actually assisted in loading a hay wain. It began that magic summer of his thirteenth year, when his father gave up trying to make a scholar of him and turned him loose with the admonition to learn how to do every task on the farm, however unpleasant. Bartlett, the manager of the home farm, had grinned mischievously when told what Edmund's plans were. "I'll take him in hand, m'lord. I don't doubt he'll be a-wishin' to be back at his books before the summer ends."

But Edmund hadn't. He took mucking out stalls philosophically, thinking that even that was better than struggling to decline Latin verbs. He learned how to curry, comb, saddle, hitch up, and doctor horses, and then moved on to fieldwork just as the haymaking began. He had sweated gleefully while wielding a scythe, earning the grudging respect of the farm workers. Then he had stood side by side with doughty old Chester Crabton, an aptly named man in his seventies who seldom had a good word for anyone, but who yielded to none in his ability to load a hay wain so high he had to lie flat as it passed under the huge barn doors to be unloaded.

He remembered thinking that in a way the loading resembled weaving, with swathes of hay lain crosswise of one another in a spiral around the wagon, narrowing ever so little with each layer. Now he followed this long-ago learned pattern, sweat pouring from him as he labored to keep up with Miss Ormhill's workers while stacking the hay so that it would hang together once it rose past the high sides of the wagon. He had little chance to observe Jason's struggles, but could not forbear to grin as he heard the youth crowing, "Nothing to it," when they began.

He'll sing another tune once the mound rises high, Edmund thought. Sure enough, after they had been at it for almost an hour, he heard Jason's voice, loud and furious, using extremely impolite language. He paused in his task long enough to watch as the boy followed a sliding avalanche of hay over the side of the wagon. What was left of the pile unceremoniously followed, covering him entirely.

The workers laughed as they dug him out, spluttering with frustration. "Leave me be," he growled, shaking them and a quantity of hay off and stalking up to his sister. "You think you've beaten me, don't you? Well, I'm not done yet!"

Edmund nodded in approbation of the lad's determination before returning to his task. He tested the load with his feet to see if there was any tendency to move in one particular direction. If so, he knew he had to alter the pattern of the next layer to knit the growing tower of hay more firmly together.

At last he stood atop a veritable mountain of hay, too high to receive any more from the workers so far below. He put his rake carefully in the center and used it to brace himself as he tested the load all around. Then he looked around to see how Jason was doing. His stack was only half as high, and leaning to one side, for which reason Jason was desperately adding new bundles of hay to the other side. Edmund had mixed emotions as he watched the youth struggle to balance the load.

It will never make it to the barn, particularly as it must go up an incline to do so, he concluded. That thought should have given him pleasure, for it meant he could learn about agricultural management from Miss Ormhill, and would have a roof over his head for a year.

This practical point of view did not keep him from regretting, when he looked at the lovely Miss Olivia Ormhill, that she would not be his bride. So he reminded himself of her tart tongue and low opinion of him.

He looked around, and found that she had ridden near and was looking up at him. "You still have to get it into the barn, you know," she said, her eyes flashing a challenge.

"True enough! Lead on," he commanded the boy who had been entrusted with keeping the pair of oxen from wandering, not that they had any interest in doing so, with all of the sweet fresh hay they could ever desire right beneath their noses.

"No, not yet," Olivia said, stopping the boy with a gesture. "I want to wait until Jason's wagon is ready to move, too." She didn't want any of the workers coaching him while she followed Edmund up the hill.

Edmund leaned on his rake and watched as Jason stacked the hay higher and higher. Perhaps the boy had caught on. He glanced down to see Olivia looking up at him, a frown on her face, and her lip caught by one eyetooth again. He smiled slowly, and gave her an elaborate bow.

Olivia had watched with growing dismay as Lord Edmund caught the hay her workers threw up to him, his movements ever more dextrous as he built up the load. She hadn't the slightest idea how the hay was made to stay in place, but it became painfully clear that Lord Edmund did. How could she fulfill her part of the bargain? She feared she would never be able to be in his presence, working with him every day, without yielding to her attraction to him. And she *was* attracted to him. She had been even before that delightful kiss last night. However she might disdain him for the cardsharp and fortune hunter he had shown himself to be, the heat still rose in her cheeks and elsewhere in her body whenever she looked at him.

Watching his long, lean frame as he caught, laid, and teased the hay into place was torture. Sweat had long since plastered the workman's tunic to his broad chest and muscled thighs. He had become a piece of moving sculpture, with a body to put those pagan statues of Lord Elgin's to shame.

As she noted Jason's improved performance with his haystack, she found herself half yearning for him to succeed, that she might be wedded and bedded by the so-tempting Lord Edmund. She gnawed at her lower lip and looked up to encounter the subject of her fantasy looking down at her, heat in his brown eyes.

The effrontery of the man! Looking at her as if he were undressing her! Olivia touched her heel to her horse and rode toward Aunt Lavinia, who sat upright in the gig beneath a wide umbrella, avidly following events.

Lavinia studied her niece's expression carefully. "Will they win, do you think?"

"I pray not." Olivia compressed her lips tightly.

"He is very handsome, is he not? And very well set up."

Very well set up. You might say so! Olivia blushed and turned to study the vast acres of uncut hay beyond the little tableau. Only two workers were scything, all she could spare this morning. Somehow she must get it all cut, dried, and into the barn or made up into haycocks before the halcyon weather changed.

"Livvy, dear?" Her aunt interrupted her worried thoughts. "Do you mean to keep your bargain? For I do believe Lord Edmund would be a very good influence on Jason."

"A good influence? The man is a gamester. Do you forget that if he had faced any other young man the other night, he would likely have taken every dime his victim had to wager? He is a penniless n'eer-do-well, a fortune hunter, a . . ." Olivia spluttered, her indignation outrunning the charges she had to lay against Lord Edmund.

"I think you are being unfair. Look, Jason has managed to load his wagon. Will you keep your bargain, dear?"

Olivia turned back, grimly noting the truth of her aunt's observation. Jason's load sat slightly off center, but it rose fully as high as Lord Edmund's. "Yes, I will, if they win, which I by no means concede. After all, they must yet take their loads up Partridge Hill. Doubtless they will both spill out there, as the others did yesterday."

As they headed for the barn, Olivia rode behind them, followed by Lavinia in the gig. Behind them trooped the workers and an assortment of children, all laughing and talking loudly. They knew there was a wager being played out, though they had no way of knowing what the stakes were. Some of the men made their own bets on the outcome, to Olivia's vexation. *My brother and Lord Edmund have set a very bad example today,* she thought, then remembered with a guilty twinge her own role in the affair.

The road to Partridge Hill rose slowly but steadily from the flat meadowland near the Sparrow River to the relatively high ground of a small bluff midway up the side of the valley. Her father had placed storage and cattle barns here, safe from the occasional flood.

Thinking of her father, she forgot to watch closely what was happening in front of her. A shout, quickly followed by a deluge of hay, caused her horse to shy and then stumble. She managed to pull it up just as her brother tumbled from his perch. He began cursing most colorfully until his diatribe was drowned out by most of the remaining load on his hay wain. He quickly disappeared from sight under the golden cascade.

At Jason's shout, Edmund turned his head just in time to see the younger man's hay separate along the fault line created when he had tried to balance his off-center load. He watched the boy slide from sight. *So much for marrying Olivia,* he thought, then consoled himself: *That rose has thorns.*

He called down to one of the gamboling boys beside the wagon, to see if Jason was okay.

"He be well enou' to say more'n what he ought," the lad responded. And indeed, Edmund could hear Jason's swearing quite clearly, and frowned at the notion of the same sounds reaching the ears of the women and children. Before he could move to put a stop to this unseemly display, though, Jason's voice fell silent.

Seeing that Jason had survived his fall, Edmund decided to continue on to the barn, mindful that his own load was very much the product of an amateur, and might follow the same path as Jason's if he continued to defy the laws of gravity by stopping on an incline.

It wasn't far to the barn, and Edmund halted just at the door, as he stood to have his head knocked if he tried to enter atop the hay. He slid down, and the young boy who had charge of the team took the wagon inside.

Not pausing to brush himself off, Edmund hastened back down the hill to see whether Jason was injured or just angry. As he moved around the second hay wain, he saw several people, including Olivia Ormhill, frantically pawing through a large mound of hay. Abruptly Jason's head popped up, quickly followed by the rest of him, looking more like a straw man than a young squire. He wiped his hand over his face, struggled to his feet, and grasped Olivia by the shoulders.

Edmund started to move faster, fearing the young man's anger would cause him to harm his sister. Jason shook Olivia and said something to her that Edmund couldn't hear, and suddenly they were both laughing. Then Jason stooped and picked up an armload of hay, throwing it at her. Soon Olivia was only slightly less covered with hay than Jason, and the sight of them made Edmund laugh, too, in amusement as well as relief.

Joining elbows, brother and sister turned toward him. "Well, my lord, it seems as if you have won your share of the bet," Jason said, catching Olivia closer to his side. "My sister will make you an excellent teacher. Do you see that you are an excellent pupil." He winked at Edmund on the side away from Olivia's view. Edmund smiled and took the proffered hand.

"That I will," he promised, looking at Olivia to see how she felt about the turn of events. She was still smiling as she nodded her acceptance. Mischief kindled in her expressive eyes.

"I collect you are vastly relieved to have won your way free of any obligation to marry me, Lord Edmund." She looked down at her hay-covered costume. "I must seem even less of a bargain just now!"

He grinned. "No, indeed, Miss Ormhill. Hay becomes you. I find myself snatching defeat from victory when I look upon such a fetching sight and realize you might have been mine!"

"Fustian." She smiled slyly at her brother. "It seems to me that Lord Edmund is not dressed appropriately for the occasion, do you not agree?"

Jason squinted at Edmund. "Indeed! But we can rectify the situation. Shall we?"

As of one mind, they scooped up armsful of the hay and

threw them at him. The golden shower briefly obscured his view. When he could see again, he returned the favor.

Abruptly Olivia stopped, merriment fading from her face. Edmund followed her gaze and saw an elegantly turned-out rider approaching down the country lane on a handsome roan gelding.

"Oh, no," he heard Lavinia mutter. She rushed up to her niece and began brushing hay from her clothing.

"Jason, Olivia, what can be the meaning of this?"

"Lord Corbright." Olivia drew herself up, combing at her hopelessly hay-bedecked hair with shaking fingers.

"Frank, you've arrived just too late to see the result of a famous wager," Jason crowed. "Come, join us for lunch and we'll tell you all about it."

Edmund was surprised at the cordiality in Jason's voice toward the man who had jilted his sister. He was even more surprised to realize who the man was.

Corbright surveyed the trio with an ambiguous smile playing across his lips. "Throwing yourself into the role of farmer again, Olivia? You look most charming in the part."

Olivia pasted a smile on her face. "Thank you, my lord. Gallant as usual. May I make known to you Lord Edmund Debham?"

Lord Corbright had barely glanced at him before, doubtless taking him for one of the estate workers. Now he stared at Edmund insolently and for an unconscionably long time before acknowledging the introduction. Edmund returned his perusal calmly. He knew this overdressed gentleman, though he had not been Lord Corbright at the time of their acquaintance. *So this is Olivia's former fiancé,* he thought. *A nasty piece of work!* A crony of his brother, Franklin Melwin had long since shown his true colors to Edmund. *Little does she know how fortunate she has been to escape marriage to him.*

"Well, Eddy," Corbright drawled at last. "I see you have finally achieved your life's ambition—to labor in the fields." He shook his head. "I suppose you have found your level—what must cannon fodder do, once the cannon fall silent?"

"Now see here," Jason spluttered. "Lord Edmund is our guest, and I won't have you—"

"Jason and Lord Edmund have just been having a bit of fun, Lord Corbright." Olivia's voice shook as she spoke, and Edmund suspected she feared an altercation.

"Did you ever notice, Jason, how easy it is for those who have never faced cannon to look down on those who have?" Edmund sneered at Corbright. If there was to be a quarrel, he would draw Corbright's fire. He did not fear the man.

"That's right," Jason snapped. "And Lord Edmund's bravery in battle deserves your respect."

Corbright flicked at an invisible speck on his coat sleeve. "Oh, do not fly up in the boughs, either of you. I referred to something Lord Edmund's brother said of him. That, of course, was before he distinguished himself as a spiker of cannon rather than as fodder for same. No offense was meant, Lord Edmund."

"Then none is taken," Edmund said, shrugging. He turned to Olivia. "Did I hear a rumor of luncheon? Haying makes one quite peckish."

"Indeed, yes." Lavinia Ormhill, standing between her niece and nephew, linked her arms with theirs and tugged at them. "All is in readiness. The trestles are set up in the shade of the barn, and I daresay our avid audience is peckish, too."

At this, they all became aware of the interested observers standing all around them: the house servants who had set up the luncheon, the farmworkers, their children, their wives, and even a pair of mongrels, though the latter were doubtless more interested in the food than the fodder for the gossip mill that they saw unfolding before them.

"I do not expect that Lord Corbright will wish to partake of so unsophisticated a meal," Olivia said, and her expression made it clear she hoped he would concur.

"On the contrary, with such a fetchingly attired maiden as my hostess, how could I pass up a bucolic feast?" Corbright swung himself down from his horse.

Lavinia directed the seating at the picnic table with Olivia Ormhill at one end as hostess, and Lord Corbright at the other as the most distinguished guest. Jason sat at Corbright's right hand; Lavinia took Olivia's right, and directed Edmund to her left.

The house servants she arrayed on one side of the table, the field-workers on the other. This odd caricature of a formal dining table might have amused Edmund at another time, but he could see that Olivia took no pleasure in looking down its length at her former fiancé. Her laughing, lighthearted manner, so briefly but delightfully displayed while exchanging barrages of hay, had been replaced by a stiffness that thrummed with some deep emotion. Edmund could not tell if it was fear or anger, sorrow or desire, that underlay her frozen manner. *Perhaps all four*, he mused. Though far from an expert, he had sufficient experience of females to know that they could be quite complicated creatures.

If he had not known Corbright for the cad he was, he might have wondered at the man for lingering where he so obviously was not wanted. Certainly he wondered at Olivia's brother, for he positively fawned on the man. It confused him to find the boy so lacking in spirit as to make a bosom beau of the man who had supposedly broken his sister's heart. That Corbright would flirt with her though he was now married, Edmund didn't wonder at. That Lavinia and Jason seemed to be delighted by such behavior confused him thoroughly.

Chapter Seven

Olivia looked around the table at the pastoral scene. It would be a fit subject for Constable's brush, she thought: the rosy-cheeked country folk with their tankards of ale, laughing and joking among themselves; the handsome, well-dressed lord of the manor at one end of the table, chuckling with one of his workers, his wife at the other, presiding over a harvest feast.

Only the man at the end of the table was not the lord of this manor, nor the woman his wife. *Nor ever shall be,* she reaffirmed to herself. She tried to catch Jason's eyes, but he seemed determined not to look her way. *I pray he does not explain all about that wager.* It would make her look pitiable in Franklin's eyes.

She glanced at Lord Edmund. *He looks as confused as I feel,* she thought. For her former fiancé to visit her, tease her, and join in their midday meal must seem very strange. Corbright's recent behavior seemed strange to her, too, though no stranger than his sudden ending of their engagement and immediate marriage to a wealthy tradesman's daughter. He had paraded Jane about, exclaiming upon her womanly submissiveness and her very proper willingness to let her husband manage her substantial fortune. After her death in childbirth, Corbright had attempted to renew his relationship with Olivia, but his recent actions had put paid to any hopes he had voiced for a rekindling of their romance.

During Jane's life he had pursued a policy of harassment of Olivia that she had been at great lengths to hide from her volatile, heedless brother, who had long since accepted Franklin's explanation of why he had broken off the engagement, and thought him the best of fellows. He had smiled approvingly at Corbright's recent attempts to renew his attentions to Olivia, as had her Aunt Lavinia.

He would have a hard time believing Corbright's recent behavior, she thought, *but once convinced, he would leap to my defense in a way that might be fatal to him.*

She shuddered at the thought. Jason's accuracy when aiming a shotgun at pheasant or ducks was much admired in the neighborhood, but he had no great expertise with pistols. As for his swordsmanship, he had little training and, she suspected, a style distinguished more by vigor and aggression than skill. Corbright, on the other hand, was widely acknowledged as an accomplished marksman and swordsman. Moreover, she feared he would delight in doing something that would grieve her.

A loud ripple of laughter brought her attention back to the present. The company was becoming entirely too jolly, and she realized they had lingered too long at the meal, drinking the ale that workmen insisted was necessary to their doing a good day's work, but which she suspected only slowed them down. She had long since learned not to attempt to wean the English farm laborer from his ale, so she provided it, but she knew better than to offer unlimited helpings. She stood, signifying that the meal was over.

Lord Corbright stood, too, rapping his tankard on the table for attention. "Before we go, I'd like to propose a toast. To the fairest, best-loved lady farmer in all of England." He saluted Livvy with the mug, then raised it to his lips. The sentiment was applauded, and the toast drunk. The servants and workers exchanged significant glances and sly nudges. Livvy felt her cheeks heat, and looked away, only to meet Lord Edmund's wondering eyes. What must he think? The very idea of such a toast in public, and to his former fiancée at that!

As the workmen and women walked away, talking and laughing, and the house servants began clearing the table,

Lavinia bustled up to Livvy. "Well, did you hear that? Very promising, I'd call it."

"Would you?" Livvy snapped. "Promising of what? My descent into infamy?"

"Of course not, dearest. It is clear that he has accepted you for what you are at last, and is going to court you again."

Livvy shook her head emphatically. "That's not it, nor would I find it cause for celebration if it were. He is making mischief again, drat the man."

Edmund had watched and listened throughout the meal, trying to sort out and understand the relationships among these people. Thoroughly confused and frustrated, he blurted out, "I think it very odd that a married man would court your niece, Miss Ormhill, and even odder that you would applaud it."

"Mercy upon us, Lord Edmund. Lord Corbright is not married. He is a widower. His poor little wife perished in childbirth over a year ago."

"Ah." He looked at Livvy, whose eyes met his unflinchingly. "That explains his behavior." What, he wondered, explained Olivia Ormhill's red cheeks and sparkling eyes? Any number of emotions could account for them, from anger to embarrassment to pleasurable excitement.

Her answer shed little light on her feelings, but made it clear she did not wish to discuss the matter further. "I do not take it to be anything but a hum. Now if you will excuse me, Lord Edmund, I must organize the workers. The hay must be put into the barn and as many more loads as possible brought in yet this day. And someone must begin cutting another meadow or we shall be at a standstill in a day or two."

"Shall I help with the unloading, load another wagon, or take up a scythe?"

Jason joined them just then, along with Corbright. "None of that," he said, laughing gaily. "Frank has invited us to look over the two stallions he recently purchased."

"Alas, we cannot avail ourselves of Lord Corbright's gracious offer, Jason." Edmond threw his arm around the boy in a companionable gesture. "We are pledged to your sister. Have you forgotten our wager?"

"You surely do not intend to hold your brother to this foolish bet, Livvy." Corbright moved in front of her, standing too close, his position such as to suggest an intimacy that she found all the more uncomfortable because it had once been so very much what she wished for. "You cannot mean to make a farmhand of the boy."

She wondered exactly what Jason had told him. If he had given away the part about trying to marry her to Lord Edmund, she would wring his neck. "I've no intention of doing so, *Lord* Corbright." She stressed his title and moved backward, firmly rejecting what his posture and use of her pet name implied.

Corbright pivoted toward her brother. "No? That is not what it seems." He plucked a bit of hay from Jason's hair. "Next I expect to see him wielding a scythe."

"I say! The very thing! Much more fun than stacking hay." Jason brushed at his clothing and grimaced humorously.

"No, brother. We'll leave the mowing to men accustomed to the scythe. You and Lord Edmund agreed to apprentice yourselves to me as estate managers, not fieldhands. You *should* have a look at Lord Corbright's horses. After all, the stud is an important part of your estate."

Jason took this notion up instantly. "Just so. Come along, Lord Edmund."

Edmund shook his head. "You seem to forget we have neither horse nor carriage at our disposal, and your sister has something of a mess on her hands."

"The workers will pick that up," Jason declared, waving this objection away. "And we can return to the manor with Aunt Lavinia, for I certainly shan't wear these clothes anywhere!"

"You go on, then," Edmund declared. "I intend to remain here. Miss Ormhill needs help getting her hay in, and I intend to do just that." He deliberately made his tone disdainful.

Jason's chin came up. "I'll stay too, then. You can explain to me how to keep it on the wagon this time."

Corbright's glance shifted from Olivia to Edmund and back again. His lips tightened, though his words were cordial. "As you wish. But you doubtless are a prime judge of horseflesh, Edmund. I would like you to take a look at a filly I think to purchase. Godolphin's line, and looks to be fast."

Edmund was tempted; there was no gainsaying that. He had a weakness for fine horses, and knew himself to be an excellent judge. But he also knew Corbright. He had been the victim of some cruel pranks into which he had been drawn, a naive boy seeking the company of his much admired older brother, by the cozening ways of Franklin Melwin. He had no wish to spend time with the man.

"I am no child to be tricked into a leaky boat now, Frank," he growled. "Nor is young Jason such a fribble as to leave his sister in the lurch when she is short of workers and has an abundant harvest of hay to bring in."

Corbright's smile twisted a little, resembling a sneer as he looked at Olivia. "You do appear to be a little shorthanded, my dear. Tch. You should realize that the haying won't wait on your whims. Your fields should be full of workers now, as mine are."

Olivia could bear it no longer. "Your fields are full of *my* workers, Lord Corbright. Hired from me at double wages, poor ignorant creatures."

"Ignorant? I think not." Corbright laughed patronizingly. "What man in his right mind wouldn't take double wages? I need their labor; they need the money. Business, my love. If you understood these things so ill, you should never have set yourself up as an estate manager."

"How dare you!" Olivia felt her cheeks flushing. Aunt Lavinia's hand was on her sleeve, urging temperance. She lowered her voice. "Do not dare to call me your love, or I shall slap your faithless face."

"Mmmmm. The lady doth protest too much." Corbright flicked her cheek briefly with his right hand. Several of the workers tittered, reminding them all once again that they had an audience.

Olivia turned toward the sound. "Get to work, all of you. Lunch is over, and we have much to do."

Corbright turned to the knot of men nearby. "Come and work for me, if you do not like being ordered about by a woman. As Miss Ormhill said, I am paying double wages this year, and—"

"See here," Jason protested.

"And who is to carry your families through the winter if you work for him?" Olivia snapped. "I have always made bread available to my workers' families throughout the winter. But I shan't be able to do so this year if my crops ruin in the field."

"The county will give us bread, Miss Ormhill," one bold young man called out.

"You men can get bread from the outdoor relief, true enough. But do not forget, as my other workers have, that your ration will feed only you, not your family."

Several of the women began to murmur and move among the men. Clearly they found this argument persuasive, even if all of the men did not. The group of workers drifted toward the pile of hay and the wagons.

Corbright snorted. "Sentimental twaddle. Such patriarchal solicitude has no place in the modern world. Jason, instead of being schooled by your sister, why do you not school her to return to her needlework? You'll be a poor man at this rate."

But Jason, feckless, heedless Jason, stood silent, fists clenched. Edmund could see that the scales had fallen from his eyes. "You tried to hire our workers right from under us. And here I thought you were hoping to regain Olivia's affection."

"That were a forlorn hope indeed," Olivia said. "Come, dear. Lord Corbright has much work to do, and so do we." She attempted to turn Jason from the confrontation.

"Your sister has no affections to engage," Corbright retorted, his face almost purple with anger. "She's turning into a harpy, an ape leader, but that doesn't mean you have to let her bankrupt you. Come, Jason, be a man. Stand up to her."

Edmund wanted to put his fist through Corbright's

scheming face, but saw no way to intervene without extinguishing Jason's suddenly kindled manhood. He stepped a bit closer, though, and knew by the tightening of Corbright's jaw muscle that his support of Jason had been noted.

"My sister is not a harpy," Jason responded. "You think to turn me against her. If you are paying double wages, you have been conspiring to destroy her, and me as well. How could I have been so blind? You have outworn your welcome, sir. I am sure my sister will join me in desiring you, in the future, to approach your estate by the public road instead of across our property."

"You are a fool, boy! She'll squander your inheritance, and then where will you be?" Corbright clapped his expensive beaver derby on his head. "Under the cat's-paw and not even married."

Jason started for him; Edmund caught at his elbow, stopping him before he had well begun the charge.

"And you are *de trop,* Franklin. I know a gentleman of your impeccable lineage would not wish to linger where he is not wanted."

Twin gasps from the Ormhill women followed Edmund's words, for they knew just how provocative they must be to the grandson of a gunsmith and son of a munitions manufacturer, whose late father had been so recently made a baron the ink had scarcely dried upon the parchment. Corbright started toward him, then checked his stride. Edmund held those pale blue eyes with his own until Corbright looked away.

"I don't need you to fight my battles," Jason sputtered, striking at Edmund's hand where it gripped his elbow.

But Corbright turned on his heel. Without another word he mounted his horse and rode away. And Edmund noted his direction with great satisfaction. "He's taking the road, Jason. You did well."

"I'd have done a great deal better to give him a facer. I'll thank you not to play nursemaid." Jason's fists were clenched. Clearly he would like to take on Edmund now that Corbright was out of reach. "Put your hand on me again, if you dare!"

"Not now. Your sister has enough on her plate."

Jason looked at Olivia's pale, drawn features. "Now, Livvy. Don't fret," he said, catching her up in a hug. "Why didn't you tell me what that mushroom was up to?"

"I . . ." Olivia leaned against him, straining to hold back tears. "I didn't want to worry you."

"War," Lavinia intoned. "Not flirting, not trying to rekindle your affections. War. I feel quite as bad as Jason, encouraging him as I did."

Edmund felt admiration at the way the family drew together. He also felt envy, and a deep sense of loneliness. He turned away, for he had a hay wain to unload.

Chapter Eight

Jason surprised Edmund by working hard alongside him the rest of that long summer day. He listened carefully to instructions on loading the hay wain, and as the workers tossed hay up to him, he became increasingly efficient at catching and placing it. He received a rousing cheer from workers and family alike when his second wagon made it to the barn without mishap. If it was not stacked quite as high as Edmund's, no one cared. The young squire basked in the praise. By the time the sun set, all of the hay that had been previously cut and dried in the fields was securely stacked in the hay barn and a good start made on cutting the next meadow.

At dinner, Edmund apologized for appearing at the table in riding clothes, the same he had worn the night before.

"I expect your trunks have gone to your brother's, Lord Edmund?" Lavinia asked.

"They are in London awaiting my directions," he replied. "I had thought to send the bulk of my possessions on to whatever estate was assigned to me for training." *They would wait there a long time,* he mused bitterly, *for such a destination.* "I will send for them tomorrow."

They would barely outrun the bills for the tradesmen who had made them, he knew. He had bespoken a small but adequate wardrobe for a country gentleman before departing London, not realizing that every bit of cash he had would be needed to pay the last of his mother's debts. *How will I pay for them?* he wondered.

A quiet in the room brought Edmund's attention back to the Ormhills. "I am sorry, my mind wandered momentarily," he apologized.

"You are both dead on your feet, I daresay." Olivia stood. "Shall we make an early night of it?"

Jason grumbled that he had no wish for bed at ten of the clock, and invited Edmund to go to the Black Lion with him for a pint.

"I will, and gladly," Edmund replied, standing. "I just want a brief word with your sister first."

Jason agreed to this with transparent eagerness, and Lavinia showed no inclination to play chaperon. "I, for one, am quite exhausted. I shall turn in now." She hastened out of the room behind her nephew.

Edmund bit back a smile at their tactics. Having given up on Corbright, they once again began to pin their hopes on him. He darted a quick glance to see what Olivia thought of the matter. To his relief, her eyes sparkled with humor. "I shall follow shortly, Aunt," she said to Lavinia's rapidly retreating back, then sat down again. She even patted the seat beside her on the sofa, indicating that Edmund should join her there.

This looks promising. Edmund sat beside her, pleased but a little unsure how to proceed. "Miss Ormhill, I—"

"Will you call me Olivia?" she asked.

Better and better. "If you will call me Edmund."

"I will. Before you state whatever it was you wished to speak to me about, please let me thank you from the bottom of my heart."

Her words and the fervor with which she spoke them took Edmund by surprise. "Thank me?"

"I am persuaded you prevented a fight between Jason and Corbright today."

Did I? Edmund decided he could take credit, which he certainly needed with the beauty who sat so close beside him. "I couldn't permit him to goad the boy into a duel."

"It is what I have feared would happen once Jason realized what that beast was doing to us. He has such a quick temper, and I am not sure just how far Corbright is willing to take this quarrel. At any rate, I appreciate your support. Now, what was it you wanted to say to me?"

"Ah, I fear I am out of turn, and telling you nothing you do not already know, but . . ."

"Yes?" Chin up, she reminded him of a boxer squaring off for the beginning of a bout.

"You cannot bring in yours and Jason's hay in time with the crew you had today."

"I know that very well. I can do only what is possible."

"Perhaps . . ." Edmund did not like to offend her, nor did he blame her for being impatient toward one so clearly inferior to her in knowledge of farming in general and her own land and surroundings in particular.

She raised skeptical eyebrows.

"I passed High Wycombe a half day from here. It is a market town. Surely you could hire some workers there."

"One would think so." Olivia's mouth twisted into a wry smile. "I went there yesterday."

"And?"

"The few who had not yet been hired by others had no wish to be hired by a lady farmer. I have largely overcome that sort of thing here in the valley, but where I am not known . . ."

"Yes. I can imagine seeing a lovely young lady such as yourself in the guise of an overseer is somewhat unnerving to the uninitiated." Edmund smiled, trying to imagine the rough country types he had seen standing in the square hoping to be hired, being approached by Miss Olivia Ormhill in a pretty muslin dress and a fetching bonnet.

"Well, railing against the stupidity of the male of the species will not solve my problem."

"Do not spare my feelings, Miss Ormhill. Speak your mind to this stupid male by all means."

"I do beg your pardon. I am all too likely to do so, as you may have perhaps observed." She seemed genuinely contrite, so Edmund smiled.

"How can I fail to forgive so charming a traducer?"

She bridled at the gallantry. "Do you have any other suggestions, Lord Edmund? If not, I feel our conversation is at an end."

Prickly female! Edmund frowned. "Perhaps if Jason or I—"

"Yes." Olivia clearly had anticipated this suggestion. "I will ask him tomorrow. He will do it, of course. Until today I could not have been sure of interesting him in the problem. I have you to thank for that."

Edmund's innate honesty would not allow him to take this much credit. "I think not. You kept your difficulties from him because of your fears about Corbright's intentions. And you are still afraid."

"After today, my fears have intensified. Would he, could he, be so evil as to force a duel on my brother, just to get back at me?"

Edmund reached for the tensely clasped hands and gently unwound them. Taking them firmly between his own, he said, "I don't know, but he will have to deal with me first if he tries."

Olivia looked from her hands, swallowed by his larger ones, to his face bending near hers. She felt herself leaning toward him. So warm, those hands, so strong. So competent-seeming, the man who sat near her. It tempted her beyond reason to put her affairs into those hands.

"Oh!" She jerked away and jumped up. "Do not!"

Edmund stood, too. "Do not what?"

"Make love to me. Use any trick you can to draw me to you. And my brother and aunt will help you in any way they can, the traitors! It won't work, though! You may as well be on your way. As I said last night, I'll not wed any man, especially one whose interest is in my land and fortune only."

At first her words angered him. But as he glared at her, her lower lip trembled, and he could see the vulnerability, the hurt in her eyes. He reached out to grasp her hands once more.

"Olivia, I find you a devilishly attractive woman. A prickly sort, to be sure, but understandably so. If I could convince you to wed me, I would, and gladly. But not by seduction. Nor by trick, nor force. It is not my way."

"Huh! So high-principled. Yesterday morning you would have wed my aunt without a murmur, thinking her the one with the property." Olivia tried to tug her hands away. Unsuccessful in escaping his grasp, she tossed up her head defiantly.

He flashed a wicked grin. "I would have, to honor my wager. But not half so eagerly as I would have wed you. But that is behind us. I am released from my wager, and have won from you the right to learn to manage a large estate. I can't do that if the estate is ruined by Corbright, now, can I?" He let her go. "So I intend to assist you in any way I can."

Olivia looked into eyes that seemed sincere. Of course, she had seen such a look in other eyes. Lying eyes. Still, in the battle against Corbright she needed allies, and however false he might be about his interest in her, Lord Edmund seemed very sincere about his desire for agricultural experience.

"Very well," she said, stepping a little farther away, because she wanted far too much to step forward into the circle of his arms. "I appreciate that. You shall accompany him to High Wycombe tomorrow, to hire additional workers."

Edmund formally bowed to her and bade her good evening, then left the room to join Jason, whom he expected to be waiting impatiently at the front entrance with their saddled horses. As he approached the front door, he found it open and the stairs and carriageway crowded with people, all seemingly talking at once. Buckman, the butler, stood in the door arguing with a rough country fellow who was demanding entry. Beyond him, by flickering torchlight, Jason could be seen standing in the midst of the crowd, trying to shout them down.

Edmund paused to survey the scene, trying to make sense of it. "What is going on, Mr. Buckman?" he demanded.

"I do not know, sir, but their sort must go to the tradesmen's entrance, and so I have told this brute, but he won't listen."

Edmund thrust past the struggling butler and grasped his

opponent by the neck of his shirt. "What do you mean by this, my man?" he yelled.

"I mean to see Miss Ormhill, I do. Got a question for her, and mean to hear her answer it."

"You know the answer, for I told it to you," a red-faced woman screamed in his ear. "If you don't work for Miss, we'll have naught to eat this winter."

"M'lord Corbright said she'd no choice but to give us bread, for it is the law."

"Lord Corbright is mistaken, Jeremiah Bleck." A quiet, yet firm voice nearby told Edmund that Olivia had joined him. At her words, Bleck ceased his struggles, so Edmund let him go.

"But it's part of the outdoor relief, ain't it?"

Olivia shook her head. "Only the single loaf of bread distributed at the Flintridge bakery is from the government. It is intended to keep the laborer fit to do work when he is needed."

At the sight of Olivia, the rest of the crowd had calmed and arrayed themselves around her on the steps. "Explain to my Jim, Miss Ormhill," the red-faced woman called out. "Explain why he shouldna be a-workin' for that new-made lord."

Olivia sighed. "I can't say what he should do, Mrs. Bleck. But I can advise him to put by the extra pay to feed his family this winter."

"Thought you wuz a Christian woman," groused another, older, man who stood just below Bleck on the steps. "Yet here ya go a-punishin' our women and children a'cause we work for someone else."

"It isn't that at all," Olivia responded once the agitated murmur that swept through the crowd at this statement died down. "It is like this: If I cannot get my hay and grain crops in before the weather turns, I'll have nothing to feed my cattle. I'll have to spend money for feed. That means I'll not be able to afford to give bread out."

"So sell 'em," grumbled Mr. Bleck.

"If I sell them, what will Dick Wilson and half a dozen others who take care of my cattle do for work? They will have to go on the county then, and you know what that means."

"The poorhouse, or starvation," Mrs. Bleck shouted.

Olivia raised her voice to overcome the murmurs of distress in the crowd. "When the enclosures took the small holdings of many of the people in the valley, my father promised to see that those who stayed and continued to work on the land would not be the poorer for it. It was not required of him. The money paid you or your parents at that time was all the law required. But he felt, and Jason and I agree, that it wasn't an entirely fair settlement, since so many would spend that money within a year or two and then be without the right to raise small gardens or gather wood, as they had previously."

"Then why don't you pay us more?" Bleck demanded.

"You'd just spend it on drink," Mrs. Bleck asserted, and several women nodded and muttered assent, or glared at their menfolk.

"Higher wages would be one possibility. But Father feared just what Mrs. Bleck says: merely giving a raise in pay to compensate would not work, because some of you would spend that money as soon as it came into your hands."

Murmurs ran through the crowd again. The women seemed ardently in agreement; the men less so, though Edmund noticed that many of them dropped their eyes or looked away.

"So we have always reserved as much of our grain as necessary to see through the winter those who worked for us—not just the workingmen, but their women and children as well. But without our crops to sell, without our hay to see our cattle through the winter, we won't be able to do that. Not from cruelty, or as a punishment, but simply because the money won't be there. Now, you may work for Lord Corbright. That is for you to decide. Only be careful with your funds if you do. Tomorrow my brother will go to High Wycombe to hire laborers, and then I will feel obligated to help them and their families through the winter. Do you understand?"

Mr. Bleck frowned, scratched his head, turned to look at the elder Mr. Jones, and at last nodded. " 'Tis fair, I s'pose. Perhaps 'at fancy lord will give us bread, too."

Mr. Jones nodded. "Surely he will, for didn't he say he'd pay us more'n Miss Ormhill, and we'd be free of petticoat governance, too."

In the twilight Olivia hoped her face did not show red, as it often did when she was angry. "That is, of course, your choice, Mr. Jones. You and your son may take yourself off now, if you please."

"Not me, Mum." The young man standing by Mr. Jones spoke up, addressing himself more to the crumpled cap he held in his hands than to Olivia. "I know I'm not safe wi' the extra coin. If I don't know it, my Sarah will be sure to remind me. A'sides, I never minded a-workin' for you, miss."

"Thank you, Silas." Olivia smiled at him, then raised her voice once again. "Tomorrow comes early, whoever you work for. Go home now and talk it over. Any who wish to return to work here should be waiting at the main barn at first light. Our wagon will transport you to my brother's north meadow."

"Aye," said Mr. Jones the younger. " 'At 'un needs cutting right soon, miss! Gonna be turnin' any day now."

Olivia nodded. "And whatever choice you make, I pray we all can still meet in the village as friends."

The workmen and their wives milled about a bit, talking among themselves. Some of these conversations were acrimonious, but most were quiet and thoughtful. Several, before they drifted away, climbed to where Olivia stood watching, and told her they would be returning to her in the morning. She smiled and shook hands with each such convert in turn.

As the last of them filtered away, Jason mounted the steps and embraced his sister. "Well done, Livvy. I hope someday I may be as wise and capable a man as you."

She pulled away a little, and jabbed at his forearm with her right hand. *"Et tu, Brute,"* she said, chuckling. "Why, oh why, is the ability to deal with such situations seen as masculine?"

"That was not my meaning," Jason sputtered.

"I know, dearest." She slanted a look at Edmund, who had observed the whole without comment. *I wonder what he thinks of me now?* Looking at his grim expression, she decided he must see her as the veriest ape leader in the kingdom.

Edmund watched the brother and sister's affection with envy. As he had yesterday, he regretted the vast difference from his relationship with his siblings. Suddenly he had lost all appetite for that pint at the tavern, and the company of the fortunate Jason Ormhill or any other human being.

"Jason, I've changed my mind," he said, abruptly turning on his heel. "I believe an early bedtime will do me more good than anything else."

Olivia sniffed the air suspiciously. The dawning day looked to be fine, but there was a hint of moisture that made her uneasy. She needed at least two weeks with little or no rain to get her hay cut and in the barns.

To her relief, many of the workers whom Corbright had lured away stood in the stableyard as they had promised, waiting their turn to mount the estate wagon that would take them to the fields.

She was glad to see that the younger Jones was there, along with his wife, for he knew the art of loading hay wains and making up haycocks. His father, as well as Mr. Bleck, had apparently returned to the employment of Lord Corbright, but Olivia noted with wry amusement that Mrs. Bleck waited her turn to sit upon the long benches of the estate wagon.

She was not the only woman, of course. It had always been the custom for females to take part in the harvest. They spread the newly scythed grass evenly across the fields, and turned previous cuttings two or three days in a row until it was judged sufficiently dry to load upon the wagons. This was a crucial part of the haymaking process, for grass that was too wet when stored could mold and make the cattle ill when they ate it. It could also ferment and even catch on fire right in the barn.

"It looks as if we have sufficient workers," Jason observed, looking to his sister for confirmation.

"If we were on time, I would agree, but it is going to be necessary to hire more to catch up. We particularly need men to do the cutting."

"I can help with that until you have your full complement hired," Edmund said.

Olivia turned a worried look on him. "Are you quite sure that you know how to use the scythe? It is hard work, and can be dangerous."

Edmund nodded. "I have not used one in years, and at the time I did I could barely hoist it. Still, I managed to cut hay as a boy, and I am sure I can pick it up again in no time."

"I should like to learn," Jason asserted.

Olivia shuddered a little at the thought of her brother lifting and swinging the long, sharp blade, but knew better than to say so. "I truly need you to go High Wycombe, Jason. As I explained last night, I need a man to hire the workers."

"You had best go with me, then. I've no idea who would be best to hire." So they left Edmund in charge, and brother and sister started on the trip. As soon as the estate wagon had delivered the workers to the field, it would follow them into High Wycombe to transport those whom they hired.

They had barely reached the main road when a rider approached them, pushing his mount hard.

"That's Corbright's livery," Jason observed.

"I wonder if he knows how his man is using his horse," Olivia responded, drawing her mount well to their side of the narrow country lane to give the rider room. To her surprise, he drew his horse up across the road, blocking them.

Jason muttered an oath as he pulled up beside her. "What do you mean by this?" he demanded.

The groom leaned forward. "I've a message for Miss Ormhill from Lord Corbright. He begs you to read it immediately, miss." He offered her a sealed note, which she took reluctantly. When it was in her hands, he turned his horse and galloped back the way he had come.

Almost as if she expected it to hold a serpent, Olivia opened it gingerly. *My dearly beloved Olivia,* it began. She almost threw it upon the ground at the sight of those words, so false and so out of place, but curiosity drew her on.

> *My dearly beloved Olivia,*
>
> *I prostrate myself at your feet with the most profound apologies for my behavior in the last few weeks. I can only plead a kind of madness since you once again spurned my offer of marriage. Somehow I must make you see how wrong you are about me, about our hopes for happiness, but I know I have gone the wrong way about it. I thought to make you see how you needed me by luring away your workers as any villain might do who wished you harm. But I see now that you think me the villain. It is not so. I do not wish you harm. Indeed, I have come to believe that you should retain your farm and the running of it, just as your father wished. When I saw how your eyes sparkled as you romped with Jason, how they darkened with worry as you thought of the problem I had caused you, I realized that you are not and never can be one of those frivolous females who decorate drawing rooms and spend their hours on clothes and cards. I have been a great fool to wish you to be so! I will not speak ill of my departed wife, but confine myself to saying that you are not she, and I am grateful for that. Please rescind your banishment of your humble suitor,*
>
> > *Corbright*
>
> *P.S. I am sending my entire enrollment of estate workers to join with yours in bringing in your hay, as I have by my foolish behavior delayed you dangerously. As you read this, they will have commenced cutting in Jason's north meadow. Do not say me nay, love, for this I owe you.*

The tender words and protestations of love, so at odds with his recent behavior, created a riot of battling feelings in Livvy. Her hand shook as she held the letter, her cheeks pink and tears in her eyes.

"What does he say?" Jason demanded. When she looked up at him, unable to respond, he grabbed the paper from her and read it. He gave a long, low whistle when he had finished. "He had proposed to you?"

"In a letter," she admitted. "Soon after his wife's death. Too soon! And then again in the spring when I encountered him while visiting our tenants."

"And then began to hire away your workers to teach you a lesson." Jason frowned. "Odd. But he obviously regrets his actions. This puts a different face on things, does it not?"

"Perhaps. But we cannot allow him to cut our hay."

"Why not? He has delayed our harvest and is trying to make up for it."

"I don't wish to be beholden to him."

Jason considered the matter for a moment, head bowed. He was torn between loyalty to his sister and his desire to see her wed. "Livvy, he is trying to end this lovers' quarrel. Why do you not meet him halfway?"

Is that what it is? Olivia wondered. *A lovers' quarrel?* She knew little enough of the masculine mind. Was it possible that love could make a man behave so basely? Had she been wrong in concluding that Corbright had never loved her, and was a villain at heart?

"This is more than halfway, Jason. I cannot accept so much from him. It might seem to commit me to something I doubt I want."

The distress in her voice reawakened Jason's conscience. "You are right. Until he proves himself, I can't permit anything that obligates you—us—to him."

"Thank you." Olivia felt tears coming into her eyes. He truly was a fine, fond brother, for all his faults. "Now will you come with me to stop him?"

Olivia was not surprised to see Lord Corbright, mounted upon a fine bay hack, waiting for them in the north meadow, which was a scene of almost frenzied activity as scythe men advanced up the field in five rows, followed by those wielding the rakes to spread the fallen grass evenly. In the distance Edmund could be seen working with the group he had led out earlier. She wondered what he made of Corbright's actions.

"Ah! My darling! You have received my missive." Corbright pressed his mount alongside hers and leaned forward. "Do say that you forgive me." He held out his hand to her.

She ignored his hand. "I forgive you, Lord Corbright, for luring my workers away with inflated wages. But we cannot allow you to cut our hay for us."

Jason chimed in, "Wouldn't be right."

"Nonsense, Jason. Why do you not go and take a look at those horses of mine, give your sister and me some time to mend our fences, eh?"

"Pressing on her this unacceptable situation does not sound like a good way to mend your fences, Frank. Don't think you can force your way into Livvy's affections."

Corbright glared at Jason, his neck and face becoming red. This alarmed Olivia, who immediately regretted involving her volatile brother.

"Jason speaks for me, Lord Corbright," she said. "While I hope we can be on friendly terms, that is all. And even that cannot be if you persist in this . . . this . . ." She waved her hand at the busy scene before her.

"You would have me think you have completely forgotten what once lay between us? That you have no desire to make up our differences?"

"I would."

"It is not to be believed. If you were not still wearing the willow for me, you would have found a husband by now. But no. Three seasons have passed and you have buried yourself here in the country. Why, you do not even attend our local assemblies or parties."

"Because I could not hire a satisfactory agent, I have been too busy for socializing," Olivia said through gritted teeth. "But as you see, my brother is at last taking an interest in learning to manage his own land, and Lord Edmund has the makings of a fine estate manager. I have already laid plans to reenter society. In fact, by spring I expect to be able to enjoy another Season in London."

Jason's eyes widened. He grinned from ear to ear.

Corbright snorted. "I don't believe a word of it. May will find you here, supervising spring planting."

"No, sir, it will not. It will find me shopping for spring bonnets! Now, if you will just stop your workers and send them on to your own fields . . ."

"No." Corbright looked at her intently. "I meant what I said. I was in the wrong, and must make amends."

Olivia's eyes flashed with fury. She drew breath for a harsh set-down, but Jason spoke first. "If they continue working in my fields, it must be for my wages, which I will pay," he declared. "It is not that I wish us to be enemies, Franklin, for I do not. But to persist in this would put my sister in a questionable light. That I cannot allow." His back ramrod straight, his chin jutting out, Jason faced the older, stronger man with all the assurance of a fighting cock.

Corbright visibly struggled for self-control, and won. "Very well. But I shall tell them I mean to take back only half of them and pay only the prevailing wage in future, so you may be easy. I need far fewer of them than I had anticipated, anyway, for I have purchased a new machine that will cut the grass in half the time with only one or two men to work it."

Nearby, one of the women engaged in spreading the grass looked up at them, alarm writ large upon her face.

Unaware or unconcerned, Corbright continued, "I have no doubt many will wish to return to your employ, so your harvest will be brought in on time. And as for me, well, my dear, I look forward to seeing you in local society, and in springtime I intend to be in London, too, admiring that bonnet!" He kissed his hand to her and turned his horse to ride across the field toward the lines of workers.

What have I done? Olivia glanced nervously at her brother. The triumphant look on his face made it clear she had really said what she had no intention of saying. *My wretched temper,* she thought. "Always keep your tongue between your teeth when you are angry," her father had cautioned her on numerous occasions when she spoke before she thought. And at twenty-one years of age, she still committed the same error over and over.

"Livvy! Darling sister! You are going to go to London! You are going to seek a husband!" Jason leaned over to hug her, half lifting her from her saddle.

"I am not!"

"But you said—"

"You know I spoke without thinking. The nerve of that man, supposing I am wearing the willow for him."

"It is what everyone thinks. Including, until yesterday, Aunt Lavinia and myself."

"Everyone?" Embarrassment flooded Olivia.

"Of course. As Corbright said, you never go about socially anymore. What else is one to believe?"

"That I have been too busy taking care of my business and yours to have time for such? For that is the truth of it!"

"Livvy." Jason shook his finger at her. "You are not being honest with yourself, much less with me."

"Oh!" Exasperated, Olivia turned her horse and galloped off, she hardly knew where.

Chapter Nine

That evening the mood at Beaumont was celebratory. With the return of the workers Corbright had lured away, the harvest would speed up considerably. Rev. Milton Ormhill, Jason and Olivia's uncle, dined with them. Busy with his own farm as well as parish work, he had not heard the full story of the two wagers. He clucked his tongue disapprovingly as he heard the details of the marriage wager.

"Knew I shouldn't have left you at the tavern," he growled, then deprived the rebuke of any sting by laughing heartily. "Not fair to Lord Edmund by half!" When he heard of Olivia's hay wain wager, he crowed, "Clever girl," and urged them to tell him the tale in all its details. Jason gladly obliged. The elder Ormhill's craggy face glowed with pleasure as he listened to his nephew tell of his efforts to stack the hay, and Olivia's chortling reminder of the inglorious outcome. Lavinia vied with her niece in describing Jason's appearance as he emerged from the hay mountain, and Olivia's once he had revenged himself by pitching hay on her.

"And poor Lord Edmund, who quite successfully delivered his own load, found himself buried in hay at their hands for no other sin than being nearby." Lavinia chuckled.

"It is a good thing Corbright came up when he did," Jason said, waggling a finger at her, "or you would have been next."

"You wouldn't have dared!"

"Oh, would I not have?"

Their uncle interrupted. "Corbright? What business had he there?"

Edmund inferred from the elderly man's tone of voice that Corbright was no favorite of his.

"Well, that is quite a tale," Jason began.

Olivia cleared her throat loudly. Her uncle shared with his niece and nephew the tendency to a quick temper, so she preferred that he not hear all of Corbright's actions. When throat clearing and a kick under the table did not stop her brother's headlong determination to retell the story, she interrupted. "Uncle does not want to hear all of that, Jason. Only you will be very happy to learn, Uncle Milton, that Corbright handsomely apologized for paying such high wages that he monopolized the valley's workers, and has promised to return to the normal price."

"What?" Lavinia looked, quite bewildered, from nephew to niece. "This is the first I have heard of it. When did this happen? For he behaved quite abominably at lunch yesterday, so much so that Jason forbade him to come on Ormhill land. And did you not have to go to High Wycombe today to hire new workers?"

Jason laughed. "You'll be pleased to know that just as we started, Corbright sent Olivia a note. And quite a note it was, too. You should have seen her blush."

"He . . . he said certain things which I am not at all sure he meant. But as I said, he did agree to lower his wages."

"Ah." Uncle Milton smiled at last. "If he keeps to that, it will be excellent, for I, too, am having difficulty getting people to harvest my acres, few though they are."

"Few! Tch. What will Lord Edmund think, our poor relation having so small a living to farm." Lavinia clucked her tongue at her brother.

"At least *I* have a crop to be harvested," the elder Ormhill retorted. "That farm of yours is all but abandoned."

"I'll have you know I have received a very handsome offer to purchase that abandoned farm."

"Purchase! You'd have to give it away."

Olivia interrupted before hostilities could break out. The sight of their elders bickering was not an edifying one, though all too frequent. "Lord Edmund will think far less of us for falling into a family feud."

"No, nor have you yet heard the best of the day's news."

"Jason . . ." Olivia's voice shrilled with vexation.

"Livvy has promised to begin going about in society again. To go to London for the Season, in fact."

Pandemonium broke out. Livvy hotly denied such intentions, Jason just as hotly asserted that she must keep her word, Lavinia exclaimed and pressed for details, and Uncle Milton shouted praise to the Lord for the working of miracles, jumped up, and bussed his niece noisily on the cheek.

Edmund could not help laughing at the scene, and the servants who had been bustling about serving the meal observed with huge grins on their faces. Olivia, mortified, finally succeeded in quieting her family by screaming at the top of her lungs, "Please, do try for a little decorum."

Astonishment stopped them all in midsentence, and though Jason muttered, "You are a fine one to talk," the elder Ormhills subsided at once, chagrin written on their faces.

"Lord Edmund already knows us for a harum-scarum lot," Lavinia said, flapping her hand at him. "What must he think now?"

"Bedlamites," Edmund responded, smiling broadly. "I have never been more entertained. Please do not stop on my account."

"Decorum be hanged. You told Corbright you would go to London for the Season, and go you must, or—"

"That will do, Jason." The reverend Ormhill, when he wished to do so, spoke with authority, and Jason instantly closed his mouth, though he sat with a mulish scowl on his face for the rest of the meal.

A change of subject was clearly in order. "But do you then really intend to remain here, working for Olivia?" Reverend Ormhill turned toward Edmund.

"I do. She has agreed to teach me about estate management. It has always been my ambition to learn about advanced agricultural practices. I had hoped one day to farm my own estate, but shall have to content myself with working for others, once I know enough to have something to offer a prospective employer."

"I see." Uncle Milton sucked contemplatively on his lower lip.

"Shall we have a game of whist after dinner?" Lavinia asked hopefully.

"The very thing," her brother replied. "I propose, gentlemen, that we forego our port and join the ladies instantly."

Jason had other ideas. "A glass of port first, I think." He waggled his eyebrows significantly at his uncle, who acquiesced, reassuring Lavinia that they would not linger. "I wanted to tell you a bit more of the events of the day," Jason said once the ladies had withdrawn. "Olivia is all in a pelter to keep matters quiet, but it may be that she and Corbright will make it up."

Reverend Ormhill took up the port and poured himself a generous glass. "You think so? It is quite a surprise to me. He clearly intended to do serious damage to her purse—and yours—just a day or two ago."

"A lovers' quarrel, is what he said. Unknown to us, he has been courting her through the mail and once in an accidental meeting. And he made amends most handsomely for the haying problem, or tried to. Had all of his estate workers out in the north meadow this morning, in an effort to help us catch up. She wouldn't accept it—descended upon him like some avenging angel—but he showed he'd learned something about her, at least. Said he had been wrong to criticize her for managing our estates, that if she'd have him, he'd leave the management of her land in her hands, that sort of thing."

"How did the decision to go to London come about?"

Jason chuckled. "You know her temper, Uncle. He goaded her into it by claiming that she has been wearing the willow for him for three years. And she has, too."

"I don't know. Certainly she was very upset at first, but I thought she had come to the conclusion she was well out of it. As had I."

"It could have been sour grapes on her part," Jason declared. "At any rate, he said he intends to court her, and I wouldn't count him out."

"I do not trust the man. What say you, Lord Edmund?"

Edmund frowned. If indeed what had gone on between Olivia Ormhill and Corbright was just a lovers' quarrel, he would not be thanked for throwing a wet blanket on their reunion. Still, he liked the Ormhills too well to withhold information that might prevent her from making a tragic mistake. "I know something of the man, from younger days. He was a treacherous friend and dangerous foe then. What mitigating effect age and a love that has survived three years might have upon him, I do not know."

"You mentioned something about his luring you into a leaky boat, yesterday." Jason put his elbows on the table and leaned forward.

"A childhood prank?" Reverend Ormhill sounded dismissive.

"Some might say so, though he was eighteen at the time. I was twelve. I wanted very much to be noticed and accepted by him and my oldest brother, Carl. I suppose I made a nuisance of myself. At any rate, I asked them to teach me to row a scull. Carl repulsed me as violently as he always did, but Franklin espoused my cause, or so it seemed. He promised to teach me when he found a suitable boat. A week later he put me up before him on his horse and with Carl following, took me to a nearby stream. I should have known from Carl's grin that all was not as it seemed. Franklin instructed me to get into a rather rickety-looking scull, then shoved it hard, out far enough from shore that it caught the current. Away I went, without oars. And it did leak. It is fortunate for me that I could swim."

"Did Corbright intend the current to take you?" Jason asked.

"Under my father's angry questioning, he claimed that he did not."

"Of course he would say that," Milton mused disapprovingly.

"Is that all you know to Corbright's disadvantage?" Jason asked dismissively.

"That was the worst of several similar incidents." Edmund shrugged, sorry to see that Jason took such cruelty lightly, or let his desire to see his sister wed blind him.

"Are you going to play whist or not?" Lavinia stuck her head in the door to the dining room and looked challengingly at the group.

They all rose and filed into the drawing room. Edmund wandered over to the piano instead of going to the table that was already set up for cards.

"Come, Lord Edmund. You must make up the fourth," Lavinia bade him.

"I will have to beg off, being quite penniless."

"Nonsense. We play only for chicken stakes." Reverend Ormhill beckoned him to the table.

"However small the stakes, remember that Jason quite cleaned me out. I have only managed to win back a few items of my clothing at billiards." Edmund smiled to show he felt no distress, and sat down to noodle at the piano.

"You misunderstood yesterday's stakes," Jason said, cutting across Olivia's equally emphatic "You should have a fat purse, according to our wager."

Edmund looked from one to another in surprise.

"Remember, I stipulated that if the two of you could not bring your wagons to the barn full of hay, you were to have your belongings *and* your winnings to the point that Jason began to drink heavily."

Edmund thought back, not remembering her precise wording. "But we changed the terms—"

"Not that part of them." Jason stalked over to the piano looking as if he meant to drag Edmund physically to the table. "I've a pretty fair idea of what I owe you, and will put it in your hands when we go upstairs. Now come along and let me win some of it back."

"But Miss Ormhill won't be able to play if I join you."

"I rarely play, and when I do, I usually manage to infuriate my partner," Olivia assured him. "I have a good deal of bookkeeping to do, and welcome the opportunity to catch up on some of it."

Edmund looked at the expectant faces of the other three

and surrendered. He would have preferred to look across the table at Olivia rather than Lavinia, of course, but found the older woman a canny partner. His fortunes had improved by several shillings when the card game broke up.

Olivia retired to her office, ostensibly to do some book-keeping. But her real purpose could have been inferred from the magazine she half hid in the folds of her skirt as she excused herself.

After lighting the branch of candles on her desk, Olivia smoothed open her aunt's copy of *La Belle Assemblée* and began studying the current fashions depicted and described therein. It had been several years since she had paid much attention to London fashions, and she knew her wardrobe was sadly out of date.

At odd moments during the day Corbright's taunt had come back to her: "If you were not still wearing the willow for me, you would have found a husband by now."

She simply could not bear that people thought she wore the willow for Corbright. She must take more care with her appearance, and begin going about in society. Was it only his taunt that made her feel thus, or his protestations of love? Or had someone else made her newly aware of herself as a woman? She knew only that, deep within her, feelings she had long suppressed were stirring. She wished to be attractive; she wished to have some pleasure in life, rather than the continual round of care and worry that had become her lot since her father's death.

"Then it is true?"

Olivia jumped, almost guiltily, at the sound of her aunt's voice. "What?" She attempted to hide the magazine under some papers on her desk.

"It is true that you are going to London for the Season?"

Olivia shook her head. "What makes you think that?"

"Don't pretend you haven't got my magazine. I sought it to take to bed with me. Even if I couldn't see a corner of it peeking out, I would know, for they don't get up and walk away on their own."

Olivia sighed and brought the magazine out into the

open. "Yes, I have it, but what that has to do with London, I cannot imagine."

"You need to begin planning your wardrobe, of course."

"If I were going to London, I would."

"Jason would have a conniption if he heard this!" Aunt Lavinia put her hands on her hips. "He talks of it as a fait accompli."

"Actually I was thinking of the Flintridge assembly."

Lavinia clapped her hands. "Even better. You are going to begin this fall."

"Begin what?" Olivia asked irritably. "Dressing?"

"Going about in society. Corbright drove you away, and now he is drawing you back."

"Do you, too, think I have been wearing the willow for Corbright?"

"Haven't you?"

"No! Emphatically no! It is true enough that I haven't gone about in society much, but does no one realize how much time these estates take?"

Lavinia held up her hand. "Pax, niece. I know how hard you work. Still, you could have found time to attend the assemblies and at least a few neighborly dances and dinner parties. You used to love to dance."

"Which is why I have decided to begin attending such again. Not because Corbright beckoned to me!" She lifted her chin defiantly.

"Humph!" Lavinia snorted her doubts. "You do mean to go to London, don't you? For Jason will be beside himself if you do not."

Olivia looked down at the magazine. "Perhaps. Oh, I suppose I must. At least this year I may leave without fear of finding the estate falling down when I return."

"Lord Edmund?"

"Yes. He seems quite capable and sincerely interested in the work. I expect he will be sufficiently prepared to stand in my stead next spring."

"That is excellent. He truly is a fine young man. Pity he is penniless. Pity your interests are fixed elsewhere."

"That isn't true," she snapped.

"Isn't it?" Lavinia looked shrewdly at her niece.

"Should it be? What do you think of Franklin? Of his behavior, and his motives?"

Lavinia dropped her eyes, fiddled with the sleeve of her gown, then popped up to go to the windows and gaze out at the night sky. At last, she said in a soft voice, "I am not at all sure of his sincerity."

"Nor am I."

Lavinia whirled around. "Then why the sudden interest—"

"When he said I had been wearing the willow for him, it started me thinking about things. It is true, I did stay at home and brood for quite a while. But then I threw myself into estate matters. Well, I had to, hadn't I, after I found that traitor Dalton stealing us blind? And then, when I went to my first dance after our broken engagement . . ."

"He was there, parading his new wife. . . ."

"Exactly! And everyone looking sideways at me, some with pity, some with cruel amusement. It just made me so angry. And so sad. Soon I stopped going out. Goodness knows there was plenty to occupy me here on our property. But it was never my ambition to spend my life as an estate manager. I wanted a home and a family. Children." She said the last word on a long sigh.

"Children." Lavinia's tone was even more wistful. "I had so hoped to have little grandnieces and nephews by now! And as it is Corbright who has restored you to your senses, I suppose I must at least suspend judgment as to his intentions."

"Oh, his intentions I have no doubt of. It is his reasons I question. Aunt Lavinia, do you think it possible that Corbright still has feelings for me? If he ever had."

"I don't know. His behavior the other day at the harvest confused me. One minute he was flirting and saluting you, the next threatening. Then the note Jason spoke of. Not having seen it, I cannot judge. . . ."

"I want you to see it." After fishing around in a desk drawer for a few minutes, she took out a small packet of letters. She withdrew Corbright's conciliatory note. "Read this, and tell me what you think."

Lavinia read the note over twice. Olivia watched her expression, hoping for some clue, but her aunt had a countenance that did not easily betray her emotions.

At last she looked up. "Livvy, it is well written. I can see why you might give him the benefit of the doubt. And there have been others, I see. Are they in the same vein?"

"If possible, more loverlike. In one of them he actually proposed! Even had I been eager to receive his attentions, I thought it unseemly to begin addressing me so soon after his wife's death."

"As do I. Why was I not aware of them before?"

Livvy looked beyond her aunt, gazing into nothingness for a moment. "I wasn't sure myself how I felt about them."

"You didn't want me pushing you toward him," Lavinia said regretfully.

"Partly it was that. Aunt, you haven't given me your opinion."

"Oh, Livvy, you know how little I understand of these things. My lack of beauty, linked with a small dowry and an overly protective father, meant I had no suitors to speak of. I've lived my life as spinsterish a spinster as ever was."

"You are an astute judge of character. Please stop avoiding the question, or I may conclude your opinion of him is even worse than I think."

"Very well. The way your father's will tied up your property could certainly have touched a prideful man on the raw."

"Father did not intend it to reflect on Franklin."

"But we are not talking about your father's intentions, but Corbright's perceptions. Still, I hardly think he would pursue you so ardently if he cared nothing for you."

"Revenge?"

"Why wait until his wife's death to seek revenge?"

"My land?" Olivia shook her head. "It is not enough to tempt so wealthy a man, is it?"

"Perhaps he speaks the truth. He loved you, loves you still, and the trifling with your workmen was only an ill-conceived attempt to make you realize you need a man in your life. I would give him the benefit of the doubt."

Olivia looked long and hard into her aunt's eyes.

"But warily," Lavinia finally added.

"I agree. To the benefit and the wariness. I will consider his suit, but I am not bound to him."

"And look about you for other eligible men in the meantime!"

"I'm not looking for a husband."

"No, but if you found one you wanted, it would solve many problems." Lavinia pulled the magazine off Olivia's desk, plopped back down in the chair, and snapped it open briskly. "I noticed today that this evening gown is of the same basic shape and material as that rose satin gown I made you last year. The one you've never worn. With a little clever trimming it can be made a la mode in no time, I think."

"Anything is within your capabilities, Aunt Lavinia," Olivia said. She came around the desk and bent to hug her aunt, who patted her arm fondly but absently.

"Anything having to do with dressmaking, at any rate. I have some lovely watered silk tucked away that I can use to make the rosettes. Shall we begin tomorrow?"

"We shall!"

While her aunt perused the magazine, Olivia drifted to the window. Once again she asked herself, *Is it Corbright who has awakened me from my long isolation? Was it just time for my heart to mend? Or has it to do with a certain someone else?* Livvy hoped not, for her opinion of Lord Edmund had not changed: He was a fortune hunter and a gambler, albeit a personable one. If she ever wed, she wanted to be sure her husband desired her, not her property.

Chapter Ten

O livia had little time for introspection over the next few
days, as she sorted out those who truly wished to work
for her from those who were there at Lord Corbright's bid-
ding.

"Franklin was as good as his word," Jason observed with
satisfaction on the first morning after Corbright's capitula-
tion. "Most of our workers have returned to our employ."

"I daresay reflections upon the coming winter had as
much to do with their decision as anything Corbright said or
did," Olivia retorted.

Jason winked at Edmund. "As you say, sister. Will we
need more workers to get the hay in, do you think?" To
Olivia's annoyance, he directed his question to Edmund.

"I have no experience on which to judge," Edmund
replied. "Miss Ormhill must be the one to say." He looked at
her expectantly.

"I intend to spend the evening after dinner calculating
how long it will take to complete the harvest. You and Jason,
if you wish, may assist me in my ruminations."

"Oh, that's all right. Plan to go to the tavern for some
cards after dinner."

"I expect we had best join her," Edmund responded.
" 'Tis an important part of our apprenticeship, after all."

Jason squirmed and fidgeted that evening while Olivia
made her calculations, but Edmund followed her reasoning
with interest, asking appropriate questions. He made no effort to insert his opinions or suggestions. He seemed to take

it for granted that she knew how long each phase of the haying operation would take, and how many workers were needed. *How pleasant to meet a man who doesn't question my competency,* she thought.

By the third day all was settled and the rhythm of the harvest was established. No new workers need be hired, she decided. It was a relief, given her practice of carrying her employees and their families through the winter.

That evening at dinner, Lavinia told them that an invitation had arrived for Lord Edmund from their neighbors the Hervilles, who had already invited the Ormhills to an evening of dinner and informal dancing the following Saturday. "I know you will wish to accept, Lord Edmund. All our neighbors will be there, so it will be an excellent time for you to meet them."

"You'll go too, Livvy," Jason crowed. "Now that you've decided to reenter society."

Olivia demurred. "I've a great deal to do the day following their party; I don't want a late night."

"You don't plan to work on the Sabbath, do you?" Her uncle, who dined with them as usual, looked at her severely.

Olivia blushed. She often worked on the Sabbath, but surreptitiously, as Uncle Milton had very strong feelings about the Lord's day. It was her practice to withdraw to her office and catch up on bookkeeping and reading in agricultural journals on Sunday afternoons and evenings. Fairly caught, she could only murmur, "I had forgotten the next day would be Sunday."

Milton grinned and wagged his finger at her. "It usually does follow a Saturday."

She giggled. "Even so, I don't wish to attend. I sadly fear I have no dress suitable. I will not reenter society and be ashamed of my appearance."

"I shall have the dress I am altering ready by then," Lavinia said, but Olivia shook her head.

"Livvy . . ." Jason fairly screeched.

"Conduct, conduct," Uncle Ormhill admonished. "Olivia must decide for herself when she is ready, Jason." His look was such that Jason subsided, muttering.

Edmund announced that he, too, would not attend, but was overruled by all the Ormhills acting in concert.

"I am but an employee," he protested. "It was polite of the Hervilles to invite me, but hardly suitable."

"You may learn from Olivia all that you wish, but you are a gentleman, living under our roof, and so you shall be treated."

"As to that," Edmund said, "there is a space for me in the bachelor quarters of the—"

"Do not say it," Lavinia cried. "You shall not live with the servants. I will not have it!"

"Nor I." Olivia's voice was lower, but her tone was firm. "Nothing in our wager deprived you of your social standing."

Edmund reluctantly agreed. His wardrobe had arrived that day from London, so he could not excuse himself on that account.

Corbright called upon Olivia after dinner. She had just settled down to reading a treatise on turnips. Aunt Lavinia sat beneath a large branch of candles sewing upon the gown she was altering for her niece. Jason, Uncle Milton, and Edmund played piquet at a card table a few feet away.

Buckman announced Corbright and immediately admitted him to the drawing room. He greeted each of them courteously before advancing on her. Seating himself beside her, he took up the small volume she had been reading.

"Turnips? Really, Olivia," he said in a chiding voice. "It is a far cry from when we used to sit of an evening and read *The Iliad* together, remember?"

The caressing look in his eyes and tone of his voice did peculiar things to Olivia. Not at all sure she wanted to once more feel the pull of his handsome face and seductive ways, she clenched her hands into fists, digging her nails into her flesh to interfere with any flutterings she might experience.

"That was long ago, Lord Corbright. I have new interests now."

"No one could truly be interested in turnips," he asserted. "Come, I'll bet you have not forgotten all of your Greek."

He reached into the pocket of his coat and drew out a small volume. "Shall we begin again?" He held it out to her. "We were halfway through *The Odyssey*."

She took it and turned the prettily bound book over in her hands. "Truly, sir, I do not wish—"

"You intend to keep me at arm's length, don't you?" There was an edge to his voice now.

"Do you blame me?" She started to rise, drawing Edmund's and Jason's attention to them. He caught at her hands and prevented her, which made Jason turn in his seat.

"Shhh," Corbright whispered. "You are alarming your hotheaded brother. That boy had best be careful or he will find that duel he seems to be looking for."

She forced herself to relax, even leaving her hands in his, but whispered a pointed question: "Are you threatening me, Franklin?"

"Ah, my name at last on your lips. I had feared never to hear it from you again."

She scowled at him, waiting for the answer to her question.

"No, of course I am not threatening you, love. Only pointing out what you may not be aware of. Your brother is like a keg of powder in search of a match. I know how it would pain you to see him hurt, and so must join you in doing all possible to bring him greater peace of mind."

She searched his face. He looked all sincere concern. "I am aware of his state of mind," she said with a sigh. "But I will not give him false comfort, nor you false hope."

"Do you give me no hope at all? No, do not answer. At least say you will be my friend."

She hesitated only momentarily before nodding her head. "Friendship would be acceptable, Lord—"

"Franklin."

"Franklin. More than that I cannot offer."

"Yet." He smiled and took her hands to his lips. "Greek, then, among friends?"

It had been a long time since Olivia had studied Greek. She had begun it because Franklin had such a deep and abiding interest in the Greek language and culture. He had sug-

gested she possessed the ability to learn the language, which
her family had not thought appropriate for the female mind.
She had already, at sixteen, been struggling with the fact that
her intellect brought her no masculine admiration, and that
she felt pressured to hide her true nature around the male
sex.

The offer to teach her had been more than flattering; it
had been an opportunity to spend many hours with the blond
Adonis who had recently moved into the neighborhood.

His father, a crony of the Prince Regent, had been too
much for her family to swallow—a loud-mouthed mushroom of a creature who shared the prince's love of coarse
practical jokes. But the young Franklin Melwin had had the
manners of a gentleman. Soon, over their Greek, she had
tumbled in love.

Now, however, she found in herself no desire to take up
the difficult language again. Without the stimulus of Corbright's presence, she had lost interest in it. Obviously he
hoped the time such a study would give him in her presence
might rekindle their love. She certainly wasn't ready for
that.

She pulled her hands from his. "I am sorry, Franklin. I
truly do not have the time right now. Even at this moment I
am late to go to my study to do some bookkeeping."

"With Edmund and Jason to help you, you should have
more time on your hands."

Olivia frowned. Corbright was an accomplished fencer,
with words as well as steel. He would explore every open-
ing, take every advantage. "They are not yet sufficiently *au
fait* with bookkeeping to be more help than hindrance."

"Well, another time, then."

Olivia rose. "Perhaps. Certainly not before the harvest
season is finished." She excused herself, hurrying to her
study.

In the intimate drawing room, the other occupants had
heard all but the whispered portions of this conversation,
and Jason threw down his cards in vexation as Olivia left the
room.

"Devil a bit. Why did you not encourage her to stay, Aunt?"

"You heard her, Jason. She has work to do." Lavinia frowned, though whether at the knot in her thread or at her nephew, no one could tell.

"Play with us?" Jason asked, for Corbright had approached their table purposefully.

"Not tonight. I would like a word in private with you if possible, though."

"Of course." Jason rose quickly. "Excuse me, Edmund, Uncle."

Edmund nodded, meeting Corbright's hostile stare without flinching. He stood. "Quite all right. I have some tracts on crop rotation to go through."

"And I, a sermon to write. I'll be off now." Milton bowed to Corbright, kissed Lavinia on the cheek, and left.

"Step outside and blow a cloud with me," Corbright commanded the boy. He steered Jason out the French doors and onto the terrace. Once under the stars, Corbright made no move to smoke, however.

"Your sister works too hard," he said abruptly.

"So I am beginning to understand. But what to do? Edmund and I are helping her as best we can, but—"

"Edmund and you are making more work for her. Now, in addition to managing your estate and hers, she is keeping school. You should get an estate agent, Jason."

"Tried that. Men don't like to work for her."

"There's no hope for her ever to marry as long as she is kept to such drudgery." Corbright folded his arms over his chest and glared challengingly at Jason, his eyes glittering in the moonlight. "I've a proposition for you."

"If it will free Livvy to marry, I'm all for it."

"Sell your land to me."

"Wh-wh-what?" Jason recoiled in astonishment. "Sell Beaumont?"

"Just so. Not the manor, of course. Keep it and a few acres around it for a country home. Invest the money in the funds. I'll give you a generous price. Don't you see? It's the only way to free her from your land. Oh, she'd still have hers to manage, but that is a trifle compared to yours. My estate manager would simply add your lands to his duties, and Olivia would find herself with time on her hands, time to reflect on what lies ahead for her if she continues to dwindle into an ape leader. She'd find a husband soon enough!"

Jason stood motionless for several moments, too astonished by the daring proposal to respond. Finally he found his voice.

"Sell my land? Land that has been in the hands of the Ormhills since the conquest? How can I do that?"

"How can you not? You cannot pretend you wish to become a country squire. To you this land is just a millstone round your neck. You'd have as much of the ready to spend as ever. Think of it, Jason. Paris, Geneva, Rome, Athens. Even the Americas. India, Africa, Egypt, all await you. Think of standing before the pyramids or the Parthenon. And when you get the wanderlust out of your system, you can settle anywhere in the world you wish, or return here and live the life of a country gentleman, without any of his cares."

The picture Corbright painted appealed to Jason. His eyes alight with interest, he asked, "But what if Livvy doesn't marry after all? Or marries someone else? You'll have thrown away a fortune."

"Nonsense. I'll have a fine addition to my holdings. I have a little plan for the valley which your acreage will greatly enhance. The plan will delight Olivia, too. Once she sees what it is, I'll be surprised if she doesn't fall right in, both with the plan and with me. But if she doesn't, at least I'll know I tried, and I'll have the satisfaction of having freed you to follow your destiny."

Jason's head whirled with the possibilities. "I'll . . . I'll give it some thought," he said. "That is . . ." He bristled at the look of scorn Corbright shot him. "Selling the land. Well. Hard for a fellow to make such a decision in a minute. But I will think hard on it."

"I suppose I must be satisfied with that. Do you think your aunt might be persuaded to sell her farm?"

Jason cocked his head to one side. "Possibly. She's cer-

tainly not making much of it. That tenant of hers! He's ruined it. She won't sell if Livvy opposes it, though."

"Oh, for God's sake, don't tell Olivia about any of this.
She'll cut up rough at the slightest hint of it. Must present it
to her as a fait accompli."

With that thought Jason was in complete agreement.
"Lud, no. Have a fit, she will! Mum's the word. Don't speak
to Aunt Lavinia till I've decided, eh? She might spill the
beans."

"Agreed. Think on what I've said. Oh, and don't say anything to Debham. He'd throw a spoke in my wheel, just for
spite. Don't care for me above half, and doubtless hopes to
win Livvy for himself. If you'll take my advice, you'll send
that fortune hunter on his way."

Jason frowned at this. "He's not like that, I don't think.
Just down on his luck. At any rate, its impossible. He won a
bet. Both Livvy and I are obligated to live up to the terms."

"Just what were the terms, Jason?"

Jason told him the whole of it.

"You ought to be horsewhipped for the first wager," Corbright said angrily. "You'll make your sister's name a byword. Already enough talk about her, without handing the
gossips such a jewel as that you had to try to force a man to
marry her. And whatever made you think Olivia would go
along with it?"

"Thought she might do it for my sake."

"Hmmmm." Corbright's brows arched speculatively.
"She loves you. She would do a great deal for you. You
thought she would marry just to please you?"

"Worth a try. Edmund seemed not to be in a position to
try to dominate her, you see. And his war record . . ."

"Yes, yes, war hero and all that." Corbright waved his
hand dismissively. "He lacks ambition, though. If he'd
stayed in the military he'd have advanced rapidly, because
Wellington likes him. But he threw that away. He's just the
sort to fasten himself upon a strong woman. But that won't
do for her. She might think so, but she'd be miserable. A
woman needs a strong hand to guide her, and a willful one

like Livvy needs it more than any other of the sex. That will of your father's is a vile thing. Ought to be overthrown."

Jason coughed uncomfortably. "He meant it for her good. Had in mind my aunt, who—"

"Yes, I know. His sister was cruelly abused by her husband. But that was an extreme case. You know I'd never use Livvy so. I would have thought your father knew it, too." Corbright's tight grimace spoke volumes.

"You thought that part of his will was aimed at you, but he planned that trust long ago for Livvy's protection, no matter whom she married."

"I realize that now. My foolish pride cost me much. Now I mean to gain it back. With your help, hopefully."

Jason nodded eagerly. "I'll help as much as I can."

"Then you'll sell me your land?"

"As to that, I will have to convince my uncle. He is my guardian until I am twenty-one."

Corbright nodded. "I know. Allow me to try to convince him, will you?"

Jason still hesitated, so Corbright changed the subject. "Do see if you can get Livvy to go about socially, will you? I know I've a good deal of ground to make up with her. Can't do it if I can never see her."

"That I will, Frank. That I will." Jason grinned as he held out his hand to Corbright. "She can't be entirely indifferent or she wouldn't have set Aunt Lavvy to sewing a new gown, would she?"

"Ah! Then that wasn't a project already begun before our confrontation?"

"Lud, no." Jason chuckled. "You hit just the right chord, saying she was wearing the willow for you. Touched her pride on the raw, that did."

"I thought as much." Corbright smiled with satisfaction. "Are you going to the Hervilles' party?"

"Yes, but Olivia does not plan to attend."

Corbright tapped his chin thoughtfully. "Don't tell her I know she doesn't plan to go. Perfect way to work on her— tell her she has to, or I will realize she lied to me. One way or another, get her to go."

Jason once again assured Corbright of his cooperation. After the older man took his leave, Jason paced up and down on the terrace, his mind whirring with possibilities. He tried to picture his life without the responsibility for Beaumont. What a difference it would make to Livvy, too! Edmund had suggested much the same thing: she would find time upon her hands once his estate was off them. He grinned at the thought. He could just picture her consternation.

He groaned and dropped into one of the veranda chairs. His uncle would cut up rough. How could Corbright hope to persuade that staunch traditionalist that he should be allowed to give up the land that was his birthright?

Chapter Eleven

Jason did not know if he could convince his uncle to let him sell his land, but Corbright had given him a very good idea how to get his sister to attend the Herville affair.

"Hullo, Liv. Still at it?" he asked, sticking his head in the door to her office.

Olivia looked up from her column of figures. "One moment," she said, and penciled in a number. "Come in. Corbright gone?"

"Yes, it's safe to come out. But something has come up. I hope I handled it as you would have wished."

Olivia's brow wrinkled. "What?"

"He asked if you were going to the Hervilles' next Saturday. I said yes."

"You did? But Jason, you know I don't—"

"Want to go? I know, but you told Corbright you had already planned to resume your social life. I thought if I let him know you weren't going, it would show you up."

Olivia slumped back in her seat. "Oh, that's right." She thought a moment. "Thank you, brother. That was clever of you. You think very fast on your feet!"

"You've no idea, Livvy. No idea at all."

"No doubt about it, Miss Olivia. 'Tis an abundant harvest!" Mr. Bleck forgot his antagonism for his female employer in his countryman's enthusiasm for a good year. He waved his hands to encompass the Ormhill lands. "Barns all full and hay cocks standing everywhere!"

"Indeed, Jeremiah. And our grain crops near ripening. We can begin cutting the wheat soon. Do you think this weather will hold?"

The old man squinted up at the August sky. "Never see'd such a year when the rain fell just as you'd wish, then held off when you needed it to, as if you'd got the Almighty on your side."

She smiled at him. "You've been a great help to me. I'm glad you came back."

"Aye, well . . ." Bleck's sun-bronzed face turned even redder. "That 'ere Lord Corbright 'n' his fancy machine'll be a long time getting in his hay! Serves 'im right, putting honest folks out o' work."

Worry clouded Olivia's eyes. Corbright's mowing machine was broken more often than working, if reports were accurate, but she had no doubt future machines would be improved. Would they do for agriculture what machine looms had done for weaving? If so, the results could be as devastating for the country folk as they had been for the weavers. What would happen then to the people who had worked on the land from time immemorial?

Jason and Edmund waved from the hill above, and she turned her mare to join them. She meant to show them the plantation project she had begun to improve Jason's woods. Her brother told her eagerly of the hares they had coursed earlier in the morning, while Edmund rode silently beside him. Olivia's attention wandered from her brother's story to wonder at the taciturnity of their guest, for such she insisted on calling him, to herself and others.

That midnight kiss might never have happened. Had her last jape at him about his seeking to seduce her offended him? Or merely convinced him it was a hopeless task? Or was he behaving in accordance with his own notions of what was proper, given their relative status? At any rate, he behaved toward her with a stiff correctness that prevented their almost constant association from being other than professional.

She knew she should be glad that, whatever the reason, he had conducted himself with perfect propriety toward her, yet she found him often on her mind, and knew she felt a disappointment at his withdrawal that wisdom would condemn.

Of one thing she had become utterly convinced: Edmund sincerely wished to know all there was to know about farming and managing an estate. After putting in long hours during the day at various farm chores, with Jason by his side, he spent the evenings reading in her agricultural library. Her brother, who had taken the physical involvement in farmwork in stride, had drawn the line at such dull study.

At least Jason had not resumed his restless rounds of local taverns, looking for games of chance and other forms of low entertainment. Lord Edmund Debham's advent and the subsequent wager had given him enough physical activity during the daytime that most nights he was content to dine at home or with neighbors, shooting billiards and gossiping.

This train of thought brought her to the Hervilles' party that evening. Lavinia had admonished her sternly to return by noon to have a bath and a rest, so she could dance late into the night. She hoped her refurbished gown would look well for her reappearance in society.

Edmund studied his image in the mirror critically. His evening clothes fit him well. Too well, perhaps? He had half hoped they might not pass muster, because he had no desire to go among the gentry of Norvale. He felt sure his lack of fortune would cause the parents of young females to look at him askance. Plus he would have to watch Franklin continue to pursue Olivia. The evening they had sat together on the couch, occasionally holding hands and whispering together, had convinced him that Olivia was open to a rapprochement with Corbright. Edmund felt sure a persistent wooing would win her again for her handsome, wealthy former fiancé. After all, hadn't she been wearing the willow for him for three years?

As promised, Edmund had been firmly suppressing any inclination to seduce Olivia or win her affections, and just as firmly suppressing any inclination on his own part to feel more than he ought. Whenever he felt any flutterings of tender emotion, as he often did as he watched her go so intently about her work, he had but to remind himself of her own harsh and accurate words summing up how little he had to offer a wife.

Still, the thought of her as Corbright's bride gave him a gut-wrenching pain that he hoped he would feel for any young woman in danger of coming under that man's power.

"It will have to do," Edmund said, dismissing Morton with a sigh. He had little experience in matters of civilian dress, but felt sure he looked ridiculous in such tight-fitting clothing.

"It will do very well, my lord," the servant who had become his de facto valet assured him.

Jason bounded into the room just then. "I say! You put me completely in the shade!"

Edmund smile deprecatingly. "Cut line. I won't shab off, even though this suit is too tight, so no need to flatter me."

They went into the hall, to find Lavinia waiting for them. When she caught sight of Edmund, she sighed. "Magnificent! Not Meyer's work. Let me see. Stultz?"

Surprised that she had recognized his tailor, he nodded.

"Edmund thinks it's too tight."

"Nonsense. Now if it were Weston, it would have taken two men to get you in it!"

Edmund shook his head in wonderment. "Glad I took Stultz, then."

The three of them started toward the stairs, when Olivia emerged from her room down the hall. "What do you think?" she asked them anxiously, smoothing a nervous hand down the side of her refurbished gown.

Edmund stopped short to stare unabashedly at the vision before him. Olivia's hair had been arranged to display all of its natural curl, upswept at the crown and with short ringlets teased forward around her face. Longer curls fell from the crown, fat dark curls that trailed alluringly over one shoulder. Her dress showed to perfection her lovely bosom and fell in graceful, clinging folds that delineated her long torso and legs. The deep rose color made her eyes seem even more brilliantly blue than usual.

Forgetting his determination to keep his distance from her, he spoke directly and from the heart. "I know nothing of fashion, Miss Olivia Ormhill," he said, "but you are paradise to look upon. May I take this opportunity to request a waltz? For the second you step in the door you will be inundated with beaux."

Her eyes shone with something he had not seen there before except perhaps briefly in the moonlit garden when they had shared that magical kiss. For a moment the usually self-possessed Miss Olivia Ormhill looked quite flustered. She lowered her eyes, and with a small, shy smile, nodded her head.

In truth, Olivia's head buzzed with improper thoughts about the man who stood so close to her. In a formfitting evening coat and breeches he looked sophisticated, cultured, and overwhelmingly male.

"Right, then." He stepped forward and offered her his arm. He supported her down the stairs, followed by her brother and aunt, strangely silent behind them.

"Olivia, my darling, you look marvelous. Not anywhere near as brown as I feared you might. And Lavinia! Not one more inch of avoir du pois. How do you do it?" Thus Mrs. Herville greeted the female members of the Ormhill party. Edmund braced himself for similar treatment, but their hostess surprised him.

"You do us great honor, my lord, to grace our humble gathering. I was never so glad as when Lavinia told me you would accept our invitation."

He scanned her puffy face for signs of sarcasm, but she seemed genuinely glad to see him. Her husband, too, shook his hand with great cordiality. As he stepped into the room, he could hear Mrs. Herville crowing over Jason. "Dear boy! You have grown a foot this summer!"

Ahead of him, Lavinia and Olivia were laughing behind their fans. Glad to see the woman's insults had not bothered them, he stepped up in time to hear Olivia saying, "No, Aunt

Lavinia. You have not won, for Mrs. Herville did not insult me in her very first sentence."

"I insist that saying you looked marvelous was the beginning of the insult, for she was being sarcastic."

Edmund chuckled. "So the Ormhill females wager, too."

"Indeed, sir, but I never bet except upon a sure thing, and Mrs. Herville's insults are that!" Olivia giggled, then turned back toward the room.

It immediately became apparent that they were the objects of intense scrutiny by the assembled guests. In knots of two or three, people stood in attitudes indicative of interrupted conversation, their eyes fixed upon the party by the door.

"Well, it begins," Olivia said, drawing herself up to her full height. "I knew my returning to society would cause comment, but this is more than I had dared to hope for." Head held high, she stepped forward. Lavinia took Edmund's offered arm and followed her niece as she made her way to the nearest group. There Olivia presented Edmund to each of the three young ladies present. As he acknowledged the introductions to the misses Herville and a sweet-faced young woman named Mary Benson, he heard Corbright's voice.

"Olivia. You look enchanting. That gown surely came from Paris?" He winked at Jason, for it was the one he had seen Lavinia remaking.

"Certainly not, nephew," another masculine voice argued. Edmund turned to see a short, rotund man of about fifty standing at Corbright's side, eyeing Olivia speculatively. "If you will but give me a moment, I will tell you exactly which London modiste made it."

"May I present my uncle, Mr. Peter Barteau?" Corbright went around the circle, introducing all of the people standing there in turn, except for Edmund.

Olivia, mouth tight, interrupted his conversational gambit upon the weather. "Lord Corbright forgot to introduce our houseguest and my brother's good friend, Lord Edmund Debham," she said to Mr. Barteau, turning her back on his nephew as she spoke.

"Ah, yes." Mr. Barteau surveyed Edmund up and down. "Coat by Stultz, what?"

"Indeed, sir. You have it, the second this evening to guess it at a glance, leaving me to wonder if this tailor sews his name somewhere on the outside of the garment." Edmund smiled at the friendly face lifted to his.

"Certainly it is, though I fancied no other but me would be able to read it. Who is my rival in fashion knowledge?"

"Miss Ormhill," Edmund responded, motioning toward Lavinia.

"Uncle, would you not like to join Mr. Perry? He is a tulip of the *ton,* and doubtless would like to learn your opinion of the latest fashions."

"Bah. A geranium is more like it. Color-blind, too. Now, Lord Edmund here has exquisite taste, and needs no padding, I'll vow. That silver embroidery with burgundy accents makes your vest an object of beauty."

"And just that touch of color makes the corbeau and white of evening dress stand out, don't you think?" Lavinia chimed in. Edmund felt like an object on display in a store window as the two perused him. Only the friendly, open face of Mr. Barteau, and the clear irritation of Corbright, kept him from excusing himself.

"Exactly. So you are Miss Ormhill?" Mr. Barteau looked at Lavinia with interest. "My nephew did not tell me his intended was a fashion maven."

"Not *her,* Uncle," Corbright growled, turning Barteau about by the elbow. "That is Lavinia Ormhill. This is my fiancée—Olivia Ormhill."

"I am not your fiancée," Olivia hissed.

"Ah, yes, she of the lovely gown," Mr. Barteau boomed. He turned immediately back to Lavinia. "You and your niece clearly have the same fine mantua maker, but I am puzzled. The fitting technique has something of Mrs. Triaud to it, but the drape speaks more of Mrs. Bean. Oh, if I could only get a glimpse of the stitching and the hem. The finishing tells the tale."

"Indeed it does." Lavinia nodded. "No matter how well cut or draped, a dress looks second-rate unless the—"

"Come, Olivia," Corbright said, taking her by the elbow. "You cannot wish to listen to this any further."

She pulled free. "Indeed, I am quite fascinated. But Mr. Barteau, I am sure you cannot guess the mantua maker, no, not even if you have a look at the construction." Her smile was mischievous. "Don't you agree, Aunt?"

Barteau bristled. "I am sure I can, young woman. It was made in London, I know that. One does not find such dress-making in the provinces."

Olivia laughed at that. "Made right here in Norvale."

"No, by Jove! You are bamming me! And your gown, Miss Lavinia Ormhill. Clearly by the same hand." Mr. Barteau hopped from one foot to the other in his eagerness to work out the puzzle. "Do tell me what local mantua maker has such ability?"

"Oh, put him out of his misery, Miss Ormhill," Corbright snapped. "She made the wretched things. Now do come away, Olivia."

"Yes, do," the elder Miss Herville, Jane by name, pleaded. "I wish you to meet some more of my guests, for I do not believe you know George and Arthur Swalen. You, too, Lord Edmund." She led the young people away from the older couple's fashion discussion, which continued unabated.

"So this is the prize of that famous wager," the elder brother, George, cried, upon being introduced to Olivia. "I have had it incorrectly, for I heard you lost, Lord Edmund, and thus had to marry her. Meeting you, Miss Ormhill, I cannot believe it to be thus."

Edmund frowned. "That drunken wager was null and void the minute it was made. Please do not further any discussion that causes Miss Ormhill embarrassment."

"Hear, hear!" Corbright threw in. "For once we are in complete agreement, Edmund. I intend to have a word with that innkeeper, to stop such talk."

"One look at Miss Ormhill will put it to the lie. At least the part about Lord Edmund losing and being forced to wed her." George smiled down at Olivia. "May I hope you will favor me with a dance after dinner?"

"And me?" The younger brother chimed in.

Olivia would have preferred to say no. She saw little to like in either of these young men, with their bold, roving eyes. Politeness dictated that she agree, however.

"Good," George crowed. "I shall have your waltz."

"I am sorry, it is already spoken for, sir. Another dance, perhaps."

A few minutes and all of Olivia's dances were bespoken, as the informal evening would include only a few sets. Dinner was announced, and Corbright, who had stood at her elbow during the entire discussion of her dances without reserving any, offered Olivia his arm to escort her to the table. She accepted reluctantly.

"It was clever of you to say your waltz was taken, Olivia. How I have longed to dance it again with you."

"You mistake the matter, Lord Corbright," she said in as chilly a voice as possible. "The waltz is reserved for someone else."

"The devil. I won't have any dances with you at all, then. Who has it?"

"Not you. And I am glad you have no dances, for you have made yourself persona non grata to me this evening thrice over."

He held her back as the others went in. "What do you mean? Why?"

"First, you insulted our houseguest by ignoring him; then you were insufferably rude to my aunt, but worst of all, you introduced me to your uncle as your fiancée. I am *not* your fiancée, sir, and I'll thank you to give no one else that impression."

Corbright's expression could only be described as petulant. "I meant no harm. I think of you that way, and—"

"Shall we go in? We are being left behind." Olivia turned her face toward the door.

"Who has your waltz? Perhaps he will give it up."

"You are forbidden to try. If he gives it up, I will sit it out with my aunt. Are you going to escort me to dinner or not?"

Corbright led her off in silence, a fierce frown on his face.

Olivia's dinner companions consisted of dull Mr. Marshmore on her left, and too, too bright Mr. George Swalen on her right. Mr. Marshmore could speak only of pigs, as she knew from previous dinners. While she could converse knowledgeably with him upon the merits of the various breed and the best means of farrowing, she did not find the topic perfectly suited to dining nor sufficiently interesting for an entire evening spent at his side.

She turned with relief to Mr. Swalen, who fixed that lively, mocking eye on her and said, "So the other scandalous rumor about you is true."

"I beg your pardon, sir?"

"You are, indeed, a lady farmer, versed in livestock and crops and caring for little else. Hard to imagine in one so outwardly feminine."

Her chin came up. "I have never understood why such knowledge renders a woman less feminine. Perhaps you will wish to reconsider your request for a dance?"

"By no means." He looked unrepentant, a disagreeable kind of merriment dancing in his eyes. "I have never paired a farmer in the cotillion before. Now tell me, do you truly find porcine management fascinating? If so, I will dig down deep and see what I can manage to say to the point."

"Perhaps we should discuss horses instead, Mr. Swalen. I expect you are just the sort of gentleman to have a great interest in that subject."

"Depends," he said after considering judiciously. "Draft animals do not fascinate me, nor yet hackneys. Now if the subject is thoroughbreds, especially those bred to race, I am your man. As to that, I am your man for any number of other purposes, if you wish it."

What I wish, she thought, *is that I were not seated next to you.* She smiled a tight little smile and asked him if he had a favorite in the fall meet at Newmarket. That distracted him from his rakish teasing and launched him on a discourse that gave her leisure to look surreptitiously about the table. Her eyes first went to Edmund, who was seated just across the table from her and down enough that she could see him around the massive epergne of fruit that was the centerpiece.

Next to him sat Mary Benson. She had her head tilted to one side, and was looking into his eyes with an expression that could only be interpreted as adoring.

So. Edmund has made a conquest already. She studied him a moment before turning back to nod and murmur encouragingly to Mr. Swalen. *I do not blame her. He is as handsome as he can stare. Doubtless her father will separate them as soon as possible, though.* Miss Benson was a great heiress with a notoriously protective father.

Her next opportunity to look around brought her aunt and Corbright's uncle into view. To her surprise, Aunt Lavinia was looking at Mr. Barteau with almost as much admiration as Mary Benson was bestowing on Lord Edmund. Moreover, Mr. Barteau showed none of the disdain or disinterest that gentlemen usually displayed with her plain aunt. He focused his attention entirely on her, and spoke with enthusiasm. She wondered if the discussion of fashion was still under way.

"Miss Ormhill. I do believe you find my horses less interesting than Marshmore's swine."

She swung her attention back to Mr. Swalen. "Not at all. You were saying that your stallion was out of Bastion by Silver Loo, and I was looking for my brother, Jason, for that reminded me he expressed an interest in adding that line to our breeding program. Have you met my brother?"

"No, I haven't had that pleasure as yet."

She gestured with her head. "He is sitting two seats down from our host, next to Jane Herville. After dinner I will introduce you. Perhaps he will wish to send you a mare to be bred."

Swalen smiled insinuatingly. "To breed into your line would be delightful, Miss Ormhill."

Olivia drew in a sharp breath and felt her face flush. "I wonder, sir, how it comes you think you may speak to me thus? I pray it will not be in hearing of my brother or friends, for you may find you have to defend yourself."

Mr. Swalen glanced down the table at Jason. His upper lip lifted in a perceptible sneer. "I am all in a quake. Your brother indeed looks formidable."

"I have friends," she snapped.

"Do you speak of Debham? Or Corbright? But to call on them would doubtless raise expectations you seem unwilling to fulfill. As you chose to conduct your life as a man, why do you not enjoy the freedom of a man, Miss Ormhill? I would be more than happy to, ah, serve you, without any expectation of marriage."

Olivia had never been spoken to in such a manner before. She turned away, blinking furiously, horrified to find that she was near tears. And the devil of it was, the obnoxious man spoke some truth. Who would take up arms on her behalf? Jason, certainly. Edmund, as Swalen said. And Corbright.

And could she bear the consequences of such an action, where failure must mean death to someone she cared for, and success might well mean being beholden to someone she preferred to keep at arm's length? *And it would mean I must admit to myself and all the world that I need a man to protect me,* she thought. This aspect of female existence had never before been borne in on her with such force.

Rather than have more speech with the man who had become so suddenly a demon in her mind, she turned back to Mr. Marshmore and smiled at him, determined to engage him in conversation about porcine matters until the dinner had ended.

Chapter Twelve

The ladies followed Mrs. Herville into her salon, named rather grandly the Queen Elizabeth drawing room, though it was doubtful the great queen had ever been near Norvale. There the conversation quickly turned to the eligible men present that evening. Olivia learned that the Swalens were former army officers who had recently purchased the Smithfield place. She parried a spate of pointed questions about her relationships with Lord Corbright and Lord Edmund, then spent the next half hour listening to the praises of both men being sung by young ladies and their mothers. Clearly her announcement that she had no claim to either of these gentlemen, nor wished to have any, had relieved them a great deal.

Mary Benson particularly sang the praises of Lord Edmund, whom she declared all that a gentleman should be. "He told the most exciting war story at dinner," she said.

This surprised Olivia, knowing how unpleasant a topic the war was to him. *She is fairly smitten,* Olivia thought. *I do hope her father isn't too rude in letting Edmund know his suit is unwelcome.* Mr. Benson was a wealthy man, heir to a fortune made in India by his uncle. Mary had many suitors, though at the advanced age of eighteen she still languished unmarried, as her father had refused all offers for her hand. She was a featherheaded young woman, as was quickly proved when Jane Herville asked her to retell Lord Edmund's war story.

Mary waved her hands distractedly. "Oh, I can't remember it all. Something about his horse joining in the fighting. It left me quite breathless, but you must ask him for the details."

It looked as if they would have the chance to do so immediately, for the gentlemen began filtering into the room just then, obviously intent on dancing with the young ladies rather than spending their time together over the port. Corbright made directly for Olivia, which she could not understand, as he had no dance to claim. Just behind him Edmund and Mr. Benson entered together, and to Olivia's surprise the men seemed on extremely good terms with one another. The older man steered Edmund straight toward Mary, and though she could not hear what was said, Olivia concluded it contained nothing to dampen Mary's spirits, and Edmund took his seat beside the girl while the father joined his peers by the fireplace.

"Looks as if Eddy has made a conquest," Corbright murmured into her ear, startling her a little, for her attention had been entirely focused upon the same little saga.

"It does indeed, and with her father's approval, more's the surprise."

"Doubtless he is unaware of Edmund's penniless status. Or perhaps Mr. Benson is becoming desperate to marry off the little hen-wit." He smiled down at her, then sat by her side. "I cannot tolerate hen-witted females, you know. Intelligent ones are much more to my taste."

She felt a wave of the old magic sweep over her as Franklin looked into her eyes, his warm approval softening the heart it had first won when she was an awkward sixteen-year-old smarting under the criticism that she was a bluestocking. His words particularly soothed her after George Swalen's insults. For the first time in several years she smiled at him without reservation. "Even if they don't care to pursue Greek anymore?"

"Ah. You will return to your true nature once you are relieved of the burdens you currently carry."

Olivia frowned, but before she could respond, Mrs. Herville began urging her guests into the ballroom, where a small band of local musicians struck up a lively tune as they entered the room. Corbright escorted Olivia there, and to her surprise made as if to lead her out. "This dance was promised to . . ." She remembered the name with a sudden blush. Her obnoxious dinner partner had taken her first dance, and she had wondered how she would get out of it without refusing to dance the rest of the evening. She didn't want to do that. It had been a long time, but Olivia had always loved to dance, and found herself yearning to take the floor again.

"To my utter surprise Mr. George Swalen approached me and asked me to take his place. He said you had taken exception to some remarks of his during dinner and he doubted either of you would enjoy the dance."

"He is entirely correct," Olivia said, chin up. "I am pleased not to have him partner me."

Corbright looked severe. "Did he insult you in any way, Livvy? For if he did, I will make him pay for it!"

"You men. Always so eager to fight! No, Franklin, there is no need to do anything more than dance with me."

"With the greatest pleasure." His pale blue eyes flashed with an intensity that made Olivia catch her breath. Corbright made good use of the little snatches of conversation they were allowed during the dance to continue the compliments he had begun in the drawing room.

"Your gown is ravishing," he said. "You are by far the loveliest woman here."

A few moments later: ". . . and the most intelligent.

". . . and the most interesting.

"The Greeks, you know, had many strong yet feminine women among their pantheon of goddesses. Men who do not find the combination of beauty and brains beguiling are fools."

His remarks almost form a counterpoint to Swalen's, Olivia thought as they were separated again in the figures of the dance. The blue-devils that had threatened after her dinner partner's disdain fled her, leaving a kind of effervescence in their place.

"You are gallant, sir," she responded.

"Honest," was his reply. "I should like to see you attired

as a goddess. Lovely as is your costume, I imagine you in Grecian drapery. Diana, perhaps, with her quiver and bow."

She laughed. "I cannot hit a target two feet in front of me."

"Athena, then. Wise as well as lovely."

"Sometimes I am not wise at all." For a moment she felt sad, thinking of her dilemma with her brother, who so yearned for her to marry and free him of his obligation to watch over her. Did the solution now weave through the formations of the dance with her?

"Or best of all, Aphrodite."

She blushed. "A rather naughty female at times, I believe."

"Yes." He looked quite serious as they moved apart once, and when they came together again he said, "Perhaps I should best liken you to Odysseus's wife, that pattern of fidelity and capability, whose name I suddenly can't recall."

"Penelope."

"That's the one! Like you, she managed his affairs quite well while he was gone, and fended off all suitors, to welcome her long-lost husband at last."

The dance had ended. They stood together, staring at one another, as the others left the floor. Slowly, reluctantly, he relinquished her to her next partner. Her mind busied itself with Corbright's comments and her own surprisingly favorable response as she gave superficial attention to her partner in the next dance.

This distraction ended when Edmund stood before her for the waltz. The warmth in his brown eyes brought her back to the present with a heart-fluttering thump. She dimly recollected seeing him dancing with Mary in the previous set. She decided to tease him upon the matter.

"It seems you have made a conquest, my lord."

He did not pretend to misunderstand her. "She is a child, and a rather silly one at that. Her father is a man of sense, though."

"I am surprised he was so cordial to you. He guards his daughter like a dog with a bone, in the general way."

"From fortune hunters, you mean." His expression darkened.

Olivia saw that she had hurt him, and regretted it. "That was not my meaning."

"Wasn't it?" He lifted a skeptical eyebrow as the music began and he swung her into the waltz.

"No, I meant—"

"Never mind, Olivia. I do not want to talk about or think about Mary Benson just now." The look he gave her sent a surge of warmth through her blood. For the rest of the dance they gave themselves up to the music and the rhythm, and the feeling of being so close.

Perhaps I am a bit too much like Aphrodite, Olivia thought as she found herself disappointed when the music ended. *To have two men create such warmth of feeling in me in one night is quite scandalous.* The reasons differed, though. Corbright had soothed her pride, but Edmund had stirred her blood.

Arthur Swalen did not appear for his dance, either, and Olivia decided to sit at her aunt's side instead of accepting another partner. She noted with amazement that Aunt Lavinia was being returned to the chaperones' chairs by Mr. Barteau. *Aunt Lavinia has been dancing!* She could never remember a time when her aunt had danced, much less danced a waltz.

Mr. Barteau bowed deeply to Lavinia, thanked her lavishly for the dance, and offered to bring both women some lemonade. As the room was warm, this was a welcome suggestion. Edmund had already left her to seek out his next partner, and she sat fanning herself as she watched both him and Franklin partner other women in a minuet.

"He dances divinely," Aunt Lavinia said.

"Who, Corbright or Lord Edmund?"

Lavinia looked a little startled. "Both," she pronounced, after a moment's consideration.

"Yes, both." Olivia sighed.

"But that was not my meaning. I referred to Mr. Barteau."

Olivia turned to give Lavinia her full attention. "I did not know you could waltz, Aunt."

"Nor did I." It was Lavinia's turn to sigh.

Olivia was speechless. Her aunt was clearly infatuated. She glared at Mr. Barteau, just returning with their lemonade. *I do hope his careless attentions to her do not arouse hopes that cannot be fulfilled, and break her heart.* From things her aunt had let drop in conversation through the years, she knew the homely woman had once yearned for suitors, for a husband, for family. Failing that, she had lived with her brother, Olivia and Jason's father. Olivia's mother had died when she was twelve. From that time until this Lavinia had been a mother to Olivia and Jason, and their affection for her was deep. Olivia thought she had been reasonably contented with her lot in life. It would be a great shame for her equilibrium to be upset to no purpose. Mr. Barteau was no paragon of physical beauty himself, of course, but Olivia knew wealthy men expected—and usually could command—a beautiful bride even when they were quite homely.

She sipped her lemonade and listened as Lavinia and Mr. Barteau continued what was obviously an ongoing conversation about fashion history.

When the dancing had ended and the party began to break up, Corbright returned to Olivia's side and remained there as the guests took their leave of their hosts; then he followed her to her carriage. "I'll call on you tomorrow," he said, handing her up.

She looked down at him and smiled. "It being Sunday, I expect I shall see you in church."

"I expect I shall, else I would not dare call at your home after, or your uncle would read me the riot act!"

"Just so. He thinks you half a pagan."

"I am." He ignored the servant trying to put up the steps, stepping up to bring his lips to Olivia's ear. " 'Great God! I'd rather be a pagan, suckled in a creed outworn. . . .' "

She tapped his cheek with her fan. "Shush. He'll hear you."

He kissed his hand to her as he descended to the carriageway. *"Au revoir."*

Olivia settled next to Lavinia, smiling.

"You both look like the cat that ate the cream," her uncle grumbled from deep in the corner of the carriage.

"A delightful evening," Olivia said.

"It was indeed," Lavinia said. "And he is to call tomorrow."

"Don't scowl, Uncle Milton. He has promised to be in church," Olivia said.

"He said nothing of it to me," Lavinia cried. "I did not think to mention it to him."

Olivia guessed her meaning, but Uncle Milton wondered, "Why should you think to urge Lord Corbright to church, sister?"

"Corbright? Why, indeed? I meant Mr. Barteau."

"Aunt Lavvy?" Olivia awakened her aunt by shaking her shoulder. "Jason and Edmund have not come home from the party."

"I expect they went to the Black Lion afterward. You know Jason always says he can't sleep after dancing."

"Yes, but it is so late." Olivia looked at her aunt's mantel clock. "Three A.M."

"You worry about him too much, Olivia." Lavinia's voice sounded weary. "Go to sleep, dear. Edmund is with him, after all."

Edmund is with him. It did comfort her a little. "Sorry I woke you." She leaned over and kissed Lavinia on the cheek. Once she was back in her room, sleep refused to come. The events of the evening played around and around in her head: Corbright's rudeness, Mary Benson's infatuation with Edmund, George Swalen's insults, Corbright's flattery, her two dances, for she did not count any of the others, only the dances with Franklin and Edmund. How she had responded to both men. And then there was her aunt's infatuation with Mr. Barteau.

As these thoughts buzzed through her head, time passed, and her uneasiness grew. She knew young men had needs they met in ways best not to think about. The thought of Jason and Edmund out whoring together did not calm her. Quite the contrary. She decided to go down to her office and get some work done, but all she did was pace the room, turning frequently to look out the window with a view of the lane. The three-quarter moon was setting, but she would soon be able to see their carriage lights when they came home. At last, past four o'clock, she saw the lights. Relief mixed with exasperation as she blew out her candles to keep Jason from knowing she had been watching for him. He already felt sufficiently tied to her apron strings without that!

She hastened out her office and up the stairs. Just as she reached the top, she heard John Baird, the sleepy footman who had waited up, greet his master with a cry. "Sir! What has become of you. Here, let me help, Lord Edmund."

Heart racing, Olivia peeped around the corner. Supported by the two men, Jason staggered up the steps. She could not see his face, but his clothes were in disarray. Foxed? Injured?

She debated making herself known, to see for herself, when she heard him say, "Shhhh, don't make any noise. Don't wake Livvy. Have a fit, she would."

"She'll find out soon enough, sir," Baird said in a scolding voice. He had been with them long enough to assume that familiarity.

"True enough." Edmund chuckled. "Can't hide that eye from her for long."

"But by tomorrow I'll have worked out what to tell her. Don't want her to know what that man said. Bad enough she'll know he knocked me senseless, without knowing why. You don't think Swalen will talk about her again, do you?"

"I think he has a well-developed sense of self-preservation."

Olivia drew back, deep into the alcove that held an ancestral suit of armor. *Swalen! He insulted me in front of my brother. That beast!* She did not want Jason to be aware of her. He did not want her to know, so she must pretend she didn't.

The three men made their way past her to Jason's room.

Once they had entered it, she couldn't resist drawing nearer, hoping to hear more. But all she heard was Turnby's sleepy voice quickly growing hysterical at the sight of his master. After a few minutes of confusion, he said, "You need someone to look after that cut on your hand, my lord. I'll ring for Morton, shall I?"

Edmund responded, "Nonsense. I can manage. No need waking up any more of the house. I'll leave you to Turnby and Baird, Jason."

"Right. And thanks again, Edmund. He'd have gotten away with his blasted insults if you hadn't joined in. But I did pop one over his guard, didn't I?"

"That you did. Bloodied his nose smartly."

Olivia retreated to her alcove as she heard Edmund leaving, knowing she couldn't make it to her room in time to avoid being seen. So Edmund had fought Swalen, too. Was he badly cut? Did he need for her to bandage his hand? She fought the urge to go to him. In vain, as it happened. Instead of crossing the hall to his own room, Edmund walked toward her hiding place.

"You can come out of there now, Olivia."

Chapter Thirteen

When she left her sanctuary, Olivia could not make out Edmund's expression in the dark hallway. A guilty conscience made her stammer out, "I didn't intend to spy. I had been working in my office when—"

"I thought I saw your light there, just as we turned into the carriageway. I confess I am surprised you did not make yourself known, especially when you realized Jason had been hurt."

"I heard him say he did not want me to know. I thought he would decide I had been waiting up for him, and take umbrage."

Even in the darkness she could see the flash of teeth as Edmund laughed quietly. "Yes, taking umbrage is something Jason is rather good at. Shall we continue this conversation elsewhere, before he takes umbrage at our talking about him behind his back?"

She let him take her by the elbow and lead her up the stairs to the long gallery. He guided her to the south end, and they sat facing one another on the banquette beneath the tall window, their only light that of the stars and the setting moon.

"What happened, Edmund? Can you tell me?"

"After the party several of the men decided to meet at the Black Lion for cards. I played with someone else; Jason sat with the Swalen brothers. The next thing I knew, Jason had jumped the table and landed the older one, Jerome, or—"

"George."

"Yes, George. Planted him a facer, shouting something about insulting his sister. When I reached him, Jason asked me to be his second."

Olivia drew in an alarmed breath.

"No, don't worry. No duel is forthcoming."

"How did you prevent it?"

"I first asked the cause, but Jason refused, saying it would only spread the insult to a wider audience. Swalen declined to apologize, so I negotiated with his brother that the matter would be settled with fisticuffs. They went outside, and with lanterns to light their way, had at one another. I am sorry to say Jason got the worst of it. In fact, he was knocked quite unconscious, at which point I . . ." Edmund paused, looking down at his right hand.

"I suggested Swalen make his apology or we would continue, as I'd no mind to let an insult to you go unanswered. A few minutes more and he agreed to regret his words."

"Oh, Edmund." Olivia gently took his hand in hers. Her eyes had adjusted to the light, and she could see that blood oozed from his knuckles. "It must hurt. I shall bandage it. I am so very grateful to you." And she kissed his palm.

"I am well recompensed, then."

She lifted misty eyes to see his tender expression. He lifted his other hand and cupped her jaw, bending almost to kiss her, then pulling away.

"Sorry. You look so lovely in the moonlight. But you'd think me an opportunist to steal the kiss I want so much."

"You won't have to steal it." She leaned forward, held her face up, and let her eyes drift closed as he pressed his mouth to hers. It was a tender, gentle kiss that sent sweet yearning sensations all through her, and he ended it before she wished.

For several moments they just sat there and looked at one another in the dim light. *What am I,* she wondered, *to want his kisses so much, when I felt earlier in the evening that I might still love Franklin?* She bit her lower lip and looked away. Edmund sighed and started to rise.

She stopped him by asking how badly Jason had been hurt.

"He's going to have a very black eye and swollen jaw, but he took no permanent harm, unless it be to his pride."

"He has such a hot temper. I wonder what it was all about?"

"As to that, he would say only that he had provocation enough."

Olivia shuddered, remembering the things George Swalen had said to her at dinner. "That I can believe."

"I take it the Swalens have some sort of quarrel with your family? For I could not help but notice how little you enjoyed your dinner conversation with him."

"I am surprised you noticed, considering how well you and Mary Benson got on."

He laughed. "That is the second time you have alluded to her. Dare I hope you are jealous?"

She tipped her chin up. "Certainly not."

"Pity."

Another long, pregnant pause ensued, which Olivia half feared, half hoped would end in another kiss. But Edmund roused himself and stood. "You did not answer my question about the Swalens."

"I never saw either of them before tonight, nor heard tell of them."

He held out his hand to her. "Come, Olivia. It will be dawn soon. You need some rest."

"And you need that hand taken care of."

"I can manage it."

"I insist."

He flashed that smile again, the one that made her feel a bit weak in the knees. "Much as I would relish your ministrations, your presence in my room at this hour might cause talk."

"We'll go to the kitchen. I've no doubt Cook will have begun breakfast by now, anyway."

Having obtained the necessary basin of water, unguent, and bandages, they repaired to Olivia's office. As she washed and bandaged his hand, she pondered Jason's behavior.

"He has always been hot to hand. I do wish he would learn to control his temper."

"A young man cannot hear his sister insulted and do nothing, Olivia."

She frowned. "No, I suppose not. Do you think I worry too much about him?"

"No. I think you do not worry enough."

This brought her head up sharply. "Now you have surprised me."

"He is no hand with his fists, though pluck to the backbone. Does he fence? Shoot well?"

"He rarely misses his bird."

"That is not what I meant, and you know it."

"No, he is an indifferent shot with the pistol. And his fencing can but be rudimentary, for he has had little training."

"As I supposed. Perhaps you thought to protect him by neglecting these matters."

She sighed. "My father took no interest in the so-called manly arts. And I thought them dangerous."

"I understand your desire to protect him. But it is much more dangerous, particularly for one of Jason's temperament, if he does not know how to defend himself, Livvy."

Olivia said nothing. The use of her nickname on his lips distracted her momentarily. She ought to scold him, to return to formality with him. And knew she wouldn't. She finished her task, rinsed her hands, and moved away from him, going to the French doors to look out at the scene beginning to lighten with the faint hint of dawn.

"Shall I take him in hand, Livvy?"

He had come to stand beside her, looking down at her with that warmth that she found so delightfully unsettling.

"I can teach him some science, though of course I've not had the benefit of the tutelage of Gentleman Jackson. Still, when in cantonment in Portugal, we filled many hours sparing and fencing. I am accounted a very good man with a sword and pistol, too."

When she did not answer, he looked away. "Of course,

Corbright is known to be accomplished in fencing and shooting. Perhaps he will take the boy in hand."

Olivia shook her head. "I do not wish to be beholden to him." He turned his head back, and she saw the quick dawning of hope. "Not . . . not yet. I do not know . . . I am very confused right now."

"Ah." He looked away again, and his mouth took on a grim line. "Nor do you wish to be beholden to me. I understand entirely, though I assure you I do not think teaching Jason to defend himself would give me the right to expect anything from you."

She looked up at him now, looked into a face that had hardened, grown wary. "I do not think you would, Edmund. I trust you. Yes, I would like you to take him in hand. Perhaps . . . perhaps you could even suggest that we go to London instead of our usual trip to Scotland for the shooting season. He could go to Manton's, and perhaps this so-called Gentleman Jackson could give him a few pointers. If the suggestion came from you . . ."

He smiled, warmth returning to his eyes. "Much better than from his sister!"

"Much! And I confess I would prefer London to Scotland for a change. For him to shoot and hunt, Aunt Lavinia and I must go, you see. He won't leave me. We go there for the grouse, then return here for the holidays, then off to Melton Mowbray for foxhunting. A tiring, boring trip for my aunt and I, but we must go, else he would fret even more than he already does. And it is always so difficult to manage things here when I am away. London will be more convenient."

How they both suffer from this strange bind they are in, Edmund thought. "Perhaps I can look after things here for a few weeks, if you think me up to it."

"I think you up to most anything you put your mind to, Edmund. That is the very thing! I shall make a list of what needs to be done. You've already gained the respect of my workers; they'll follow your direction quite as well as mine. Perhaps better." She smiled ruefully, a smile that turned suddenly into a massive yawn.

"I hope you can stay abed this morning," he said, looking worried.

"Alas, I cannot. Uncle would be very disappointed if I missed services. I can nap this afternoon, though." She turned back to the scene before them. "I love being up at dawn, though I rarely see it at the end of the night, rather than the beginning of the day." She looked out at the river, now echoing the pink streaks in the dawn sky. "It's beautiful."

"A beautiful sight indeed," he agreed. But he was not looking at the scenery.

Corbright startled her by appearing just after breakfast the next morning. He asked to speak to her privately, and immediately launched into a tirade. "I shall call George Swalen out," he declared. "Any insult to you will not be tolerated."

"I wish no duels fought! The matter was dealt with at the time."

"Hmmmph. Fisticuffs. Not a gentleman's way of dealing with such a matter."

"Better a broken nose than a death. Edmund flattened the man. That is enough."

"And that is another thing. It is not for Edmund to protect you," he shouted.

"It is not for you to protect me, either. It is none of your affair."

"And it *is* Edmund's, I suppose?" Corbright spoke through clenched teeth, a vein throbbing in his temple.

Olivia shuddered. "A tavern brawl is all it was, and best forgotten. How did you know about it?"

"Servants seem to know everything," Corbright said, waving his hand vaguely. "Olivia, I beg you to marry me right away. I will protect you, and Jason can go about his life."

Olivia snapped, "I cannot accept. I would prefer that you not come here if you cannot refrain from pressing me this way." She turned her back on him. "Please go."

There was a long silence behind her. At last she heard

him sigh. "Very well, Olivia. I will go. But whether you will have me or not, no man is going to insult you with impunity."

She whirled on him. "A duel will make me a byword in the community and cause a lifetime of scandal. I forbid it."

"There are other ways, and I will find them. For now, I bid you good-bye before we quarrel further." He took her by the shoulders and pressed a quick kiss to her lips, striding away without acknowledging her protest.

Whether because of his annoying possessiveness, or because of the memory of Edmund's tender kiss last night, Olivia couldn't have said—all she knew was an intense relief that he was gone, and satisfaction that it would be Edmund, not Corbright, who would teach Jason to defend himself.

After Sunday services Uncle Milton accompanied them home and joined them for luncheon, where he inspected his injured nephew and hollow-eyed niece closely. He glared sternly at Jason. "Once we are alone, I expect you to be more forthcoming with me about exactly what was said. If it was some minor taunt, you have by your actions exposed Olivia to scandal for little reason."

"I will gladly tell you, sir, in private." Jason held his head high. Olivia found it painful to look at him, with his purpling eye and swollen jaw, but she knew as she looked into his eyes that the comment had been as bad as what Swalen had murmured in her ear at dinner. She wondered, if Edmund knew the full truth, whether he would still think it had not been a killing matter.

"There goes Corbright. Looks as if he just came from Beaumont." Jason peered down at the tall, elegantly dressed rider on the road that rose toward Flintridge.

"You did better on that shot." Edmund strolled to the edge of the bluff and looked down. "Calling on your sister, I suppose." Corbright had called several times since the Hervilles' party. He looked at Jason, wondering what the boy thought of the man's attentions to his sister.

Jason smiled. "Yes, looks like it's on again. I did better, you say? Does that mean I actually hit the target this time?"

Edmund laughed. "Tipped the edge. Here, I've reloaded for you. Have another go. This pistol throws to the left, remember."

As he watched Jason aim and fire the pistol, Edmund pondered his situation. After their kiss the night of the Hervilles' party, Edmund knew his heart was in serious danger from Olivia Ormhill. He could have seduced her that night. She had been vulnerable, and she was attracted to him. He had promised her he would not do so, however. He wouldn't want her with anything less than her full consent, which meant mind and heart as well as body. Would she ever want him that way? Or was her heart still Corbright's? The thought sent pain lancing through him.

"Come into my study, please. Betty, have tea sent in, if you will," Milton Ormhill instructed his maid before closing the door to his study. "Now, what brings you here today, my lord? Not spiritual guidance, I suppose?"

Corbright flashed a quick smile at his host. He seated himself and regarded the man as if not quite knowing how to begin. "Recent events relating to Olivia underscore my purpose in coming here today. I wish to purchase Jason's land."

Ormhill almost dropped the pipe he had begun to fill. "You what?"

"You see, sir, Jason has no interest in it. He wishes to travel. You cannot deny that Olivia's management of the land occupies her far more than is good for her. It would be in both their interests if he sold and placed the money in the funds. His income would be secure, he could do as he pleases, and Olivia's cares and burdens would be sufficiently reduced that she might well consider marriage."

Corbright leaned forward, looking earnestly at his astonished host. "I hope she will marry me, sir, but whether me or someone else, she must marry. It is not right, not safe even, for a woman to be on her own. Eventually she will be, you know, if matters go on as they have."

Ormhill templed his hands, forcing himself to consider this request calmly. "Jason is younger than she; he'll always look out for her."

"Unkind, though, to tie the boy down so, wouldn't you say? And this recent quarrel with George Swalen—well, don't think it will be the last. A hot young blood like Jason, cooped up as he is—"

Ormhill interrupted him. "We all feel the same on this subject. And I agree Olivia should marry. I must say I am impressed that you express yourself as wishing her to do so, even if it is not to you."

"Naturally, I hope and believe it will be me. But I truly care for her. I want her free to find someone she can love and trust, and live a woman's life as God intended."

At this the vicar rose and went to his window, which looked out upon the main street of the tiny village of Flintridge. "I am not entirely sure what God intended for women. The Bible praises female industry, you know. Are you familiar with the verses in Proverbs praising the woman who purchases a field and plants a vineyard?"

"But the woman referred to in that passage is a married woman, under the protection and guidance of a husband, is she not? I would not deprive Olivia of her interests in husbandry, nor her dominion over her own estate, even if her father's will did not prohibit it. He did not know me well, if he thought I would."

"He didn't aim that will at you. It had been planned for a long time, since our sister . . ." Ormhill's voice broke and he covered his eyes briefly.

"I bitterly regret not understanding that three years ago. What do you say, sir? Will you not consider my offer? As I told Jason, I will be most generous as to price."

"Jason has agreed to this?"

"He wished to think it over. He thought you'd never allow it, but I know you to be a man of reason."

"Still, to sell Ormhill land . . ."

"I know it would be hard. Perhaps . . . perhaps a lease," Corbright offered, brow furrowed. "Yes. Perhaps a lease. Five years, with an option to purchase if Jason still has no interest in it. Once his estate is out of her hands, I think Olivia will marry. He can then see the world and yet return to his land if and when the wanderlust is satisfied."

Milton Ormhill beamed upon the man regarding him so imploringly. "You surprise me, Lord Corbright. I think perhaps I have underestimated you. I will discuss the matter with Jason, but the offer of a lease seems to me to be an excellent idea."

Chapter Fourteen

"For goodness' sake! It looks as if all the county is here." Lavinia leaned forward to look out the window at Corbright Manor, which the late summer twilight revealed to be surrounded by carriages.

"So it does." Olivia shrugged. "So much for an intimate dinner!"

Lavinia smiled archly at her niece. "Did you wish for one, dear?"

Olivia shook her head briefly. "Certainly not. But I expected one, merely a return of our hospitality to him and his uncle last week." Corbright's uncle had practically lived at their house since the Hervilles' party two weeks before, courting her aunt even more assiduously than Corbright courted her. "Such a fete as this surely took some planning. Isn't that Lord Dalway getting out of that carriage? He is not the type to accept a spur-of-the-moment invitation."

"I'm sure I don't know, but I suppose Corbright might have planned this without inviting us, then added us to the list as the two of you seemed to be getting along so well. Or perhaps the surprise he mentioned in his invitation has something to do with it?"

"I don't like surprises," Livvy fretted. She certainly hoped tonight's surprise didn't involve her.

Jason tugged at his cravat. "Are you quite sure this is tied right, Livvy? I don't want to appear the gudgeon, and Turnby does not approve of elaborate cravats, so he was no help."

"It is the loveliest waterfall I have ever seen," Livvy assured him.

He looked at her suspiciously. "Have you ever seen a waterfall?"

"Yes, certainly."

"Ah. That's all right, then."

Olivia smiled at her brother. In some ways he seemed a different person than he had been before Edmund came to them in late July. He had developed a more muscular physique, and a more mature outlook on life, but he still seemed impossibly boyish sometimes, and this was just such a moment.

Edmund went to the dinner party with Uncle Milton, as five would crowd Jason's carriage. He had been a bit surprised to be invited to Corbright's party. On the way, Mr. Ormhill sought additional information about his childhood experiences with Lord Corbright.

"I have told you the worst of several incidents. I believe at the time Franklin was much impressed by our family's title and history. For a cit's son to have been taken up by the scion of a noble family must have been heady stuff. I thought he would do anything to ingratiate himself with the aristocracy. Perhaps his behavior toward me echoed my brother's attitude, for Carl hated me cordially, but I can't help feeling it also reflects a vicious disposition."

"Certainly his father yearned to be accepted into the *ton*. I confess I have always wondered why Franklin chose Olivia, rather than a member of a more tonnish family. Ah, there it is. A grand spectacle, is it not?"

Edmund leaned forward to see past Mr. Ormhill. Ahead stood a majestic home with massive Ionic columns on a broad portico, gilded by the late evening sun and ablaze with lights. "Quite something. It looks new."

"It is. A lovely Elizabethan manor, Corbright Hall, was torn down to make way for it."

Edmund settled back against the squabs again. "So that is where the Corbright title comes from—the manor. Apparently Franklin's father thought using his family name might unnecessarily remind the *ton* of his plebeian origins."

"Apparently he also thought the Tudor home insufficiently grand for his new title, for he had already begun its transformation when he died." Ormhill's scornful tone made Edmund laugh.

As they approached Corbright's palatial home, Edmund pondered his relationship with the woman he now knew he loved. Olivia seemed to have accepted him, laughing and joking with him or talking over the latest agricultural journal quite as if he were her peer in knowledge as well as interest. There had been no more romantic interludes, though. She guarded her heart carefully. Did it still belong to Corbright? *She certainly can't fear that Franklin wants her just for her possessions,* he thought sadly as he looked at the ostentatious display of wealth that was Corbright Hall.

"You are right; he must have had this planned for some time," Lavinia whispered into her niece's ear as she noted the guests, many of whom were not local at all, but had arrived from the four corners of England. They stood in the magnificent entryway waiting their turn to be announced and exchanging nods and greetings with acquaintances.

"Yes. Gracious, there is Cynthia. Fancy Lord Bower coming all this way for a dinner." She smiled a greeting, and the lush blonde tugged her husband toward them.

"Olivia! Are you Corbright's surprise, then? For I am indeed surprised to see you here. Is there to be an interesting announcement tonight?"

"Not concerning me, I assure you. We are here as neighbors and friends, nothing more."

"Hmmmm. Well, it is wonderful to see you. You have kept well away from town, and have been missed. Is it not so, my love?"

Lord Bower bowed his assent to this observation. He had been one of Olivia's suitors during her season. A taciturn man, he had chiefly signified his interest by standing near her whenever possible. When she became engaged to Corbright, he had courted Cynthia the same way. Olivia could

not but wonder in what manner he had conveyed his proposal. She did not wonder at Cynthia's acceptance, though.
Beautiful though she was, Cynthia's chances at a good
match had been severely limited by a small dowry. Lord
Bower's wealth and title must have spoken quite eloquently
for him.

"I understand you are become a great political hostess,"
she said to Cynthia.

"Oh, yes. Bower is going to be a part of the ministry next
year, I shouldn't doubt, and I take a great deal of credit,
don't I, my love?"

Lord Bower nodded. "Charm," he allowed.

Olivia supposed that Bower had the ability to converse
more fluently about politics than he had to make idle
chitchat, else he would not be a rising star among the Tories.

A stir in the group of people around them directed their
attention to the open front door, where a footman was bowing Edmund and her uncle into the entryway.

"Who is that gorgeous man?" Cynthia whispered in her
ear.

As if answering her, Lord Bower muttered, "Edmund
Debham!"

"Lord Edmund is our houseguest," Jason volunteered. "A
friend of mine."

"Heslington," Bower said.

Cynthia cocked her head at her husband. "Ah, yes. Lord
Edmund's brother. Bad blood there, I understand. Should
add a certain interest to the evening."

"Lord Heslington is here, then?" Olivia felt a stirring of
unease.

"As you see." Cynthia nodded toward a tall man a few
feet ahead of them.

When their party was announced, Corbright's perfunc-
tory politeness to the others gave way to effusive praise of
Olivia's beauty, and expressions of joy at her arrival. He
drew her aside, in fact, for a tête à tête in defiance of all the
rules of hospitality.

"Livvy, dearest, I can't tell you . . . I am almost overcome. To see you here in my home! I wish all my other

guests at Jericho. But alas, this evening was planned long ago, and will be a great triumph, which your presence only makes the more delightful for me. In fact, I wish that you would consent to make it a double triumph. What do you say, shall we announce our engagement? Many already expect it."

Olivia drew away, irritated. "Impossible."

"Oh, it's possible," he said confidently. "But you still require more time. Well, you shall have it, my love. You have waited three long years for me; I can't deny you a generous and ardent courtship in return. But the outcome shall be the same. I won't let you slip away again." His look of burning intensity brought a flush to Olivia's cheeks.

She lowered her eyes and responded lightly, "You must let me slip away and give you back to your guests." She led him across the room. "I see that Heslington is here."

"Indeed. It should be interesting to see what he makes of his brother's new career."

That Corbright and Olivia went apart for a private conversation at such a time seemed unpleasantly significant to Edmund. His opinion was shared by others. Jane Herville asked him if he thought there would be an engagement announced that evening. Mary Benson allowed that surely the surprise mentioned by Corbright in his invitation could be nothing else.

A chill went through Edmund as he remembered the wording of the invitation: *Please join me for dinner. Afterward there will be a surprise which will be of great interest to all who live in Norvale.* Could the surprise be the announcement of their engagement? Though she had received Corbright's visits politely, she had not seemed to Edmund to behave like a woman in love. Nor did she seem the type to keep such a secret from her family. However, he had not been present the night Corbright and his uncle dined with the Ormhills. He had decided it was a good time to accept Mr. Benson's invitation to dine with them. Had something happened between Olivia and Corbright that night?

He steeled himself for the possibility. If Olivia accepted

Corbright, he firmly told himself he would think no more about the matter. He had learned in the army to control his emotions, to submerge them in his work, and he would do so now.

He noticed his brother standing with a small knot of people by the fireplace. They were all looking at him, and at something his brother said, several laughed. He frowned. Heslington must be dealt with soon. He had no intention of taking any sort of insult lying down, not from such an unnatural brother.

No time like the present. He approached the group just as Olivia and Corbright did.

"Olivia, you remember Lord Heslington." Corbright proceeded to introduce her to those she did not know in the group. Edmund stood back a little, waiting and watching.

"I understand you are my brother's employer now, Miss Ormhill." Heslington glanced briefly at Edmund. "I'd not waste too much time and energy on him, for he always was an ungrateful lad. I purchased his colors, kitted him up for the army at great expense, and made it possible for him to succeed resoundingly at the only career open to one so disinclined to learning, and here he is, having sold out and thrown it all away."

"Lord Edmund is not an employee, my lord, but a valued friend of my brother," Olivia responded hotly.

"What? I heard he spent his days loading hay wains. 'Twas the height of his ambition when a boy, was it not, Edmund?"

Edmund bowed. "Today my aspirations are a bit higher. Miss Ormhill has kindly agreed to school me in the art and science of running a large estate, something my father had intended for me to learn."

Heslington stiffened at this, but said nothing.

Corbright chuckled. "That may be a bit harder than that of the loading of hay wains. I remember well how your old tutor used to complain of your scholarship. Tell me, *did* you ever learn to read and write?"

"Well enough to read and write dispatches to and from

Wellington," Edmund said calmly. "Latin and Greek I confess I never quite saw the need for."

"One does not need them to go into battle, that is true enough. Which is why I thought you so ideally suited for a soldier, brother." Heslington rocked back on his heels, looking very self-satisfied.

"Yes, your kindness toward me has been duly noted. I will be glad to spread the word of it around, if you wish. *All* of it."

Heslington flushed. "Did I not say he was ungrateful, Miss Ormhill? I hope you will spare me a few tips, by the by. I hear that you have developed a type of *sang froid* suited to dry land."

Olivia thought it a very good idea to change the subject before the brothers came to blows, so she allowed Heslington to turn aside with her. "I cannot take credit for developing a new strain of alfalfa, my lord, but I have found that it actually prefers poor soil and dry conditions. I have improved my upper pastures amazingly by planting it." They began to discuss the merits of various crops for grazing cattle.

Edmund understood her intentions, but regretted that Heslington had had the last word. He looked at Corbright, who smiled, eyes half-lowered, like a cat who had just finished a dish of cream.

Dinner passed without incident, and afterward Corbright insisted the men join the ladies immediately, promising champagne after his surprise had been announced. They all trooped into a large, empty salon lavishly decorated in the Greek style, with Ionic columns and faux marble friezes on the walls. Gods and goddesses enacted various legends, and satyrs and nymphs sported on an ornate, gold-trimmed ceiling. If the ladies had studied the scene depicted there they might have blushed. But all eyes were on the two objects in the middle of the room. What appeared to be a large painting and a long table were both draped in white muslin.

When all had entered the room and were ranged around these two objects, Corbright moved to the painting. A footman took up position by the table, ready to remove the drapery.

"Though I cannot make all the happy announcements I wish I could make," he began, bowing to Olivia, "I called you all here to show you a project I have in mind, one which will be of great cultural benefit to Britain. My friends know of the admiration I have for all things Greek. Lord Elgin's marbles have been a source of admiration for me for some time. Someday I hope to travel to see the real thing, but what with banditti of both Greek and Turkish persuasion making the area dangerous, I have decided to bring the Parthenon to England."

With that, he whisked the drapery from the painting. At first no one made a sound. All gazed at a less than excellent rendering of the Parthenon, done in the same florid, over-colored style as the fresco on the ceiling. It stood on a promontory overlooking a valley. Beneath it a Greek village gleamed white in the sunlight. Lesser temples dotted the valley and the hills on either side.

To Edmund there seemed something familiar about the landscape. As he puzzled over it, Jason almost shouted, "That's Norvale."

As a buzz of speculation swept the room, Edmund realized that the scene depicted the entire valley from the viewpoint of Wren Hall, Olivia's property. The bluff on which the Parthenon stood was the one that could be seen across the river from Olivia's office. They had watched the early morning sun gild it after the Hervilles' party.

Corbright raised his hand. "You have the right of it, Mr. Ormhill." He motioned to the footman, who lifted the drapery from the table, revealing a detailed scale model of the same scene depicted in the painting.

Edmund looked at Olivia as she leaned over it. Her expression gave nothing away. Aunt Lavinia was quite another matter.

"One of your lesser temples seems to occupy Sparrow Hill, where the Ormhill hay is stored, Lord Corbright. And where is Beaumont?"

Corbright glanced sideways at Jason. "My artist left them

off, feeling that pastoral simplicity better displayed the magnificence of the scene. That temple on Sparrow Hill is a model of a temple of Persephone."

"As you cannot possibly mean to transport the real thing from Greece, do I understand," Lady Bower asked, "that you propose to build a life-size model of the Parthenon here in Norvale?"

"Precisely." Corbright beamed and appeared to await the approval of his guests.

It came quickly from those not native to the area. Calls of "Bravo," and "I can't wait to see it," could be heard above the less approving murmurs of the local gentry. One of the latter, a red-faced man of nearly sixty, after a hasty conference with some others, said, "That Parthenon of yours occupies the spot where Mr. Smithfield's barns stood."

"The very place." Corbright's smile slipped a little.

"But the Swalen brothers own it now," Mr. Herville objected.

"Not anymore. They sold it to me."

"Deuced odd," Herville said. "Only just bought it. Told me they planned to settle here."

"Yes, well, I decided they were not the sort of people we want here in Norvale." Corbright's jaw jutted out. He looked intently at Olivia. "When I had expressed my opinion to them forcefully enough, they agreed to sell to me. I intend to pull the farm buildings down to make way for the Parthenon, and below it I will build a model Grecian village. It will house visitors to the area, for I am sure there will be many."

"On Ormhill land?" Lavinia looked at her nephew, expecting him to object.

Jason turned beet red. He had not intended to reveal his plans to Livvy in this public way. Indeed, he had scarcely given Corbright's proposed purchase any more thought. He looked to his uncle for help, but the elder Ormhill's complexion was equally high-colored.

"Yes, well, it is speculative, of course," Corbright responded smoothly. "I am hopeful I can work something out

with the young squire, but if not, then it can be relocated on
my own lands."

"What do you think, my dear . . . ah, Miss Ormhill?" He
looked at Olivia expectantly. Every other eye in the room
turned to her, too.

"I scarcely know what to think. It quite takes the breath
away." Olivia flushed deeply. Everyone who lived in Norvale knew why Corbright had decided the Swalens did not
belong here. She wondered how far the tale had spread, and
what embellishments it had received. She hardly knew
whether to thank Corbright for getting rid of them or to
scratch his eyes out for making her the object of such attention. As for building his village on Jason's lands? One
glance at her brother's embarrassed face told her something
was afoot.

"I hoped you would be pleased, being as devoted to
Greek culture as I am."

Olivia lifted doubtful eyes to his. He looked so proud, so
hopeful, she felt she must say something positive. "This
should be educational. Many who can never hope to travel
to Greece can visit this. Though I cannot think the gentle
green hills of Buckinghamshire very close to the pictures I
have seen of the bare limestone cliffs of Athens."

"True, but this area is close to London, so many will visit
on their way to or from the city. Just think of the employment the building of it will offer to workers in the area. I will
schedule construction in the off-season, when agricultural
workers are underemployed. You have recently made me
aware of the problems they face during the winter months."

"That would be excellent." Her doubts still showed in her
voice. Her brain was racing, her slight trust in Corbright
rapidly crumbling. Mr. Smithfield had refused to sell his
land to Corbright for some reason. Now he had it, thanks to
the Swalens. A nagging question suddenly surfaced: how
had he known she would be free to dance with him at the
Hervilles' party? Thinking she had no dance free, why had
he not reserved a dance with some other woman? Had the
insults by George Swalen been planned in advance? Corbright had known of the fight very early the next morning.

Had there been an intentional provoking of Jason that night? With what purpose? Her mind was so busy she scarcely heard Corbright's continued explanations.

"And when the model village is built and begins accepting guests, there will be work there too, of course. I know Miss Ormhill will like that, as she has such tenderness for the welfare of the valley's laboring sort."

"Quite a good idea, I think," Sir Comfrey said, beaming at his host. "It will be the talk of England."

Corbright bowed toward him. "Just so. And here is the champagne, as promised." He gestured to the door, where footmen bearing trays of champagne were entering. "I hope all of my friends will join with me in a toast to the success of this venture . . . and of another I have in mind when I can convince the fair one of its merit."

Murmurs, chuckles, significant looks, and elbowing accompanied this public declaration, putting Olivia to the blush again. The company accepted the champagne and drank the toast enthusiastically. Most of them, that is. Reverend Ormhill did not refuse the toast, nor did Edmund, though both drank it with no sign of pleasure. Only Jason Ormhill did not lift the glass to his lips, but stared at the painting as if transfixed.

Olivia and Aunt Lavinia quaffed the sparkling wine, then turned aside to listen to the cluster of females who surrounded them. Edmund watched Olivia, wondering what she really thought of this ludicrous scheme. *Her smile looks strained,* he thought, but then he gave himself a mental shake. *Wishful thinking,* he cautioned himself. She had not objected to Corbright's very public attentions. He turned away and took another glass of champagne from a servant's tray and downed it. As he drank, he noticed that Jason was in deep and animated discussion with several of the local gentry. He had a rather wild look in his eye. *Have to keep an eye on him,* Edmund thought. *Whatever Olivia thought of that scheme, Jason did not like it by half.*

Olivia slipped away from the crowd of excited guests and headed for the terrace, where she stood looking at the moon shining brightly over the site of the projected Parthenon.

Thoughts and impressions tumbled together in her mind, and she tried to concentrate on the beauty of the night to gain some control. But a memory kept shattering her composure: Mr. Smithfield had come to her shortly after his barns had burned, offering her the purchase of his farm.

"Selling out? But Mr. Smithfield, your barns can be rebuilt. I know you feel badly about the loss of your prize cattle, but . . ."

"No, I won't be doing that. I've had it in mind for some time to try my luck in . . . in Canada."

"For some time? Then why did you put in the new fences this winter? And make those improvements to the cottage?"

"I . . . thought it would fetch me a better price."

Reluctantly she had refused. "I am dreadfully sorry, but we cannot purchase it. We lack the funds. Why do you not offer it to Lord Corbright? Part of it marches with his land, and—"

"No, I will not sell it to Corbright," he had almost shouted. "I will leave it fallow first."

He had stopped abruptly. The look in his eyes, which would not quite meet hers, had been so uneasy, his manner so fearful, that she had not pressed him further. Soon everyone in the valley knew he was going, knew, too, that he had refused to sell to Corbright, but no one knew who had purchased his farm, which had sat idle this last year.

Now Corbright had the land Smithfield had sworn not to sell to him, through the Swalen brothers. Speculation filled her mind with unease. There had been other odd incidents around Flintridge recently—fires, livestock mysteriously stolen or dying suddenly, wells gone bad. At least two other freeholds had been sold and left fallow. *I must look into their ownership.*

"A penny for your thoughts." Corbright joined her at the balcony.

She looked up into eyes filled with longing—and longed to know what thoughts really lay behind them.

Chapter Fifteen

S ince she could not know all of Corbright's thoughts, she had no intention of letting him know all of her own. But one thing she could not forbear to tell him.

"I was thinking how much you have embarrassed me tonight with your pointed attentions. I have told you repeatedly I could offer you only friendship."

"You are looking so beautiful tonight. So fashionable. Another new gown, delightfully designed to show off your charms. Who else did you think to charm with your beauty tonight, if not me?" His mouth tilted up in that confident, arrogant smile that had once made her heart race.

She responded hotly, "You are not the only eligible male here!"

He looked around. "Hmmm. Did you know such a large group would be here?"

"No, I—"

"Did you think the Swalens would be here? Are you displeased that they are gone?"

"No. Though I wish you had not spoken of it in public."

"I will always defend you, Olivia. Now, if it was not the Swalens you hoped to impress, who was it? As far as you knew, there were only the usual local people, mostly married men, boys still in leading strings, or men with one foot in the grave." He slid his hand along her jawline in a possessive caress. "I think you dressed with such care for me tonight."

She spluttered, "I knew Lord Edmund would be here."

Corbright dropped his hand. "Edmund!" He spat the

word. "Edmund Debham is so far beneath you in so many ways, I scarcely have the patience to list them. For one, he is almost illiterate. He is a bearer of tales—exaggerations of the truth and outright lies. And lately, a gamester. Surely an intelligent young woman like yourself would not throw yourself away on a penniless fortune hunter? Look." He turned her toward the room where most of the dinner guests stood talking. "He is making sheep's eyes at Mary Benson. Her fortune outweighs yours, so do not think to capture him with it." He stalked to the balcony, which he gripped tensely, swaying back and forth.

"Edmund Debham is my brother's friend; that is all." She turned away from the sight of Edmund smiling warmly at Mary Benson.

"Good. Walk in the garden with me."

She shook her head. "I have some questions I must ask you."

"About my project?"

"Yes."

"What do you think of it?" His eager, almost boyish look momentarily disarmed her. She could not quite bring herself to snap at him as she wished, *Why is it set on land you didn't yet own? Why a village on Jason's land?* She temporized.

"It will be an astonishing feat. And as I said, it will be educational."

"Olivia, stop fencing with me. I thought you would be thrilled. I surprised you with it, sure that once you saw it, you would be swept away and wish to join with me. . . . Never mind. I was obviously mistaken. You do not like it."

"It isn't that. I am wondering about its location."

"That's easy. The artist, Pierre Montrose, put it there. While he was painting the frescoes in the manor, he also roamed the valley, which he pronounced quite picturesque, making sketches for paintings he planned to do later. One of them was from Wren Hall, which everyone knows has the finest view in the valley. On a whim he put the Acropolis where Smithfield's barns stood, and showed it to me. It fascinated me. I asked him to work it up into a finished oil painting. He added other temples, the village—just let his imagination run riot."

"And you had a model made up from it."

"Yes. But before you begin to see deep plots and dishonesty, let me assure you that the location of the Acropolis can easily be changed, if you object to it."

"I don't object to it; it just seems odd that now you own that land."

He scowled at her. "You don't think I had anything to do with Smithfield's problems?"

"You must admit it looks suspicious, particularly when he told everyone he would never sell to you."

"He went a little crazy after his prize cattle burned. Surely you can't imagine I had anything to do with that, though?" When she did not reply, he moaned. "I deserve for you to suspect me. After all, I jilted you. I must win back your trust. Olivia, if you object to the location of any of the buildings, I will place them elsewhere. Indeed, if you wish, I will abandon the entire scheme. It is you I want. Greek temples are made of marble and would not warm my bed at night as I hope you will."

Abruptly he took her arm and half dragged her down the terrace, out of the line of vision of the guests in his house.

"What are you doing? Let me go!"

"No, I must show you, must convince you." He pulled her behind a hedge. "Oh, Olivia, I love you so much. Can you have forgotten how it was between us?"

She tried to flee, but his hands held her just above her elbows.

"Remember that night when we shared our first kiss?" He leaned close to her. "We were in your aunt's rose garden. The air was heavy with their perfume. You came into my arms so sweetly, so trustingly. You had never been kissed before, but I think you quite liked it."

Olivia relaxed a little. His hands had gentled on her arms, and his voice had taken on a crooning tone. "Yes, I remember. You proposed to me afterward."

"And you accepted. Oh, Olivia, don't let my one rash, foolish act destroy what was so perfect and could be again."

He lowered his head and, when she did not draw back, pressed his lips to hers. Olivia allowed it, wondering if indeed the old magic was still there. *No, be honest,* she told herself. *You wonder if his kiss will affect you as Edmund's did.* She waited for the sizzle to begin in her veins, but it didn't.

His arms went around her, molding her body to his. His lips grew hard and insistent, as if he would compel her to respond to him as she once had. The pressure was painful rather than pleasurable, and she began to push against his chest. He only intensified his efforts. Olivia frantically struggled, kicking him with one foot, with little effect.

Then suddenly it was over. He was stumbling backward, and her brother was between them, charging at Corbright, raging at him. "Get your hands off my sister. Do you think she is some doxy, to be taken behind a hedge? You'll answer to me for this!"

Olivia almost fell from the violence with which her brother had shoved them apart, but she found a pair of strong arms supporting her from behind. She looked over her shoulder into Edmund's concerned eyes.

Corbright put his hand out to prevent another shove. "Take it easy, Jason."

"Take it easy! While you manhandle my sister?"

"My fiancée! Or would be again, if you had not so inopportunely interrupted us."

Jason sneered scornfully. "After you had raped her?"

"Don't be ridiculous. We were kissing one another; that is all."

"She was struggling for all she was worth. You are a lying, deceitful, scheming bastard."

"Take care what you say, Jason."

"I know what I am saying. You are never to go near her again."

By this time Olivia had come to stand by Jason's side, terror thrumming through her. Corbright looked at her, his eyes hard. "You had better rein in this cub, Olivia. I won't tolerate such slurs on my character."

"I am not a cub," Jason snarled. "Name your seconds!"

"No!" Olivia gasped.

"Take care, Corbright." Edmund moved to Jason's other side. "I've known boys of his age to kill grizzled veterans. And you should know I also believe that you were forcing yourself on Miss Ormhill. If Jason fails to convince you of the error of your ways, I shall have to do so."

"Stop it, all of you," Olivia pleaded, looking from one to the other in panic. She saw on Edmund's face that same fierce implacability that she had seen the day he told her why he had always fought with such ferocity. Jason's young features echoed the same harsh determination.

Abruptly Corbright's expression changed. "This is ridiculous. Olivia and I shared a romantic moment in the moonlight. I will admit I became carried away. Jason, you have the right of it. You are not a cub. You know enough of passion to know a man may be overcome by it, don't you? And I'm sure Olivia will agree that at first she was a willing participant."

Even if she had not permitted the kiss, Olivia would have agreed, so desperate was she to prevent a duel between her brother and Corbright. "Yes, yes, I did. We . . . we were talking about old times. About when we became engaged."

Jason's mouth still looked grim with purpose. "You won't marry this man, Livvy. You don't know all of it. When you do, you will never consider him."

"Don't tell her, Jason. Not yet. Let me." Corbright held out his hand to Livvy. "Please, my dear. Come aside with me. I have something to say that you must hear from my lips only."

"On no account." Jason knocked down Corbright's hand. "Go up to the manor, Livvy. Tell Uncle to escort you and Aunt Lavinia home."

"I will not!" Olivia drew herself up. "I am an adult, and this is a ridiculous quarrel."

"Yes. As if I would duel my beloved's brother." Corbright laughed hollowly. "She'd never forgive me, never marry me then, whatever the outcome."

"She never will, anyway."

"I will decide whom I marry. Come, Lord Corbright. We'll step just out of their hearing." Olivia took Corbright's arm, and threw Edmund a pleading look as she moved away with him. She heard Jason's protest, and Edmund's low-voiced response. Whatever he said must have convinced her brother, because he stayed where he was.

When they had gone about ten feet away, Olivia stopped and looked up at Corbright. "What is it that you want to tell me?"

"You know I never meant to force myself on you, Olivia. I became overcome with—"

"Yes, yes, I know, with passion. My father used to say a gentleman never allows his emotions to control him."

Corbright drew back as if she had slapped him. They glared at one another for a long moment; then he sighed. "I suppose I am not a true gentleman, then, nor ever will be."

"Perhaps you had best tell me what it is that Jason started to say to me."

Corbright turned away, looking at the river placidly gleaming in the half-moon's light. "I offered to buy his land."

Olivia gasped. "You *what*?"

"Or lease it, if your uncle would not approve of the sale."

Olivia felt as if she had been dealt a blow to the stomach. "Sell Ormhill land? Did he agree to this? Did my uncle?"

"He hadn't decided. Neither of them had. Olivia, I thought to relieve you of the huge responsibility the management of his estate entails. Now, of course, he thinks I wanted it for my project. I should have realized that construction might have been placed upon my offer. Stupid on my part." He struck his forehead with his hand, then turned to her. "But I swear to you, Livvy, by all I hold sacred, I never did it for that reason. As I told you, I can move the Acropolis to another site, one that we have owned since we first came to Norvale. You can see it from the other side of those shrubs." He held out his hand to her.

"No." She drew back. "Jason wouldn't permit it just now."

"That hothead is going to get himself killed someday. . . ."

"He is my brother. He has a right and a duty to protect me."

Something odd came into Corbright's eyes. "And you, to protect him?"

She felt cold, suddenly. Cold and afraid. "I had best go."

"Olivia, wait. I will cancel the project. I will! I'll sell the manor and all my land here. Anything to convince you and Jason that all I want is you."

Olivia looked into his eyes. He seemed so sincere. He was so dangerous. Suddenly all the turmoil in her mind overwhelmed her. Her head began to buzz, and for the first time in her life she felt she would faint. As she swayed, Corbright caught her, then took advantage of the moment to put his arms around her. She clung to him a moment until her head cleared, then pulled away. "I am going to go home now. I feel a bit tired."

"But you haven't said . . . you do believe me, don't you? Oh, God, how I wish I had not promised myself to the Comfreys. I am to leave with them tomorrow after my guests have gone, to look at an alabaster quarry he owns in Staffordshire. But I can't. I must stay here and convince you somehow—"

"No, go on with your trip. It will give Jason time to cool down."

"Yes, perhaps that would be best. After all, I'll see you in Scotland in a few weeks, when grouse shooting begins, won't I?"

"I . . . we haven't made our plans yet, but I expect so."

"That is all right, then. We'll meet there, and spend time together. Lots of time. We'll talk, become reacquainted, make plans." His eyes seemed feverish in their intensity. Olivia could only nod, wishing to be away from him.

"Good. Then *au revoir*, my love." He took up her right hand and kissed it fervently, then strode back toward the manor. Olivia noticed that he gave Edmund and Jason a wide berth. She slowly approached the two herself, her mind reeling with all that had happened.

"How could you let that man embrace you again?" Jason demanded as she approached.

Olivia did not bother to disabuse him of this notion. "You were going to sell him your land? Without telling me?"

When he heard this, Edmund started as if he'd just heard cannon go off.

Jason looked sideways at him before reluctantly responding to his sister. "I hadn't decided yet. I wanted to free you of the burden. . . ."

"So I would be more likely to marry."

"Well, yes, but . . ."

Olivia sighed. "Oh, Jason." She looked up into his eyes, and saw pain and confusion that echoed her own. "We'll discuss it tomorrow. I am tired. I am going to collect Uncle Milton and Aunt Lavinia and go home. Will you . . . will you come, too? Soon?"

"I've no desire to stay here!" He offered her his arm. "Edmund?"

"Yes, I'll leave, and gladly."

On the way home, Lavinia dominated the conversation, talking with more animation than Olivia could remember her showing before. She had spent the evening in the company of Corbright's uncle, and quoted him endlessly on matters of fashion and garment construction.

"Mr. Barteau plans to establish a museum of fashion," she said. "He is looking for a property where he can suitably house his own collection and add to it. Think of it—he has costumes from the reign of William and Mary! He wants the gown our mother wore to George the Third's coronation. I don't see why he shouldn't have it, do you, Milton?"

As they conversed, Olivia barely listened, commenting as required, while in another part of her mind she turned over and over the events of the evening.

Just as they pulled into the Beaumont carriageway, her uncle called to her: "Olivia? Odd, isn't it, about the Swalens selling out and moving so suddenly?"

"I gather Lord Corbright took my part rather forcefully," Olivia said. "I cannot like his making the reason so public, but I am pleased that they are gone." She leaned her head back against the squabs and closed her eyes.

"Olivia, are you feeling poorly?" her aunt asked, finally noticing her niece's uncharacteristic lack of animation.

"Just a touch of headache. I shall be fine tomorrow." She opened her eyes and looked directly at her uncle. "Then we shall discuss Corbright's land acquisitions in greater detail."

Milton drew back, brows arched. "Ah, so that is it."

"Yes." The door to the carriage opened, and the footman put down the steps.

"Olivia, I—"

"Tomorrow, Uncle. Please? We'll go home with you after church." She hastily departed the carriage first, instead of letting her aunt go ahead of her, and dashed up the stairs to her room.

"What was that all about, Milton?"

Lavinia's brother shook his head. "Tomorrow, Lavvy."

On the way home Jason raged about the way Corbright had manhandled Olivia, about the hints of foul play in his dealings with other landowners, and his scheme, which Jason did not hesitate to call mad, for building Greek temples in Norvale.

"Now I know why he broke it off after he learned of Father's will. He wants Wren Hall. He wants her land. I shall forbid her to ever see him again," he declared.

"A most unwise suggestion," Edmund observed.

"You take his part?" Jason's lip curled.

"Indeed not. I am more convinced than ever that he is a throughly rotten individual. But Olivia is a rather willful young woman, and not under your control. You and she seem to brangle a great deal. Any attempt to force her decision might just drive her into Corbright's arms."

"Surely now that she knows he has tried to buy my land, she will recognize his interest in her for what it is. He wants this valley, Edmund. Not Olivia. He always has. There's something demented about it. Other landowners have also received offers for their land. There have been barns burned, wells poisoned—it's incredible. Several small landowners have sold out and left."

Edmund felt a cold chill run down his spine when he learned the extent of Corbright's scheming. "Did you tell Olivia this?"

"I haven't had a chance yet. As for selling my land, Corbright suggested it be presented to her as a fait accompli. He suggested the same thing you did, that she might consider marriage once she was not so taken up with my estate. At that time I only wished her to marry—him, or you, or anyone. But now I no longer trust Corbright. Will you speak to her, Edmund? As you say, she will oppose me, but she might listen to you."

"No, I most certainly will not seek to dissuade Olivia from marrying Corbright. She thinks me after her fortune, so what credence would she give to me when I try to discredit a rival? Besides, you must consider the possibility that she loves him still."

"She tried to fight him off tonight. You saw!"

"And I saw her, a few minutes later, go willingly into his embrace."

"That truly surprised me," Jason mused. "I thought once she knew he'd tried to buy my land, she'd slap his face and walk away, never to listen to his lies again."

"A woman in love does not find it easy to believe evil intent of her beloved."

"I can't believe Olivia would be such a nodcock!"

"Nor I. Perhaps she just needs time to think things through. Tell her about these other incidents, by all means. But do not try to force the issue, Jason. That is the wrong way to go round with her. Do you remember my mentioning going to London for training in fencing and boxing from the experts? Perhaps if you took her there this fall, she might meet someone else. But remember, if she does love Corbright, don't set yourself up to be his enemy, for then you become hers. And she will need all the friends she can get once she is his wife."

"God forbid."

The two men spoke no more, each staring bleakly out the windows of Uncle Milton's carriage as it carried them back to Beaumont.

Chapter Sixteen

The next morning Olivia avoided her brother's and aunt's questions at breakfast by taking toast and chocolate in her room. She came downstairs just in time to go to church. Edmund was waiting with them at the foot of the stairs. She wondered if he should be invited to their family meeting. He had taken her and Jason's part last night, and yet she hesitated to call upon him to further embroil himself with a man as jealous and dangerous as Corbright. The matter was out of her hands, however.

"Shall we postpone our meeting?" Jason asked when she came into view. "Before our confrontation last night, Edmund had accepted an invitation to dine with the Bensons today."

Corbright's words from the night before about Mary Benson came back to her: *Her fortune outweighs yours, so do not think to capture him with it.* She lifted her chin proudly. "It is a family meeting, Jason. I do appreciate your help last night, Lord Edmund, but we can't ask you to involve yourself in our affairs."

"Nor would I wish to intrude upon them," Edmund responded in as chilly an accent as she had employed.

The trip to church was a silent one, and when they arrived Edmund allowed himself to be taken in charge by a triumphant Mary Benson, to be led to their family pew. Olivia heard scarcely a word of the sermon, instead planning what she would say to her family. Corbright had been right. She did have a duty to protect her brother. She must marry before Corbright knew she meant to refuse him; otherwise Jason might forbid him to see her, which could lead to a duel. When they convened in Uncle Milton's parlor after church, she had a speech all ready, but Jason forestalled her by immediately launching into a litany of Corbright's heavy-handed attempts to buy out several landowners in the last three years. There were more than Olivia had known of, and she shuddered at the fury on her brother's face as he talked.

She had to defuse his anger. "There's nothing wrong in trying to buy land. You planned to sell him yours, too."

"I said he offered to buy it. Never said I'd sell it."

"Or lease it," his uncle put in. "He suggested a five- or ten-year lease."

"He said it would free you to look for a husband."

"Very disinterested of him," Olivia snapped.

"I thought so at the time, but now I have serious doubts," Uncle Milton said.

"Oh, he's interested, all right. In Livvy's land. Finest view in the valley, indeed! Well, he shan't have it, or mine either." Jason slammed his fist into his palm. "Scheming creature. He wants to marry her, buy my land, doubtless has his eye on Lavinia's through that uncle of his."

"Oh, no." Lavinia gasped. "Surely not Peter. He wouldn't be a party to something so devious."

"Peter! You are on a first-name basis with Mr. Barteau?" Olivia looked pityingly at her aunt. How cruel of that man to court her to further his nephew's schemes.

"Surely you do not wish to marry him now, Olivia," Uncle Milton said. "He will not like it, to be sure, but—"

"Like it or not, he shan't even so much as see her again," Jason declared, Edmund's good advice forgotten. "When next he shows his face here, I shall personally throw him off the property."

Olivia put her hand to her mouth. The thought of another physical confrontation between Jason and Corbright made her blood run cold. She knew who would prevail, if ever Corbright thought he had no hope of marrying her. She knew Corbright's temper too well, and now feared his very nature. It would be death for her brother.

"You most certainly shall not," she declared. "I am shocked that you would think to sell your land, Jason, but I do not appreciate your assumption that it is for my land that Franklin renews his courtship. Do you think no one will have me except for my dowry?"

"Certainly not!"

"Then why did you feel you had to force Lord Edmund to marry me? You dragged a fortune hunter home, thought to sell your land—anything to see me wed." Bitterness laced her voice. "Well, I may indeed marry Lord Corbright. . . ."

"No, Livvy . . ." Too late Jason remembered Edmund's suggestion that his opposition might push his sister into Corbright's arms. "Please think about it first. We've told you many incidents that raise questions as to his veracity, his intentions, his very honor. Just don't decide until you've given them more thought."

Livvy continued as if she hadn't heard him. ". . . or I may marry someone else. But one way or another, I *will* be married by this time next year, to someone of my own choosing. You *shall* have your freedom, brother. But do not go picking any more fights with Corbright. I'll have your word on it."

Jason thrust his jaw forward. "I am not afraid of him, Livvy."

"No one doubts your courage. Your sense, perhaps, but not your courage. But you are no match for him, Jason."

At Jason's kindling wrath at this slur on his abilities she hastened on, "But that is not the point. I . . . I may still love him. And after all, nothing has been proved against him. As he said last night, if his intentions had been insincere, would he have announced that scheme before he had your land safely in his pocket? Please don't kill the man I may love, or let him kill you. I couldn't bear it!" Olivia's pleading tone and teary eyes moved Jason to take her in his arms.

"No, dearest, of course I won't. But—"

"There, then! That's settled." Olivia pulled away and launched into her set speech at last. "I have been thinking perhaps I would like to go to London as soon as the harvest is complete. Now, this will doubtless displease you, but Lady Bower has invited me to a ball she is giving in October. She says every important political person in the kingdom will attend. Meeting other men may help me to better understand my feelings toward Corbright. I know it will mean giving up your shooting, but . . ."

Jason could scarcely believe his good fortune, though he pretended to be dismayed. "Go to London? Hunh! Give up my shooting? You ask a lot, sister!"

"But it is in a good cause getting rid of me! Who knows, I may marry a politician. I shall become a great London hostess and never . . . never bother with agriculture again. Your estate agent can run my property along with yours." The crack in her voice gave away her true feelings about this notion, but Olivia hastened on. "You can at last be rid of your encumbrance and live your life as you see fit."

"Livvy, I do not see you as an encumbrance. I've been a selfish twit!"

She put her hand to his cheek. "But please, please don't sell your land. Once I am off the scene you may engage a male estate agent who will doubtless do a better job than I."

"Perhaps Lord Edmund," Jason mused.

"Ha!" Olivia's eyes flashed. "I think Lord Edmund will be long gone by then. Have you forgotten where he is dining today? He has his eye on a richer prize by far. Aunt Lavinia, you'll enjoy visiting all the shops, I daresay."

Lavinia's woeful face did not reflect any joy. "Well, I never thought *I'd* be the target of a fortune hunter. I must say, it is not a pleasant thought."

"No, it is not!" Olivia stood, suddenly aware that tears were near. "Come, let us go into the garden and begin planning what to pack."

"Ah, I've hurt her feelings, haven't I?" Jason asked his uncle as the women left the room.

"There was no easy way to say it. The worst of it is, we could be wrong. Corbright may love her deeply."

"Then he'll still want her when he learns he's not to have

my land or hers, won't he?" Jason growled. "For I will tell him if he marries her, I will exercise my right to take it."

"Don't say anything to him yet," Uncle Milton advised. "I wish to make some inquiries into these other incidents young Hinson-Jones told you about."

"I don't trust him. I'll see him dead before he marries my sister."

"Jason, you always go to extremes. Let this play out as it will. You know how contrary she can be. And she is right about one thing: in a duel you will be no match for him. "

Jason had the grace to agree. "I'll make good use of my time in London. Edmund says my science is improving, but I should try to get further instructions from Gentleman Jackson. And he says my fencing is only adequate. I'd never beat Corbright at swordplay. I'll go to Angelo's and study fencing from the master. And to Manton's every day for target practice. While Livvy is looking for a husband, I'll be preparing to do what I must to protect her, if need be."

His uncle wiped his hand over his face. "I cannot like such violent plans."

"It is the way of the world, Uncle." Jason sat by him and threw his arm around the older man's shoulders. "You know what I wish?"

"What?"

"That Livvy and Edmund would fall in love. I heard how her voice broke as she spoke of giving up her land. She loves the country, and so does he. And I would swear that they had become quite attached to one another lately."

"Friendly, at least."

"Well, on his part it is more. He follows her with his eyes whenever he thinks she is not looking. And as for his sniffing at that feather-witted Mary Benson, I don't believe it. I think he'd have Livvy in a heartbeat, if she'd encourage him."

His uncle looked quite struck by this. "And her remarks about Mary seemed like jealousy to me. She 'doth protest too much,' do you suppose?"

Jason withdrew his arm, a thoughtful look on his face.

"Yes, that could be. But we've only a month left here. Will that be enough time, given how wary she is?"

"We can only hope."

"At least we can count ourselves fortunate in one regard: Livvy did not jump into Corbright's arms when he unveiled that stupid Greek thingamawhirl. Guess she's not as Greek-mad as she once was. Did you ever see anything so foolish as the Parthenon in Norvale?"

"No, nor more pagan."

As Edmund walked in the Bensons' elaborate garden after dinner, he could not concentrate on what Mary was saying. Her idle chatter could not drive out the memory of Olivia's frozen, disapproving look when she had learned he was to dine with the Bensons. *She still thinks me a fortune hunter. She just believes that now I am after a larger fortune.* He looked down at the pretty, animated young woman who prattled away about gowns and balls, and shrank from the thought of having to listen to that for a lifetime. But how to convince Olivia? Now that Corbright had once again wounded her, she would be doubly shy of any man who sought her, thinking it was her land that attracted her suitor. *Damn the man,* he thought. *I should call him out just for that reason.* But just as quickly came the realization that Olivia might still love Corbright. After all, hadn't she gone into his arms quite willingly before parting from him the night before? He wished heartily that he had been able to attend that family meeting. While Mary Benson tried to lure him into kissing her, he could think of nothing but how to keep Olivia Ormhill from Corbright's clutches. When he returned to Beaumont that evening, he eagerly allowed Jason to fill him in on the conference.

"And so we are to go to London," Jason concluded triumphantly. "Olivia is to look about her for a husband. I want you to go with us, Edmund. Squire her to some balls, dance with her. She is warming to you, I know, and—"

"How can I do that?" Edmund sighed. "I haven't the funds for such an excursion, nor an excuse for it."

"You care for her, don't you?" Jason said. "I know you do."

"More than you can guess. It is a great relief that she is willing to consider someone other than Corbright for a husband, but if I cannot get her to look my way before she departs for London, my cause is hopeless."

Edmund determined to spend every moment of the next month with Olivia that he could. Little did he know how difficult this simple plan would be to accomplish.

"Your hot bath is ready, miss."

"Thank you, Mary." Olivia shed her robe and shift eagerly and lowered her aching body into the tub. She had been in the saddle for hours this day, and was exhausted. Always a busy time, late summer had been particularly frantic this year, partly because their crops had been so successful.

Jason had conceived an enthusiasm for proving he could do any job on the estate, and Edmund had proved as willing a worker as ever. Olivia would have resented any effort on either man's part to assume supervision of the harvest overall, but she gladly accepted that in addition to providing two much-needed extra hands, their presence also kept the crews at their work when she had to be elsewhere. She felt a little guilty that she had not had more time to spend with Edmund, discussing the whys and wherefores of the tasks she assigned him and Jason, but the other activities of the estates did not cease just because harvesting of hay and grain was going on. The dairy still had to be seen to, hens must still be set, and eggs crated. Jason's tenants took a great deal of her time, too.

Then the stud farm must be managed, though Jason had always taken a lively interest in it. She hoped he might soon take it óff her hands entirely, but for now she was too thrilled to see him forced to learn about the rest of the estate's functions to risk taking him away to consult upon its operation.

No silver lining is without a cloud, Olivia thought as she contemplated her toes peeking out of the water. For the last month she had worked from dawn to dusk. Often she had not even dined with the family, just taking a simple collation in her room and collapsing in a heap after a hot bath, as on this evening. The worst was over at last, though. With the sale today of the year's crop of beef cattle she could officially consider summer at an end.

It is just as well I have not had much time to spend around Edmund, she thought, sinking lower in the water. Each time she was with him, she felt ever stronger the pull of attraction to him. She did not want to be attracted to him, not when he was in full pursuit of Mary Benson. Not only had Mr. Benson invited him to dine with them twice, he had invited the entire Ormhill family on another occasion, and Mary Benson had scarcely left Edmund's side that evening. When Aunt Lavinia had invited the Bensons in return, the same pattern repeated. Edmund and Mary's father were on excellent terms, so there was no need for Edmund to fear rejection.

I suppose the only reason he has not proposed to her as yet is that he truly wants to learn what I have to teach him before he leaves us. Again she felt that twinge of guilt, and decided that she would have to begin his formal tutelage once more. Tomorrow would be a good time. Michaelmas was almost upon them, so she must prepare for quarter day, when she would pay all of her workers, collect rents, and pay her bills.

She also liked to use that occasion to evaluate the summer's profits and the general finances of the estates. Jason and Edmund had learned a great deal about the practical side of farming, but now they must deal with what she found to be the most tedious side: bookkeeping. To know what profits had been made, it was very important to keep extensive and accurate records, particularly when one was experimenting with different crops, methods of rotation and fertilization, and breeding of livestock.

Estate duties had not managed to distract her from her greatest worry: what to do about Corbright. From various shooting spots he had sent her a barrage of letters. She read each one nervously, often shaking her head and frowning at the excessive passion voiced in them. They both depressed and alarmed her, spurring her to increase her preparations to go to London and seek a husband. Each time she had this thought, a fugitive part of her mind whispered Edmund's name. But she ruthlessly suppressed it.

At least Corbright had no inkling she planned to go to London instead of Scotland. Although Mr. Barteau had remained at his nephew's home for some time after Corbright's departure, and had called upon Lavinia almost every day, they had kept their London plans from him. Olivia thought her aunt enjoyed these visits far too much, and had been glad when the man announced he had some business interests to see to. He had said he eagerly looked forward to seeing them again when they came to London in the spring. *I hope to have a husband by then*, she thought. *But alas for Lavinia. And he* will *loose interest in her when his nephew realizes his schemes for getting control of the valley have come to naught.*

Not the least of your sins against us, Franklin. There had been another letter from Corbright this morning, plaintively asking her when she meant to join him in Scotland. She clenched her teeth at the memory of his florid protestations of love. *Never!* She rose from the rapidly cooling water, intending to send a note down to Jason and Edmund asking them to join her the next morning. The sooner her bookkeeping chores were out of the way, the sooner she could get away to London.

As she looked for them the next day, she mentally girded herself for the task ahead, for Jason had always hated anything to do with mathematics, and according to Corbright and Lord Heslington, Edmund had had little formal schooling. But she had put off their tutelage in this important aspect of estate management far too long. The late-afternoon light coming through the French doors was not sufficient to illuminate her office on such a dreary day, so she gave orders for the candles to be lit, then went to the billiards room, where Jason and Edmund were engaged in a desultory game.

"Oh, there you are, Liv," Jason said. "Come to drag us to the schoolroom, eh?"

Olivia smiled. "Just so. Complete with chalk and slate."

Lord Edmund put down his stick and donned his coat, which he had placed on the back of a chair for the game, depriving her of the stirring sight of his well-muscled body straining against the fabric of his shirt. "Lead on, fair instructress," he said, smiling at her. She wondered if he felt any trepidation at having his mathematical skills on display. If so, he did not show it, but rather appeared quite at ease, even eager.

She soon found out why, when she began to explain how her bookkeeping system worked. He grasped the concept immediately, whereas Jason appeared completely at sea. She then showed them stacks of notes about crop yields, receipts, expenses, and so forth, and set them to recording sums in the appropriate ledgers. "Add each page up and then to the total carried forward," she instructed. "Then place this number at the top of the next page."

Jason groaned. "May I get foxed first, Livvy? Then I'll have them done in no time."

She smiled fondly at him. "No, you may not. You may do sums speedily when drunk, but your handwriting becomes illegible."

Jason grumbled, but set to work. She began some bookkeeping of her own while they did this, and was startled when Edmund brought her his work in about half the time she expected. She frowned over the ledger he handed to her.

"Didn't I write it neatly enough?" he asked anxiously. "I confess mine is not the easiest hand."

"Nothing is wrong with your handwriting," she assured him. She had no choice, she felt, but to add the columns herself, for it was information that she needed, as well as important for him to understand that this would be a crucial part of managing any estate.

Working on a piece of scrap paper, she found to her relief that her figure tallied with his at the end of the first page. She looked up, meaning to give him an encouraging smile, and surprised a look of fond amusement on his face that made her bristle and blush at the same time.

"What is so funny, Edmund? You have indeed added this correctly, but I do have to make sure, for—"

"Your lips move as you add," he observed.

"And what of it?"

He held up his hands. "Pax, Olivia. I realize not everyone can add in his head as I can. And you look quite charming as you work on the sums." Olivia felt her innards warm at the light in his eyes.

"Add them up in your head?" Jason broke into the moment with a wail.

Olivia cocked her head to one side. "Edmund is a mathematical prodigy, it seems."

"I think you did not believe me capable of simple addition," he responded. "Surely after all these weeks you have realized that my brother and Corbright overstated my lack of education."

"I know you are an intelligent man," she assured him, feeling her cheeks pinken at being caught doubting him.

"But not a literate one. Well, it is true enough that I learned little Latin and Greek, but that is because I did not want to, not that I couldn't. I simply didn't see the point. But my father made sure I knew how crucial mathematical skills were to farming. Simple arithmetic came easily to me, so he gave me bookkeeping tasks on the farm. In addition he taught me to survey land, which sharpened my interest in geometry and algebra, as well. It was a practical education, true, but one well suited to my temperament."

Jason returned to the simple but to him stunning fact that Edmund could add in his head. "Can you also subtract without using paper?"

"Assuredly. And multiply and divide, if the sums are not too large."

Jason blew out an indignant huff. "It isn't fair, Livvy. You've given us the same amount to do."

Olivia laughed. "The important thing is not the amount, but the process."

"Here," Edmund said. "I'll trade you the receipts from the dairy for those from the stud. You'll be interested, no doubt, to see how much profit your breeding operation is bringing in."

"That is more like," Jason said, gathering the items Edmund passed to him. He fell to work with a will, and Olivia looked at Edmund, letting her gratitude show in her eyes. He bowed to her briefly, and she blushed at the warmth of his smile. She left the two of them in the study working away while she went in search of her aunt.

It is good that I am going to London soon, she thought. *I find Lord Edmund's smiles too attractive. That way lies calamity. Bad enough to fall in love with a fortune hunter— it would be even worse to do so when he seeks another woman's fortune.*

That evening when they discussed plans for their imminent departure for London, Jason seemed surprisingly happy, looking forward to his own plans for improvement in the manly arts.

"I shall become an expert," he said. "And Edmund, I don't think you ever miss a shot. We shall find some ignorant souls and wager upon it, eh?" Jason looked hopefully at his friend, who scowled.

"I've told you, I won't be going. Olivia has already agreed that I will see to matters here."

Though none of them were surprised, Jason and Lavinia had not given up hope of convincing him. "Of course you will go," Lavinia asserted. "We consider you one of the family. And Milton will be here, after all, to see to any crises at Beaumont, as he always does during the shooting season."

Edmund smiled sweetly at her. "Thank you, Lavinia, for saying that. But I am *not* one of the family, and my purse won't lend itself to London life just now."

"Besides, I expect Edmund has certain interests he would not care to abandon," Olivia said with a sniff. "The Bensons, after all, never go to London before May."

Edmund glared at her. "I did not know that, but I thank you for telling me. All the more reason to remain in Norvale."

She stood abruptly. "You are very welcome, I am sure.

And now I have some work I must do." She fairly ran from the room.

Edmund got to his feet and bowed politely to Aunt Lavinia. "If you will excuse me, a fortune hunter needs his rest. I believe I will turn in early." He stalked from the room, leaving Lavinia and Jason staring unhappily after him.

Chapter Seventeen

"Oh, bother!" Jason bit his index finger and slumped low in his chair. "The game is over if Edmund doesn't go with us. Aunt Lavinia, I think he is perfect for her. They have the same interests, yet he can talk to her about crops and cattle without setting her back up. He would take much of the work from her shoulders without trying to dictate to her."

Lavinia shook her head. "I fear it is a lost cause. She is utterly convinced he is a fortune hunter, and perhaps he is."

"I don't believe that. This morning matters seemed quite promising. They were flirting, in fact, and he looked at her so fondly."

"Well, if they are separated, nothing can come of it." She sighed and bent once more to her sewing.

Jason stood and walked over to the window of the drawing room. "Wish it weren't the dark of the moon. I'd like to take Moonstone for a good gallop." And then, in a flash, he saw what he had to do.

"I know how to get him to go to London with her."

Lavinia turned to him, her needle suspended in midair.

"If I were ill or injured and couldn't go, who would escort you and Olivia to London, Aunt?"

"Ill or . . ." Lavinia's eyes widened. For an instant hope dawned, then faded. "You wouldn't let her go. You never do let her go anywhere without your escort."

"And she scolds me endlessly for it. So I would relent this time, provided Edmund would escort her in my stead."

"I doubt she'd agree. She'd stay with you if you were ill or injured."

"Something minor, of course. And if she stayed here, she would be near Edmund. But much better if they went off to London. Away from the farm, away from Mary Benson, with leisure to spend together, perhaps they would discover their feelings for one another."

When they presented his scheme to the reverend Mr. Ormhill the next morning, he glared at his nephew. "A broken ankle? That's a harebrained notion!"

"Not really broken, of course. A severe sprain. Perhaps a slight fracture. Mr. Plimm won't be sure."

Brother and sister looked at one another. Higgens was the local apothecary, and since there was no nearby physician, he was generally consulted for illnesses. But for broken bones, people in the valley turned to Mr. Plimm, the blacksmith. His powerful yet strangely gentle hands had set many a broken limb.

"Plimm would never be able to lie. Or to grasp why he should do so," Milton objected.

"Brother, brother. Can't you see? Plimm won't have to lie."

"Trust me, Uncle. A few scratches here and there to show that I've taken a fall, and a good deal of moaning and groaning are all it will take. Plimm will believe it's at least a bad sprain, if not a slight fracture. I've never been one to complain, so Olivia won't suspect me of malingering."

"That's true." Lavinia beamed at her nephew.

"I shouldn't sanction a lie," her brother said, frowning.

"To save Olivia from Corbright?" Lavinia demanded indignantly.

"Surely this is a white lie?" Jason suggested.

"Don't wheedle me, boy. I must think on this."

Jason seemed to concede. "Doubtless you are right. Perhaps you can convince her she is needed here or something." He winked at his aunt as he stood. "It is a beautiful day. I am going to take Moonstar for a nice long gallop."

"Tell Cook to set the meal back half an hour, and then serve it whether my brother has returned or not." Olivia's brows knitted in concern. It was unlike Jason to be late for dinner, particularly when they were having guests. She had decided to return the hospitality of several families in Norvale with a large dinner party before they left for London. All were assembled in the drawing room awaiting Jason.

Lavinia and her brother exchanged worried glances. "Do you suppose . . ." she whispered.

He whispered back, "I hope he's just lost track of time."

Just then Buckman opened the door with some appearance of haste. "Miss Olivia, would you step out here a moment?"

Her heart in her throat, Olivia excused herself and stepped into the entryway, followed by her aunt and uncle. Her head groom, Richard Cox, stood there, his seamed face working with emotion.

"Begging your pardon," he said with a darting glance around at the trio. He tugged at his forelock. "We've had a message from the young master, you see. His horse came in without him a few minutes ago, with this tied to one of the stirrups." He held out a torn piece of cloth, which Olivia took in trembling hands as her aunt and uncle drew near.

"Is that blood?" Lavinia fairly shrieked.

Olivia's mouth trembled. "It appears to be written in blood on a torn shirtsleeve." She read the message aloud. " 'Robin Creek, foot hurt.' "

"Have you started someone in that direction yet?" Edmund demanded of Cox, alerting Olivia that he, too, had joined them.

"Yes, m'lord. Sent two men out. Thought I orta let the family know, though."

"Hitch up a wagon, get some rope, wood for a splint, and something to carry him on," Olivia directed. "He's hurt badly, perhaps has broken something, to send this instead of riding home."

Cox tugged at his forelock and started on his errand, closely followed by Edmund.

Olivia turned to her aunt. "Why don't you take our guests in to dinner?" she asked.

"But my dear—"

"It will keep everyone occupied. Don't explain just now. Simply say that something has come up. Uncle, will you act as host? I am going to go with the wagon."

He nodded, his face grim. "Send word as soon as you know something?"

"I will." She gave him a brief hug, then started toward the rear of the house. By the time she reached the stable, Edmund had mounted Storm. He saluted her briefly and rode off while she waited for a wagon to be hitched and loaded with equipment. With Richard Cox driving, they set off at a spanking pace toward the creek that ran to the north of the estate, a favorite fishing spot for Jason and Olivia.

As they approached the spinney through which the creek wound, Edmund emerged and shouted at them, waving them on. By the time they had drawn up as near the trees as possible, he came back out, carrying Jason. He staggered with the load, for a summer of hard work had added muscle to Jason's already considerable height.

Olivia's heart turned over at the sight of her brother lying there so limply in Edmund's arms. She jumped from the wagon and ran toward him. "Is he . . ."

"Barely conscious," Edmund replied in a tight voice. "Get those sticks out and I'll stabilize his ankle before we go any farther." He bent with his burden, laying Jason carefully on the ground. The boy groaned as he did so.

"Oh, Jason. What have you done to yourself?" Olivia sank to her knees beside him.

"Hullo, Livvy." He turned a white face toward her, his eyes crinkled in pain. "Something stupid, if you must know. Went wading barefoot in the creek, and slipped in a hole. Wedged m'foot under a tree root."

"Wading? It's almost October!" She shivered, for though it was a sunny day, it hardly seemed warm enough to be dabbling in the water. "You're soaked," she exclaimed.

Edmund knelt on the other side. His clothes were wet where he had held Jason. "He was in the creek for some time, apparently."

"Yup. Told you it was stupid." Jason began shivering violently.

Mr. Cox stepped up, three sturdy sticks in his hand, along with some rope.

"Get the blankets," she told him, taking the items from his hands and passing them to Edmund, who was examining Jason's left ankle and foot carefully.

She looked at his ankle and gasped. It was swollen, covered with scratches, and oozing blood. "Oh, Jason. You poor darling. Do you think it is broken, Edmund?"

"I can't tell for sure, of course, but I feel no protruding bones. It seems to be mostly bruised and cut."

Through chattering teeth, Jason explained, "Had the devil of a time getting it out, and all the time water sluicing around me! Hurts like the devil, Edmund. Must be broken. And Moonstar just kept twirling around when I tried to pull myself up to mount. Fool horse!"

The blankets arrived, along with the door the men had taken from the stable to carry him on. Olivia tucked the warm woolens around her brother once he was positioned on the flat surface. Edmund wrapped the injured ankle in his own neckcloth, then fastened one of the sticks on either side for stability. He and the grooms then carried Jason to the wagon, Olivia alongside, holding his hand.

"S-stupid of me," Jason muttered. "Hate to make such a fuss."

"Hush, dearest. It is nothing to worry yourself about." She climbed into the back of the wagon and rode home with her brother's head in her lap.

After a long, confusing evening that saw first Mr. Higgens and then Mr. Plimm examine Jason's ankle, and pronounce in turn that they did not know whether it was broken or not, Aunt Lavinia chased the others out of Jason's bedroom so she could clean and bandage her nephew's foot.

"Olivia, you look like death," she announced firmly, almost pushing her niece out the door. "Have Cook prepare a tisane for you, and get some rest. And Edmund, go change. You'll catch your death in those wet clothes."

Uncle Milton looked on, his face grim, as the bandaging went forward. Once Olivia was gone, he said to his nephew, "Had to go ahead and do it, didn't you, sprout?"

"You'd have said no, Uncle. Or if you didn't, your conscience would have bothered you forever."

"Took it all on your own soul. Don't you know morals are like muscles? Use them and they'll grow strong. Abandon them and they'll weaken from disuse. Then when the important moral decisions come along, you'll have no muscles to use to resist evil."

"Yes, Uncle," Jason said, then winced at his aunt's ministrations.

"You're well served for your wickedness, you know," Milton barked.

Jason responded between clenched teeth, "If you mean my ankle is truly injured now, you have the right of it."

"You overdid it, I think," Lavinia agreed, straightening from spreading a healing unguent on his bruised, torn flesh.

"Not on purpose. Just meant to scrape it up a bit. I really did get it wedged under there. As you say, Uncle, I am well served. But now the trick is getting matters to fall out as we intended."

"Don't say we, you varmint. You are on your own!"

"You aren't going to tell?" Jason looked anxiously at his uncle's severe face.

"He feels feverish to me, Milton. What do you think?"

Milton laid his hand against Jason's cheek. "Don't you get sick on us and die, you wretch! I'll never forgive you."

Jason smiled ruefully. "Nor would I forgive myself." He grabbed his uncle's wrist. "Say you won't tell, please?"

"No point in that now. It's done. As you say, the trick will be to get Olivia to leave you, especially if you come down with an ague."

"She won't, if he does that. I'm going to have some willow-bark tea sent up." Lavinia stepped to the door to summon Jason's anxious valet.

Once outside Jason's door, Olivia felt a mild attack of the vapors coming on, the events of the day having finally taken their toll on her nerves. She had been forced to bear up while politely dealing with her guests' solicitousness when they brought Jason home. Mary Benson had fallen into near hys-

teria. It was Lord Edmund she required to calm her. Olivia
had watched this blatant flirtation irritably, telling herself
she only wanted to be done with the girl and all the other
guests so she could go to her brother.

When at last all of them had left, she had hurried upstairs
to watch first Mr. Higgens and then Mr. Plimm twisting and
turning and handling Jason's ankle over his loud objections,
until she thought she would scream. She had been almost relieved when Aunt Lavinia insisted on doing the treatment
and bandaging.

Instead of going to her room and sending for a tisane, as
Lavinia had suggested, she went to the drawing room, intent
upon a glass of brandy. There she found Edmund pacing
back and forth. He poured her brandy while questioning her
about Jason's condition, and stood next to her, a concerned
frown on his face, as she lifted the glass to her lips with
shaking hands.

When the fiery liquid rushed through her veins, she
found her shakes replaced by weakness that made her knees
buckle, and Edmund helped her to a sofa, then sat down beside her, chafing her cold hands as she babbled.

"I've never seen Jason take on so. Edmund, you've never
seen him injured, so perhaps you think he's overdramatizing."

"That is not my assessment of him. I expect that ankle
hurts like the devil."

"I am sure it has a crack in it, as Mr. Plimm said might be
the case. I am just glad he could not mount his horse and
ride home. He might have made it worse. But, oh! He shook
so. And looked so pale. What if he comes down with a
fever? Just last year the Melbys' boy was carried off within
a day of a fever caught after a wetting."

She began to cry, and Edmund put his arms around her,
drawing her close to him in a comforting hug.

"He's a strong, healthy young man, Olivia, not a child."

Olivia bit her lower lip, trying to bring the crying to a
halt. "I know." She sniffled. "It's just . . . he seemed half out
of his head on the way home. He said over and over that I
must still go to London. As if I would leave him when he is
ill! When he is hurt!"

"Of course you won't. But he'll bounce back more quickly if he doesn't think your trip is scuttled."

"He wants me to go so much. He wants to see me married so badly! I am surprised he no longer pushes me to marry Corbright."

The bitter tone in her voice caused Edmund to move so he could look into her face. "Don't you want to marry Corbright, Olivia? I had the impression you still cared for him."

"I don't know." She wouldn't look into his eyes. "I haven't decided. Poor Edmund, you shouldn't have to shoulder our family's troubles."

"I care deeply for . . . for every member of this family. If I can help you in any way, I will. Above all you mustn't let yourself be pressured into marrying anyone you don't want, including Corbright."

"You don't like Franklin, do you?"

"No." He looked down at her, at the way her head was cocked to one side and her blue eyes still glistening with tears, and yearned to tell her that he would hate any man who might win her heart. But she would not welcome such a declaration. Right now she seemed to trust him, to accept him almost as a brother. He had gained that much ground with her. She no longer regarded him as a scoundrel, and he would certainly be one if he used her present vulnerable state to advance his own cause. Moreover, he was mindful of the advice he had given Jason, not to arouse her contrary spirit by trying to manage her.

"My dislike of him is of long standing, but I can certainly see why a woman might find him . . . eligible."

What precisely she had hoped to hear, she did not know. But this cool, dispassionate response to her question wasn't it. She remembered the way he had comforted Mary Benson earlier in the evening, and stiffened. "Thank you for giving me a shoulder to cry on, Edmund. I won't pester you anymore."

"I won't go to London without you!"

Jason groaned. "You must, Livvy. Please!" Jason had battled a cold for the last three days, and his throat still sounded hoarse.

"How can I, when you are ill?"

"I'm fine. It is just a cold, almost gone. Just because my ankle is hurting, that doesn't mean I need you here."

"We can delay our departure until you are feeling up to the trip."

"You'll miss Lady Bower's ball if you don't go on. You know you want to attend, and she really wants you to be there to celebrate her husband's new appointment to the cabinet."

"Her ball will be a success without me, though. And Aunt Lavinia and I can't go unescorted." She glanced at her aunt, who with her uncle and Edmund were ranged about Jason's bed.

"Uncle—"

"Oh, no you don't!" Uncle Milton exploded. "You young chub! You know I detest London. And besides, I've got my duties here." Everyone knew how seriously Milton Ormhill took his ministry, so Jason ventured no reply to this.

"I expect Edmund would escort us, dear," Lavinia said, looking at him for confirmation. He nodded assent.

"No, indeed." Olivia lifted her chin. "Edmund didn't agree to act as a substitute brother. He wants to learn how to manage an estate. He won't learn that in London. And besides, who *will* manage the estate if he goes?"

"Are you saying I can't keep track of things for two or three weeks? That I've learned nothing this summer?" The gravel in Jason's throat made him cough as he almost shouted his protests. "Won't the instructions you wrote out for Edmund serve well enough for me, too? You think I'm too stupid to follow them, don't you?"

"No, that was not my meaning."

"And it wouldn't be as if I were asking Edmund to stand in my stead for long. I shall join you as soon as I am well enough to travel. I can practice at Manton's with a bad ankle, I daresay. Then, when I have completely recovered, I can begin my training with Gentleman Jackson, and a good fencing master."

Olivia frowned, touched by her brother's distress, but

puzzled, too. "You have never before agreed to allow me to go farther than High Wycombe without your escort."

"Oh, Livvy!" Jason threw his arm over his eyes in a despairing gesture.

"If you will allow me to escort you, Olivia, I would be happy to do so." Edmund held out his hand to her. "I'd like to speak privately with you for a moment." He led her across the room. "He'll fret himself into a fever again if you persist," he half whispered. He looked into her blue eyes and felt his heart contract with longing. He knew he should resist this assignment. But the conversation he had had with her about Corbright the night of Jason's injury had given him renewed hope. The scorn in her voice when she spoke the man's name had contradicted her insistence that she was undecided about her feelings for Corbright.

Olivia looked into Edmund's warm brown eyes and knew a moment of panic. *Why do I feel so fluttery around him? When he touches me or speaks to me, I want to throw myself at him. This could be a disaster, to be in his company even more.* It was a pointless attraction, for Mary Benson was now his object.

Yet she knew she could not deny her distraught brother what he appeared to be so set on having. And in fact it might be an excellent idea to encourage this tentative step by Jason away from his strict interpretation of his father's deathbed charge. Moreover, she really needed to be at the Bowers' ball to meet the eligible men there.

I will just have to be very careful to keep Edmund at a distance.

"If you truly do not mind," she said.

"I truly do not."

She returned to her brother's bedside. "Very well," she told him. "We will go on to London. When you join us, Edmund can return to look after Beaumont and his . . . other interests here."

Because she was looking at Jason as she spoke, she did not see the hurt that flashed across Edmund's face. But Lavinia and Milton did, and looked at one another in consternation.

Chapter Eighteen

"They make a charming couple." Olivia was proud of her steady voice as she remarked upon Mary Benson and Edmund, stepping their way lightly through a waltz. Finding that the Bensons had also traveled to London for the Bowers' ball had not been a particularly pleasant revelation for her. Seeing Mary and Edmund so very much in step with once another hurt her more than she had expected. When Edmund had asked Mary for this waltz, Olivia had declined a partner and retreated to the wall, where Mr. Benson joined her, his eyes on his daughter and the handsome man who partnered her.

"Yes. It is a pity, really."

Olivia looked sideways at Mr. Benson, surprised. She had seen no evidence that he objected to Edmund prior to this moment. "A pity?"

Mr. Benson nodded. "I have run off dozens of men as fortune hunters who were a great deal wealthier than Lord Edmund. He hasn't a feather to fly with, yet I feel he would make my Mary an excellent husband. I know I could trust that he would never neglect her, mistreat her, or waste her fortune." His solemn voice and depressed manner only added to Olivia's perplexity. He turned and encountered her surprised look.

"Will she not have him, sir?"

"Not have him? Of course she would have him. Mary would have any half-presentable young man of whom I would approve. She falls in and out of love with the seasons.

This season it is Edmund. Thank goodness for her fickle nature, for this failure to attach him cannot cause her much pain." Mr. Benson rounded on her, suddenly angry. "Can it be that you believe he is dangling after my daughter?"

"Why, I . . ."

Mr. Benson gave a bark of humorless laughter. "No, indeed. I fairly threw her at him, but he gave me to understand his affections were otherwise engaged."

"Otherwise engaged!" Olivia felt as if she had been hit by lightning. "But who . . . ?"

He frowned at her, then smiled crookedly. "Who, indeed, Miss Ormhill? For an intelligent woman, you are being remarkably obtuse."

He is mistaken. That was all Olivia could think as she watched Edmund smile and bow to Mary at the end of the dance. He was the very pattern of a polite suitor as he led her back to her father. She had discounted as mere show his look of surprise at finding the Bensons at the ball. Of course he had known they meant to go to London. Why else had he been so willing to escort her in Jason's stead? But if Edmund actually told Mary's father his affections were engaged, what could it mean? Olivia's heart thrummed with a painful sort of excitement.

Seeing her partner for the next dance searching for her, she ducked out of the ballroom and made her way to the withdrawing room. She was not alone there, but the chattering women who clustered in the outer chamber primping at the mirrors were strangers to her. She went to the window and looked down at the rainswept street below.

Suddenly tears began to flow as she thought of all the times she had accused him directly or indirectly of being a fortune hunter.

"What is it, dearest?" Lavinia hurried to her side.

"Oh, Aunt Lavvy! He doesn't want to marry Mary Benson!"

"No, I didn't think so."

"But she stands to inherit one of the greatest fortunes in England. Oh, Aunt. When I think of all the times I hinted . . . How it must have hurt him."

"Yes, I think it did," Lavinia said, gently blotting at her niece's tears with her handkerchief.

"He told Mr. Benson his affections were otherwise engaged. Who do you think he meant?"

"Now, Livvy, don't be hopelessly dense."

"How long have you known? Why did you not tell me?"

"I only just now learned it for sure, from you. But anyone who has seen how he looks at you when he thinks he is not observed would have suspected. If I, or anyone else, had told you, would you have believed them?"

"Likely not. I have become too suspicious, haven't I?"

"You have reason, dear," her aunt said, giving her shoulder a comforting pat. "Do you . . . is it possible you feel the same for him?"

This gave Olivia pause. She was attracted to him, and had enjoyed the trip to London with him enormously because of his gentle humor and good-natured tolerance for the demands two women travelers put upon him. Could it be their friendship might ripen into something more? Had it already, and she had simply not been willing to see it? She pulled out of her aunt's embrace. "I . . . I am not sure. Oh, I am so confused. Why has he not courted me? No, don't tell me. I have treated him so!"

"It is not too late, Livvy."

"Do you think not?" Olivia wiped at her tears.

"If it is not too late for this old maid, it is not too late for you. You must make the first move, though. Edmund is a proud man, and his lack of fortune weighs on him, as do all your aspersions on his character. But do be sure how you feel before encouraging him, for I like Edmund so much, I would not wish to see him hurt."

"I don't wish to hurt him either." Olivia sighed. "Nor do I wish to be hurt again. You can't know what it feels like. . . . Oh! Speaking of someone being hurt, I mislike your allowing Mr. Barteau to continue to court you. It is a great pity he turned up here tonight, for I fear he will write Corbright and bring him to London."

Lavinia's mouth turned down. She drew away from her niece. "I don't believe that."

"But Aunt . . ."

"We must have this conversation another time, Livvy. We are attracting a good deal of attention. Besides, Peter awaits me downstairs. Dry your eyes, dear, and come down with me." She bustled out of the room before Olivia could respond.

Olivia entered the ballroom with trepidation, knowing her eyes were still red. She had promised the supper dance to Lord Pilter, a young man particularly recommended to her by Cynthia Bower as a rising star in the political world. Since Olivia had reasoned that a wealthy, powerful husband would be less likely to be a fortune hunter, she had given him considerable encouragement. Now she regretted it. Even as he approached her, her eyes sought out Edmund, wondering whom he would take in to supper. And during the meal, she could scarcely keep her attention on Lord Pilter, for studying Edmund as he entertained a handsome older woman she did not know.

Because she had her eyes on him so often, she realized that he often looked over at her. The third time this happened, her heart lifted with pleasure and she smiled and nodded to him. Instantly his face changed. The polite smile he had worn became genuine as he nodded to her in turn. After supper was over he sought her out.

"Is it possible that you have a dance available?" he asked, looking adorably unsure of himself.

Shamelessly ignoring her partner, who was just behind him, she laughed. "This one, as it happens." And she joyfully danced a spirited Scottish reel with him.

This time Edmund's dance caught the eyes of another man, markedly more hostile than Mr. Benson. Lord Heslington stood next to Cynthia Bower, avidly watching the interplay between his brother and Miss Ormhill.

"Corbright will not be pleased," Cynthia purred insinuatingly.

"No, he won't. What is she doing here anyway? Thought she was to join Frank in Scotland."

" 'Tis my opinion that his suit is in vain. I think Olivia came here to find a husband."

"Nonsense. She loves Corbright, has since she was six-teen," Heslington snapped. "My little brother shouldn't poach on another man's preserves." He left the ballroom with a determined glint in his eyes.

By the time they returned from the ball, it was so late there was no opportunity for Olivia to speak to Edmund that night. The next day they were to go shopping for clothes, and Mr. Barteau insisted on accompanying them, so Ed-mund excused himself to conduct some personal business. He had looked at Olivia challengingly, as if daring her to hint that he sought out Miss Benson. And Olivia felt shame at knowing she would have suspected just that before last night.

That afternoon they had many callers, and that evening they attended a lecture on mesmerism, again with Mr. Barteau. Once again Edmund took the opportunity to absent himself, saying he had been invited to dine with friends he had encountered at the War Office that morning.

Olivia was vexed by her inability to find a moment with him to formally apologize for her insulting belief that he had been after Mary Benson's fortune and, more important, her own. Determined to have her say, she crept back downstairs once her aunt had gone to bed, and settled down in the drawing room of their rented Mayfair town house to wait for Edmund's return.

She had a long wait. At length she sent the sleepy foot-man to bed and took his place in the chair near the door. The hall clock was chiming four A.M. when she awoke to a knocking at the door. She opened it and sleepily blinked at Edmund, who stood on the stoop looking somewhat di-sheveled.

"Olivia!" He grabbed her arms and pushed her inside ahead of himself, closing the door. "What is wrong?"

"N-nothing." His nearness, his touch, awoke her fully.

"Then why are you here?"

"I have something to say to you."

He had not released her. If anything he drew her closer. The scent of cigar smoke clung to his clothes, and brandy perfumed his breath. Was he foxed? Aware suddenly of the impropriety, nay, the downright danger of this moment, she pulled away from him, though she wanted nothing more than to close the distance, not widen it. She started walking toward the stairs.

He accompanied her, a worried look on his face. "Something is wrong. I know it!"

"No, but perhaps we had best discuss it tomorrow. It is late, and I—"

"Sorry about that. I met some men I served with on the peninsula and we went to White's to catch up on one another." He lightly touched her arm, anxiety furrowing his brow. "Please don't leave me in suspense until morning! And I have a piece of news, too, which I am eager to share."

Judging him to be sober, she decided to go ahead with her planned conversation. After all, she might not have another opportunity to be alone with him for some time.

"Very well. Will you step into the drawing room?" She sat down on a settee in front of the banked fire, and he sat at the other end, somewhat tentatively. "You go first," she said. Her heart lurched erratically. Had Mr. Benson been mistaken, or simply toying with her? Had he in fact proposed to Mary?

"No, you go first."

"No!" She said it so emphatically he jumped a little.

His brow knitted again. "Very well. It is just that I have received a rather handsome offer. I may not take it, but at least it proves to me that I am not utterly without value in the scheme of things."

Olivia couldn't speak, so she nodded. *He refers to Mary Benson,* was all she could think.

"You may not know just how useless and hopeless I felt when I arrived at the Black Lion that evening in July and fell into that fateful card game with Jason. You pretty well summed me up the next day." He smiled, rather sadly. "A penniless gamester, cast off by his family. A fortune hunter. Well, I really wasn't a gamester, exactly, but . . ."

Olivia felt tears tickling the back of her throat, knowing she had helped contribute to his sense of worthlessness.

"At the time I met you, I hadn't much of a future. You and your family took me in and gave me one. For that I shall always be grateful."

He looked away, cleared his throat, then looked back at her. "The long and the short of it is, I told my friend the Earl of Marcoombe what I was doing. Described your estate system and how much I was learning from you. He has just inherited, you know. Viscount Baringdon during the war. Knows next to nothing about estate management and has little desire to learn. He has offered me employment!" he finished on a triumphant note, his eyes gleaming with pleasure.

"Oh! Oh!" Livvy put her hand to her mouth. She wanted to share his joy, but this would take him away from her.

"Of course, I won't leave you beforetimes. I committed myself to you for a year, and I'll keep that promise."

She swallowed hard, took herself in hand, and replied, "Nonsense. You aren't bound to stay. As if Jason and I would hold you to that agreement, which was intended for your benefit. One cannot force a winner to take his winnings, after all." She tried for a smile.

"I don't want to leave early. Told Marcoombe even if I accepted, I'd a great deal to learn yet. He was vastly intrigued that a young woman could be so accomplished an agriculturist. Wants to meet you, in fact." He looked down and sighed a little. It would cost him dearly to introduce the woman he loved to so eligible a man as Marcoombe, but if she would marry him instead of Corbright, she would be much better off. Of course, in such a case he would not work for Marcoombe, for he could not bear to be that near to Olivia and her husband, any more than he could accept Jason's offer that he work for him, if she married Corbright. Her repeated references to his being a fortune hunter had convinced him that he stood no chance with her. *Though last night she seemed different somehow,* he thought, studying her face for some sign of her thoughts.

Livvy had by this time gotten herself well in hand. "I think that if you go to work for Marcoombe he will have the best of the arrangement. You will be a valuable asset to any great landowner."

His eyes grew warm. "Ah, Livvy. It is a balm to my soul to hear you say that." *Though I could wish you were not so willing to let me go,* he thought, then thrust the notion aside. He had learned to face hard realities in the peninsula; he could do so now. "So, tell me why you are up at such an ungodly hour, waiting for me."

"Actually, I have already begun." He quirked an eyebrow in question. "I once apologized for insulting you the first time we met, but it wasn't the only time. I have said things I shouldn't, several times. In particular, I have made disparaging remarks about your relationship with Mary Benson."

He jumped up, fist clenched. "There is no relationship with Mary Benson. You still think me a fortune hunter!"

Livvy leaped to her feet, too. "No, no, Edmund. That was not my meaning. I wished to say that I know you are *not* a fortune hunter. That you in fact have passed up the chance to marry one of England's richest heiresses. And to say I am heartily ashamed that I ever thought it of you."

Edmund still stood stiffly, regarding her with suspicion. "What has caused this change of opinion?"

"Well, nothing *you* did," she snapped. "You positively encouraged me to think so!"

"Then what?" He relaxed a trifle.

"Mr. Benson told me himself."

"Ah." This did not seem to please Edmund, who frowned down at her. "What else did he tell you?"

"N-nothing." She couldn't interpret his look, but it didn't have the aspect of a man eager to declare himself. "But I realized how wrong-headed I had been, and I wanted to apologize."

He nodded, studying her face carefully, waiting to see if there was more.

"And to ask if we could begin again."

"Begin again?"

"Yes. I wish to know you as you are, without this veil of prejudice between us. And I hope you will no longer feel the justifiable anger that has kept you so distant from me. In short, I hope we can be friends."

Low, almost throbbingly tender, came the question: "That is all, Livvy?"

She met his eyes, his soft brown eyes, which just now seemed darker than dark, his pupils were so dilated. She felt she could drown in them. She swayed toward him, in fact, before recollecting the place, the time, and her own as-yet-unresolved feelings. "That is all, Edmund. For now."

His smile grew slowly into a joyous and sensuous sideways grin. "Ah, Livvy."

Mindful of her aunt's warning not to hurt Edmund, she answered firmly, "That is all. For now."

"I understand. For now."

"Well, then. Good night." She started to turn, but he put his hand out, lightly touching her arm.

"Shall we begin this friendship by doing something I have yearned to do ever since I returned to England?"

Remembering what had followed on another occasion when he had said something similar, Olivia's heart began to race. She felt warm all over, and knew it was desire. She knew she should run, would run, if he tried to kiss her. And knew she hoped he would stop her.

"What, Edmund?" It came out a hoarse whisper.

"Go to Week's Mechanical Museum. I have long wished to see the mechanical jumping spider."

She lifted her chin. The look in his eyes was a bit too knowing for her comfort. "That would be a perfect place to begin."

Chapter Nineteen

The next two weeks were the most enjoyable of Olivia's life. She and Edmund went to the Tower of London, Westminster Cathedral, and various other sites around London like the veriest tourists. They were usually accompanied by Aunt Lavinia and Mr. Barteau. Olivia had given up trying to prevent Corbright's uncle from escorting her aunt, though she still mistrusted him.

The restraint that had lain between Olivia and Edmund from the first melted with their new understanding. Though she often yearned for time alone with him, Livvy avoided it, and Edmund did not appear to seek it either. Instead, as if by explicit agreement, they concentrated upon knowing one another as friends before any more kisses could turn them into lovers. They found they shared not only agricultural interests but a similar view of society in general. They laughed at the same things often, and brangled without rancor about those areas where they disagreed. These, however, were surprisingly few. Edmund joined her in deploring the state of the poor in the country, and feeling that the rich and powerful spent far too much of their time and treasure on frivolities. While they both could and did laugh often, they found they shared a fundamentally serious turn of mind.

By the time Olivia received a letter from Jason that his ankle was well enough to join them, she hardly wished for it, and wrote him back to take his time. His previous letters to her had been full of his activities on behalf of the estate, and a simple pride in his ability to manage glowed through in them, which satisfied Edmund as much as it did her, when she shared them with him.

They occasionally came across Lord Heslington, and he appeared to take little pleasure in these meetings, barely acknowledging them and then frowning sourly upon them from afar. Thus, when Heslington was announced just as the two couples prepared to leave for a visit to Kew Gardens, all four of them looked apprehensively at one another.

"Show him in, Kittrick," Olivia told the butler they had hired for their stay in London. The earl entered the room stiffly, greeted Mr. Barteau and her aunt perfunctorily, then asked if he might speak with Edmund and Olivia privately.

"We will promenade on the square while you talk," Lavinia said, and left on Peter Barteau's arm, glancing back worriedly at Olivia as she did so.

"They are smelling of April and May," Heslington observed disdainfully.

"They have grown to be fast friends," Olivia responded.

"As have you and my brother, Miss Ormhill. I should warn you that some people have drawn the same conclusion about the two of you."

"Did you come here to retail gossip, Carl?" Edmund's voice vibrated with anger.

"No, I came here to warn both of you. Miss Ormhill, you should know that your relationship with Lord Corbright is in serious jeopardy because of your presence here in London when he expected you to join him in Scotland."

"That is none of your affair, Lord Heslington."

"Perhaps not. But Corbright is my friend, and I know the affection he holds for you. I do not like to see him betrayed."

"I cannot betray him, for I owe him nothing. We have no understanding, sir." Olivia's voice rose with anger.

"Do you mean to marry my brother, then?"

"You go too far, Carl," Edmund growled. "I think you should leave."

"Leave you to lure this innocent creature away from a man who adores her and can give her everything, into the hands of a man who can give her nothing?"

"Nothing but himself," Olivia corrected, looking at Edmund tenderly. "Which, if a woman should be fortunate enough to attach him, would be a great deal."

"What of your father's will? He required you to marry a titled man."

"Really, Lord Heslington, this is outside of enough."

Edmund stood, fists clenched. "Come, Carl. I will show you out."

"Not quite yet. Miss Ormhill needs to know the risk she runs. If you continue to pursue her, I will do what I should have done the day my father died: seek to have his marriage to your mother set aside. In case you don't know the law—"

"Oh, I know it. You taunted me with it enough when I was younger. Such a marriage is not void but voidable."

"Quite. In such a case, Miss Ormhill, my brother's title would not be Lord Edmund, but Bastard Debham."

Edmund sprang across the room and hauled his brother out of his chair. "You made my mother's life a misery with that threat. I don't fear it! Go on. Make an ass of yourself in front of the *ton* by declaring your brother a bastard ten years after his father's death."

Heslington struggled and finally broke Edmund's grip upon his coat with a violent upthrust of his arms. "If I must, to save Miss Ormhill and you from a great mistake."

"Then do it! If there were an inheritance to consider, I doubt not many would support you, property being near to a god among the *ton*. But dredge up an old scandal merely to spite your brother? I think you will find yourself no small target for ridicule."

Heslington frowned. "I doubt you would credit it, Edmund, but I am thinking of your welfare."

"And why do you concern yourself with my welfare, Carl?"

"We are family, after all."

"No, we are not. Never were, even before you expelled me from the fold this summer. I now know what a family is, you see, having known the Ormhills. They quarrel occasionally, but they stand by one another and care about one another. Your only interest in me is to thwart me."

"I am not surprised you don't credit me, but I am truly

concerned for both of you. In the end she won't have you, Eddie. Or if she does, she'll be miserable and make you so. She loves Franklin, you know. That so intelligent and capable a young woman would look to a man so beneath her in intellect and fortune only shows her motives to be revenge. Ultimately she will discover that to be a cheap and unhappy substitute for making it up with her true love. You would be much happier with sweet, uncomplicated Mary Benson than with this woman. As for you, Miss Ormhill, you had best send Edmund back to his haystacks before you lose your inheritance and Corbright forever."

"My feelings for Edmund, whatever they might be, would not be altered by your actions, my lord."

"But your property would be, Miss Ormhill. Correct me if I am wrong, but if your father's will is abrogated in any way, all of it goes to your brother, does it not?"

Edmund drew in his breath sharply. "Olivia, is that true?" He knew her father had tied up her property for her benefit, but this was news to him.

"It is." Olivia regarded Heslington calmly.

"You see how shocked he is, Miss Ormhill? He seeks your estate, not you. What's the matter, Edmund? Benson turn you down?"

From his tone, Heslington clearly felt he had delivered the coup de grâce to Edmund's hopes, but to his astonishment Olivia only laughed. "You have not the knowledge I have, sir. Mr. Benson would have been delighted to have Edmund offer for his daughter. Frankly, Lord Heslington, I pity you. You have a brother who is a fine, upstanding man, a delight to know, and a good one to have on your side, but you have alienated him and made yourself dyspeptic, too, all for nothing."

Heslington looked from one to the other, clearly perplexed. At last he shrugged. "I have done my best to do my duty by you, Edmund. Now I wash my hands of you." He turned and walked from the room, leaving both Edmund and Olivia stunned and embarrassed. Edmund spoke first.

"Thank you, Livvy, for defending me."

She continued to stare at the door through which Hes-

lington had just disappeared, hardly able to believe such en-
mity between brothers.

"My brother is a great fool. He has embarrassed himself
and us for nothing."

She turned slowly then, looking up at him uncompre-
hendingly.

"He thinks we have an understanding, but we are not
bound together by anything but friendship."

"Oh, Edmund." Her face crumpled. "Don't!"

"Livvy, don't cry. Please don't look at me so." He sat
next to her on the sofa and put his arm around her. "I will do
nothing to take your inheritance from you."

"Never think I prefer it to you, nor believe you will not
have me without it." Tears coursed down her cheeks. "I love
you, Edmund Debham, with all my heart."

Joy replaced Edmund's consternation. He gathered her
closer, the quality of his embrace changing entirely.
"Livvy!" He traced the tears on her cheeks with his lips, out-
lined her mouth with their moisture, then covered her lips
with his own in a kiss of such tenderness it made Olivia
quiver all over. She melted further into his arms, her hands
circling his neck to draw him closer.

When finally they drew apart, she asked shyly, "Does this
mean you love me, too? I think you do, but you haven't said,
you know."

"More than life itself! I have done since—oh, I don't
know when exactly, but for ages now."

She laughed, a deep, wet chuckle. "We haven't known
each other for ages." Her hand caressed his cheeks, where
lurked a suspicious moisture. "Are you crying, too, love?"

He took her hand, lowered his head, and pressed a deep
kiss in it. "With joy. Oh, Livvy. You will marry me, won't
you?" Then he pulled away. "But how can I do that to you?"

She tugged him back to her. "Heslington's spite cannot
part us. Jason will do the right thing by me, I know. And if
for some reason he does not, why, you will be well able to
afford a wife on what Lord Marcoombe will pay you, won't
you?"

If possible he looked even more adoringly at her. "He

told me a snug little manor house goes with the offer. We'll be partners there, love. He'll get two estate managers for the price of one."

Once again she ducked her head shyly. "Now, Edmund, I should be glad to be of assistance to you, but . . . that is, would there be a nursery in this manor, do you suppose?"

Wordlessly he drew her to him and kissed her deeply. She put her arms around his neck and kissed him back with all her heart. When he drew away he tucked her under his left arm. "Do you know what I have been wanting to do ever since I laid eyes on you?"

"I do hope it is not to take me to see any more jumping spiders."

He chuckled. "No. This." He put his right hand on her chin and began exploring it gently. "I have wanted to touch that entrancing cleft in your chin."

"Entrancing! It is a flaw. . . ."

"No, indeed. You are perfect."

"I am not! Oh, Edmund, when I think how often I have hurt you! I have a hasty temper, you know. I shudder to acknowledge it, but I may yet scold you again. How can you stand to live with such a flawed wife?"

"I can't stand to live without you. And I do not think of your prickly nature as a flaw, just as part of what makes you . . . you. Doubtless you will discover my flaws soon enough, if you haven't already."

"No, I have seen no sign of any. That is why I almost fear to inflict myself on you."

"I have too much pride, Olivia. Odd, in one who felt so worthless, but I suppose because of that, I was too sensitive to your criticisms. I should have courted you flat out from the beginning and never let Corbright near you once! My foolish pride kept me from letting you see how much I cared."

"I did wonder why you seemed so detached at times. You must never again believe anything I or anyone else says against you!" She cupped his head in her hands and pressed on his lips a tender kiss that soon turned passionate and brought his arms around her, drawing her onto his lap.

It was thus that Aunt Lavinia and Peter Barteau found them.

For only an instant did her aunt look indignant. Then she clapped her hands together. "Does this mean what I think it does?"

"Indeed, ma'am!" Edmund looked up, not releasing his treasure. Then his eyes slid to Mr. Barteau. "At least . . ." He straightened and set Olivia away from him. "It means my brother upset Olivia."

"That vicious young whelp. I'll bet I can guess why." Peter heaved his bulk into a nearby chair. "He's trying to scare you off, isn't he? He told me the other day he wouldn't stand for your poaching on Corbright's territory."

"N-no," Olivia said, putting even a little more distance between herself and Edmund. "That wasn't it at all. It just upset me so to see how cruelly and hatefully he speaks of Edmund." She dried her cheeks ostentatiously, accepting the handkerchief Edmund offered her. "C-come. We shan't let him ruin our outing. It is a sunny day, and there won't be many such left." She bounced off the sofa. "To Kew Gardens, shall we?"

Aunt Lavinia looked at Peter, then at the couple facing them, forced gaiety on their faces. "You can trust him, you know. He has told me a great deal about his nephew, none of it good."

Barteau leaned forward, fists clenched. "He is an insolent, arrogant, false creature. Hate to say it of my own nephew, but it is true. He hadn't a word to say to me, indeed seemed somewhat ashamed of me until my son died two years ago. Since then he has cultivated me assiduously. Wants to be my heir, you know. A clothing manufacturer is not someone that mushroom wished to know until there was a chance of inheriting a fortune. Now, I won't pry, but don't you dare see me as an enemy in your camp!"

Olivia and Edmund relaxed a little. "We won't, then," Livvy said, "but do let us go out into the lovely day."

Later, as they walked several feet behind Lavinia and Peter, Edmund told Olivia sotto voce, "We may be able to trust him, but I'm not sure."

"Nor am I. Do you know what Cynthia called him? A tailor! That could explain his interest in fashion. Perhaps he is not the wealthy man he pretends to be. I do hope he is not after my aunt for her property, as part of Corbright's scheme to get the whole valley under his control."

"How long have you believed that?"

Olivia's face grew grim. "Once I heard he had acquired Smithfield's land and offered to buy or lease Jason's, I knew my worst suspicions were correct."

Edmund whistled softly. "And here I thought you still considered marrying him."

"I meant for you to think it, you and Jason, until I found a husband. I feared a confrontation between Jason and Corbright if Jason forbade him to court me, as he threatened to do. I still fear it. Only once I am married will I feel that Jason is safe from Corbright and his own temper."

Edmund stopped walking, a look on his face she couldn't interpret.

"I didn't mean I want to marry you just for that reason," she hastened to reassure him."

"That's not what I was thinking. You are right about the potential for conflict. Corbright is ruthless and cunning, and Jason is impetuous and hotheaded. I have an idea that might work, but I am afraid you might once again believe me a fortune hunter."

"No. Edmund, whatever happens, I have learned what kind of man you are. I trust you completely."

He reddened with pleasure. "Oh, Livvy!"

"No, don't kiss me here."

He glanced to where Lavinia and Peter stood waiting for them to catch up.

"I will tell you my plan tonight."

"No, I can't wait. Whisper it to me now, as we walk."

"I know my brother, Livvy. He will do as he threatens, just to spite me, even if he isn't acting for Corbright. But such suits in the ecclesiastical courts take a long time. Your father's will says you must marry a lord, but I doubt he thought to require that your husband remain one. Surely he could not have anticipated so peculiar a circumstance. If we act quickly . . ."

Her eyes danced. "I am so happy to be marrying such a clever man! We shall get a special license and be married before your brother can do much more than file to have your parents' marriage set aside, and before Corbright can do any mischief."

"Just so. I will apply for a special license tomorrow morning."

"And I will write Uncle Ormhill and Jason, telling them. We'll go home as soon as possible. I do wish my uncle to marry us."

"As do I."

"Aren't these lovely, Olivia?" Lavinia called her attention to some small shrubs with bright red berries on them. "I wonder what they are, and if they would thrive in Norvale?"

"We must ask the curator, Aunt. If they will, I know just the place for them." She leaned forward and whispered in her aunt's ear, "At Wren Hall. I expect to be taking up residence there soon." When Lavinia looked about to break into joyful speech, she shushed her, looking at Mr. Barteau. "Not yet, Aunt."

"You still suspect him," Lavinia huffed indignantly.

"Only being cautious. I will explain later. Also, I think I should tell Jason and Uncle Milton first, don't you? Please, Aunt. Say nothing."

Lavinia agreed reluctantly, and led Peter off to give her niece and Edmund privacy.

Edmund seemed to have drifted into a brown study. As they walked along silently, Olivia could see the furrows in his brow that were so expressive of worry or unhappiness. "Won't you tell me what is troubling you?" she asked.

"Olivia, if your suspicions of Corbright's motives proved to be untrue, how would you feel about him? Would you be looking for another husband, or turning to me, if . . ."

Edmund's heart sank as she hesitated, obviously thinking his question over. "You do have a great deal in common, you know, with your love of Greek, and—"

Olivia burst into a peal of laughter. "I don't love Greek. I loved being recognized as intelligent enough to learn it. I loved studying it with a handsome young man. Remember when he came over and gave me that copy of *The Odyssey*?"

Edmund nodded. "And made me feel a dunce!"

"Well, I tried to read some of it, and found I had quite forgotten all my Greek, and had no desire to learn it again. At that time, I still thought I might marry Corbright, and I wondered how I would manage to escape studying it with him."

"Well, I hope that you are sure, for I shan't study it with you." Edmund shook his finger at her, laughing.

"I am so glad you asked me about that, Edmund. I had never put it to myself quite that way before."

"What? Whether you want to study Greek?"

"No, whether I would want to marry Corbright even if he were as innocent as a spring lamb of all the things I suspect him of. I wouldn't. Nor would have, even before I knew I loved you. Whatever drew me to him died a long while ago." She threw her hands in the air and spun around in a joyful little dance. When she stopped, dizzy, and let Edmund steady her with his strong arms, she smiled tenderly at him. "Now, I want you to stop worrying that I still have an attachment to Corbright, do you hear me?"

He laughed at her exuberance. "I hear and I obey."

Chapter Twenty

"How many men does this female intend to marry?" Mr. Peter Barteau's eyes goggled as he grasped the import of the archbishop's clerk's question.

"Do you mean to say someone else has applied for a license to wed her?"

"Two others, in fact. One last week, and the other yesterday morning. Ormhill. Unusual name, Ormhill. Wouldn't mistake it, much less when I see it for the third time in a week." The clerk began to search through a large stack of documents.

"Ah, that explains it. There are two Miss Ormhills. My fiancée's first name is . . . Did you say the *third* application?"

"Indeed, sir. This Miss Ormhill is obviously running some kind of a rig. Doubtless she has taken expensive gifts from each of you. I should have her up before the magistrate if I were you."

Peter Barteau mopped at his brow. He understood well enough the clerk's confusion of Lavinia's and Olivia's names, and had guessed that Olivia and Edmund meant to marry, so two applications would make sense. But three?

"I don't believe you," he exclaimed. "May I see those documents? I don't want to accuse my beloved falsely."

"Well, it is irregular, but I do hate to see a decent man being taking advantage of by some doxy." The clerk's mouth twisted in distaste. "Here is the one from yesterday."

Peter Barteau studied the application. As he expected, it was for Olivia and Edmund's license.

"As for the other," the clerk continued, "it was approved.

The prospective bridegroom called for it this morning. Seemed to think she was to marry him in Saint George's this very day. Too bad I didn't remember the other application in time to stop him."

"Let me guess. A tall blond man? Lord Corbright?"

"That sounds right. If you know him, I hope you can succeed in warning him off. Hate to think of him getting wed to such a scheming hussy."

Peter explained that he wished to marry the aunt of Olivia Ormhill. "The names are often confused," he said. "And as for Miss Olivia Ormhill running a rig, she has no knowledge of Lord Corbright's application. He is my nephew, you see, and as far as anyone knew, he was in Scotland. Nor does Miss Olivia have the least inclination to wed him."

"He apparently doesn't know this," the clerk said, fascinated.

"Obviously not. She wishes to marry Lord Edmund. Please process his application as expeditiously as possible, will you?"

The clerk scratched his head. "If you are quite sure the young lady is what she should be . . ."

"She is very much a lady, a woman of property, too. She will choose her own husband, and that choice will fall on Lord Edmund. My nephew has exerted himself in vain."

"When you return to collect your license you must tell me how it all comes out." The clerk smiled at Barteau and placed Edmund's application on the top of the stack.

"I'll see if Miss Olivia Ormhill is at home, my lord," Kittrick said, bowing reverentially to Lord Corbright on the basis of the card he had been handed.

"No need. I'd like to surprise her."

When Kittrick made to object, Corbright flashed a golden guinea. "I'm her fiancé, you see. She won't mind."

"In that case, my lord, she is in the drawing room." The butler palmed the coin, though his eyes followed Corbright uneasily as he dashed up the stairs.

"You look so charming, my love." Corbright sailed into the room and straight toward the small writing desk where

Olivia sat penning a letter to her brother. He spared but a glance toward Lavinia.

"Lord Corbright!" Olivia stood, hastily hiding the letter under another sheet of paper as she did so.

"*Lord* Corbright. Must you, Livvy?" He bent to kiss her. She dodged his kiss and stepped away.

"Why did you not tell me you were in London? I thought to have you join me in Scotland at any moment." He smiled pleasantly down at her. "Naughty girl, to lead your fiancé such a dance."

"You are not my fiancé, sir."

"By that flush on your cheeks I see you are irritated with me. Come, take a drive in the park with me and explain why, for it is such a beautiful day I vow you must take the air."

"What I have to say to you can be said here." Olivia drew herself up, fists clenched.

He looked puzzled and worried. "So solemn." He glanced at Lavinia. "Hullo, Aunt Lavvy. Pardon me for not noticing you before. So excited to see my sweetheart again, you see."

Lavinia was on her feet, bristling. "How did you know of Olivia's presence in London?"

"Why, I have just come from Beaumont, that is how. I returned to see what was keeping you. I have a message for you from Jason on me somewhere." He began patting at his pockets.

Olivia felt the hair on the nape of her neck rise. Why would Jason send a message by Corbright? "Please be seated, won't you? Aunt Lavinia, might I be private with Lord Corbright for a few moments?"

Lavinia reluctantly left the room. "I shall return in ten minutes," she assured them.

"Gad. What have I done to make the pair of you treat me as a stranger?"

At that moment Olivia almost pitied him. He looked so worried. *Perhaps he is sincerely attached to me, after all,* she thought. *I must go gently with him.* She seated herself beside him on the sofa.

"Franklin, I—"

"Now that is better! My name never seems to suit me so well as when it falls from your lips."

"Listen to me, please. I must remind you I that have not given you leave to regard me as your fiancée. I have held steadfastly to the position that we might be friends only."

"But you did not mean it. As I told Heslington when he wrote me, I know a woman as true as you gives her heart only once." He tried to take her hand, but she jerked it from him.

"I see I must be very plain with you. You are wrong, for I have given my heart again. I love Edmund Debham, and intend to marry him."

This news did not stun Corbright the way she had expected. Instead, he merely laughed shortly. "So Heslington thought. I am grateful to him for writing me, for it is clear that Edmund has found some way to ingratiate himself with you. But whatever you feel, it is but a passing fancy."

"It is not!" Livvy glared at him. "I love Edmund with all my heart. Please give it up, Franklin. My love for you died long ago."

His voice was low and gentle. "I won't accept that, Livvy."

"You must."

He regarded her silently for a long time. She held his eyes steadily, unwaveringly. At last he sighed. "So you won't have me."

"No."

"I think you will change your mind. I had hoped not to have to give you this, but . . ."

She watched his hand go unerringly this time to the pocket inside his morning coat. With a sense of impending doom she saw him take out a thin sheet of paper, unsealed, and hand it to her. It had a reddish streak across the edge. She opened it and immediately recognized her brother's handwriting, though the message was smeared in blood.

"My God! What is this!" Livvy recoiled away from Corbright, turning toward the window to make out the short message.

Dearest Livvy,

Do not be alarmed. I am somewhat bloodied but otherwise unharmed. The Swalen brothers have me. They say they are holding me for ransom. They have not named their figure, but say they will be in touch with you soon.

All my love,
Jason

Olivia put her hand to her mouth.

"Don't cry, dearest. I am sure we can raise the ransom." Corbright tried to pull her into his arms. She jumped to her feet and turned on him.

"You villain! Do you take me for a fool? You are behind this! The ransom is me, isn't it?"

Corbright dropped his solicitous manner. "In a manner of speaking, yes. I would have liked to have your love, too, of course, but I *will* have your land. Yes, and your brother's, too. And Lavinia's, of course."

She shook her head. "You know my father's will. If I am forced into marriage—"

"Or afterward find it disagreeable, or even if your trustees have reason to suspect that you do so, your land goes to your brother." Corbright stood, too. Suddenly he had never seemed so tall, and as he stood too close for comfort, that height became menacing. His eyes were cold, so cold they glittered like blue diamonds.

"But you won't admit to being forced, and afterward you won't admit to finding our marriage disagreeable. Your father thought himself very clever, Livvy, but he misunderstood one thing, something I only came to realize after I married: A real man can find a way to rule his wife, and rule you I will. If anyone, *anyone*, ever suspects you are less than delighted with our marriage, those you love will pay the price. Your brother will be released once we are wed. You will tell him I helped you raise the ten thousand pounds for his ransom. The Swalens will disappear, but others are in my employ. Any missteps on your part, and harm will occur to

Jason, or your uncle or aunt, or . . . did I understand you to say you love Edmund with all your heart?"

She gasped.

"Ah, yes. Your very words. What pleasure it would give me to have his life snuffed out. And I will do it, Livvy. Never think to escape me. If you call upon the oh-so-brave Edmund for rescue, then Jason will suffer."

Olivia tried to still the trembling that overtook every limb in her body, but could not.

"If you refuse me, or afterward complain of me, then as long as I have breath in my body, I will delight in tormenting you and yours. Not death for Jason, I think. Not right away. So young, so vibrant, so eager to travel. It will be difficult for him to travel with bullets through both knees, won't it?"

"You are a monster. No, you are insane! Franklin, no amount of land is worth this. Nor any amount of revenge, for whatever reason you feel you are owed revenge. Think how miserable your life will be with a wife who hates you."

"Not at all. You've read *The Taming of the Shrew,* haven't you? Outward conformity to love is all I ask, just as Petruchio did. Who knows, you may even learn to love me again. For I mean to be a generous, considerate husband, Olivia."

She snorted, anger steadying her. "Considerate!"

"Indeed, yes. In truth, I do not particularly enjoy bedding unwilling women. A weakness, I know. But there it is. I will bed you only until I have an heir and a spare. Then, if you are very, very good, I will allow you to live with your children."

She pressed her hand to her chest, where her heart seemed about to scramble out of her breast. "You'll fail, you know. My family will know you mistreat me then, for they know I would never desert my children."

"Ah. Well, that is another plan of mine. Really, I should have been a military man, for I am a genius at tactics, if I do say so myself. Do you think for one moment that your brother would take your land or refuse to sell his own to me, if he knew his sister or her children were to suffer if he did not?"

Livvy swayed on her feet, and he caught her to him. It was in this posture that Aunt Lavinia found them as she entered the room, saying, "Your ten minutes are up, and . . . Livvy!"

Corbright turned around, his left arm firmly around Olivia's shoulders. "Ah, there you are, dear Aunt Lavinia. You may wish us happy."

Lavinia took one look at Olivia's face and charged at him. "Oh, no you don't. Get away from her, you beast!"

"Why, what can you be thinking of, to behave so uncivilly to your future nephew?" Corbright held her off easily with his other hand.

"I see the tears on Olivia's cheeks. She won't have you, not willingly. Let her go!"

Corbright looked down at Olivia, squeezing her shoulder so painfully with his hand that she gasped and looked up at him. "Tears of happiness, aren't they, my love? She is—we are—so happy that all our disagreements have been settled and we can be together at last. Isn't that true, Livvy?"

Olivia turned great, tear-filled eyes to her aunt. "That's true, Aunt Lavinia. I . . . I am quite ashamed of myself for doubting him. And I feel terrible about hurting Lord Edmund, as I know this will. You must explain to him for me."

"That I never shall, for I don't believe it. Not for a minute!"

Olivia knew she had to pull herself together and put on a performance worthy of a Siddons. She smiled at Lavinia. "Now, Aunt Lavvy, please. I am so happy, I wish my family to share in my happiness."

"There. Didn't I tell you?" Corbright released Olivia and nudged her toward her aunt.

Olivia reached out for the distressed woman and hugged her. "Please, please try to understand. I never stopped loving him. So much of what I did was based on the pain his marriage caused me, and a desire to repay him. But I know now how wrong that was."

"And your fears about his real intentions . . ."

"All laid to rest. He has explained all." She pulled back, looking pleadingly into Lavinia's eyes. "Please," she whispered.

Lavinia looked no less troubled, but stepped back. "If

you are quite sure, my dear. But . . . but you won't rush into anything, will you? I mean, only yesterday—"

Olivia half screamed, "Don't remind me of yesterday. I am so ashamed. Oh!" She began to cry in spite of all her efforts. Corbright took her in his arms and patted her back.

"There, there. Edmund will get over it. He is young and handsome. I understand he has a very good chance at a much greater heiress than you, that Miss Benson. Doubtless he will be married before we are, if your family has its way." He turned once again to Lavinia, wagging a finger at her.

"But I, for one, do not promise to let you have your way. We have been separated too long. I hope to persuade you to marry me as soon as may be. Now, my love, why do you not come for that carriage ride with me? Such a lovely day for late October. And we've a deal of talking to do, plans to make, haven't we?"

Olivia looked up and forced herself to smile. "That would be delightful. I shall get my shawl."

Corbright followed her out into the foyer and took her arm. "Let your maid bring it out to you. I want to show you my new pair of matched blacks. Lavinia, *au revoir* for now."

Edmund returned to their town house from his visit to the War Office with information that did not much surprise him. He wondered if he should tell Olivia that the Swalens were deserters, wanted for numerous crimes, or if it would just worry her unnecessarily. After all, the two had not been seen since Corbright sent them on their way. He dashed up the steps, eager to see her, but found a distracted, distressed Lavinia Ormhill pacing the drawing room instead.

Lavinia cast herself into his arms, wailing, "Oh, it is terrible. I don't believe it, not for a minute, but she said . . . Oh!" Her tears flooded his waistcoat as Edmund tried to coax her into some coherent speech.

"What is it, Aunt Lavvy? Tell me. Here." He led her to the sideboard and poured a generous measure of brandy, then virtually forced it down her throat. She choked and gasped as he led her to the sofa. "Has something happened to Olivia? Where is she?"

"Oh, Edmund. I don't know how to tell you this." Lavinia gulped back another sob. "She has gone for a drive with Corbright. He has won her back."

"Won her . . . If that pup Jason has been wagering again, I'll hang him by his ears. But no. That can't be your meaning. Livvy wouldn't abide by any such wager, no more than she did when I—"

"That is not my meaning. Oh, dear boy. I know it will break your heart, but she said she loves him, always has. That it was all spite and revenge. That now he has answered all her doubts and they are to be married."

Edmund stiffened. "I don't believe it."

"Neither did I, but she swore it was true. She . . . she hugged him, and smiled at him, and . . . she asked me to break it to you, to say she was sorry if you were hurt."

"*If* I were hurt!" Heslington's words came back to him then, as the taunts of his older brother always had, cutting him into ribbons too many times to remember. *In the end she won't have you, Eddie. Or if she does, she'll be miserable. She loves Franklin, you know.*

He slumped backward in his seat. Words would not come.

Lavinia longed to comfort him, but how to do it she did not know. "To think that only a few minutes ago she was composing a letter to Jason and my brother, to tell them of your engagement." The clock on the mantel ticked into a painful silence. "It isn't like Livvy," she mused.

Edmund lifted his head. "No, it isn't. If true, I can understand why she wouldn't want to face me. But she will have to, eventually. I am not going to just slink away. I will hear this from her own lips before I accept it." Just then Peter Barteau, red-faced and sweating, burst into the room.

"Where is Olivia?" he demanded.

"She is with your nephew," Lavinia said bitterly. "She has decided to marry him, after all."

"When did they leave?"

"Why, not fifteen minutes ago. Just for a short drive in the park, they said."

"When did she decide to marry him? Last night it was—"

"I know. Apparently when she talked with him this morning—"

"I don't believe it!"

"That makes three of us, Peter." Lavinia sighed.

Edmund sat up straight. "Why did you rush in here looking for her in such a manner, sir?"

"Because I just learned that last week my nephew took out a special license to marry her. It has been granted, too. He collected it this morning."

"How did you . . ?"

"I . . . never mind. I think we had best go and find them."

Lavinia screamed, "He has a license with him?"

"This gets smokier by the moment. If he applied last week, he was far too sure of himself for any encouragement she had given him, at least that I am aware of." Edmund looked at Lavinia for confirmation.

"Indeed, no. You know her suspicions! I don't like to tell you this, Peter, but she even thought you a part of a plot for him to get all of the land in Norvale."

"How?" Peter's eyes narrowed.

"By marrying me." Lavinia's eyes stayed on Barteau's face, hope mixed with fear.

"Balderdash! Don't you believe a word of it! My nephew shall never see a penny of mine nor a clump of dirt from your land. Come now, Edmund. We must go after them. My curricle is at the curb."

"Where do you think—"

"Saint George's. He told the archbishop's clerk that he was to be married this very morning at Saint George's. How he has managed to get her to agree, I don't know, but we must be sure she isn't being forced."

"Let's go." Edmund took Lavinia's elbow, but she pulled back.

"No. You go ahead. Peter's team will not go swiftly enough with the three of us in that curricle. I shall call for the carriage and follow. Just hurry and stop them, please!"

Chapter Twenty-one

"Was it always about my land?" Livvy asked Corbright as he tooled his curricle through traffic.

He shook his head. "Not entirely. You are a choice morsel, Olivia. And I do admire your mind. You will add luster to my project, quoting Greek to our visitors and dressing the part of an Athenian matron. But yes, since you ask, I always wanted your land. Otherwise I would have looked higher for a wife. The vision was originally my father's, you see. He said Wren Hall was the key to the whole thing. The plan is to put a palace fit to entertain royalty right there, overlooking the valley and the best view of the Parthenon.

"Even though he was made a baron, my father was still snubbed. But Prinny is a patron of the arts, especially architecture. He'll be mad for this project. Wouldn't be surprised if he wants to build his own palace nearby. I'll be made an earl. You'll be a countess, Livvy, and no one will look down on me again, ever."

The fanatical look on his face as he spoke told Livvy more than she wished to know about his state of mind. The busy London traffic passed by in a blur as she listened to Corbright outlining the behavior he expected of her. She hardly knew where they were until they were nearly upon Saint George's church. A small knot of people stood outside, obviously waiting. To her astonishment, she knew most of them, and the expressions on their faces told her it was she and Corbright they awaited.

"Oh, no! What is this? You cannot mean—"

"To wed you this very day? Indeed, yes. No more delays, remember. What delight I have had in planning this surprise wedding for you, asking everyone to keep my secret. Many skeptics claimed you would never show; I even have some substantial wagers resting upon your appearance. Now smile, Livvy, and act the excited, happy bride."

"I can't. Oh, I truly can't. See, I am crying again. If you must marry me today, it should be in a place where we are unknown. Too many people here know me well enough to guess at my feelings."

He scowled at her. "I believed you would come willingly. I truly thought you would want me. That hurts me, you know."

"Think again, Franklin. Remember that you do have feelings, and they can be hurt. Do not saddle yourself with an unwilling wife."

He shook his head, his mouth grim. "Too late to draw back now. I'll have no more embarrassment at your hands, do you hear? Not to mention the wagers I would lose. Those tears are tears of joy, do you understand me? Unless you wish to cry tears of grief over your brother's grave."

Olivia shuddered all over. But she fixed a smile on her face as they drew even with some dozen members of the London *ton.* Cynthia Bowers stood closest to the curb, waving to her with a bouquet of flowers.

"Livvy, you did come. We could not believe it, but here she is, my love!"

Olivia glanced at Lord Bower. His skeptical expression put her on her mettle. "Yes, I am here. It is most amazing. What a romantic surprise my love has arranged!"

By this time Corbright was helping her from the carriage. Once on her feet she turned to embrace her friend. "You are to be my bridesmaid, I hope?"

"Yes!" Cynthia giggled nervously. "But Livvy, have you been crying?"

Olivia hugged her. "Tears of joy, dearest. You have no idea how I felt when I saw Corbright again this morning. My heart suddenly knew its mind at last."

"Ah! That is all right, then."

"Did I not tell you how it would be, Miss Ormhill?"

Olivia turned to find Lord Heslington at her elbow, an arch look on his face.

"Very prescient of you, my lord." She wondered just how much of Corbright's villainous scheme Edmund's brother knew.

"How did my brother take it when you told him?"

"I have not told him, my lord. I doubt not you will enjoy having that pleasure." She turned her back on him, only to encounter Corbright's icy eyes.

"Lord Heslington is to be my groomsman, my love."

Olivia turned back and met Heslington's golden brown eyes, so like her beloved Edmund's in color, so unlike in expression. "Perfect. You are the perfect choice for this wedding, Lord Heslington. I thank you." She curtsied to him. He returned her a deep bow, but his expression altered to a frown.

A swirl of well-wishers engulfed them then. Olivia felt she stood in a minefield as questions were fired at her, such as the barbed compliment of one woman on her choice of wedding dress. "As I did not know I was to be wed, Mrs. Tillersby, you will excuse me for wearing a carriage dress. I thought only to go for a drive in the park." Her voice quavered a little at this. The drive was to have been with Edmund, to select a wedding ring.

"Why are we all milling about out here?" Corbright looked sharply at Heslington. "Let us go in."

"Not just yet. There is a wedding ahead of ours."

Corbright muttered under his breath and glanced up and down the street. "Perhaps we should go to Saint Peter's instead."

"Nonsense, Lord Corbright. How should we get there?" Lord Henry Aversley asked. "We sent our carriages on, to return later, and you can hardly expect us to walk."

"No, indeed," Mrs. Tillersby exclaimed. "In fact, my feet are hurting already."

Corbright had come to Olivia's side and held her firmly against him with one arm. His eyes scanned the streets, and when Olivia felt his grasp tighten painfully, she followed his gaze with dread in her eyes.

"It looks as if we are to have your uncle and my brother join us," Heslington said, also staring at the approaching curricle.

At the same time Cynthia said in a gasp, "Oh, Livvy, how embarrassing for you. Bower, will you not go and tell Edmund he is de trop?"

Lord Bower's jaw tightened. He looked at Corbright and Heslington, then down at Olivia, who was shredding the bouquet she had been given into tiny pieces. "Is he?"

"If he ruins this, I shall call him out," Corbright growled. "I think a word from Olivia will be sufficient, however."

Olivia knew she must speak the words that would send Edmund away. She prayed as she approached Peter Barteau's carriage that her beloved would believe her.

Edmund alighted before the curricle had stopped, and raced toward them.

"Come, Olivia. Get into the carriage. Peter will take you home while I deal with Corbright."

"No. Edmund, listen to me. Look at me." She forced herself to meet and hold his eyes. "It was as your brother said. When I saw Corbright again this morning, it all came back to me: our courtship, our quarrels, my desire to be revenged. We talked it all over, and I faced what I did not wish to face, that I was throwing away my chance to marry the man I have always loved."

Edmund looked from her to Corbright, and then to his brother. "I don't believe you." He raised his voice so the others would hear. "She is being forced into this. He has threatened her with something truly terrifying, to make her do this."

"Go away, Eddy. You are making a cake of yourself." Heslington moved forward and put a hand on his brother's arm.

Edmund shook it off, giving him a look of such loathing that the onlookers gasped. "That you would do what you could to injure me, I have long since accepted. But to be a party to such cruelty to an innocent woman—well, all I can say is that you will soon be known by the company you keep, and once that happens, few will care to keep you company."

A chorus of sound came from the onlookers, from jeers to nervous laughs. Aversley spoke for many of them when he said, "Do go away, Edmund. You are putting a damper on things."

"Do you really want to be a party to this travesty? I had thought you a decent man. And you, Lord Bower. You know Olivia. Do you really think her so fickle?"

"If he does, I do not." Peter Barteau joined them, having secured his curricle. "Nephew, I suggest you give this up now. You stand to lose a great deal if you do not, and I refer not merely to your reputation."

"What makes you so sure she doesn't wish to marry him?" Aversley asked Peter.

"Well, for one thing, her family isn't here. Deuced odd, don't you think? You know how close that family is. You remarked on it to me at my nephew's party, remember? So where is her aunt? Her brother? Her uncle, whom I certainly would have expected to be the one to marry her, seeing that he is a vicar."

"Her brother is ill in Buckinghamshire. I brought a note from him this morning, did I not, love?" Corbright proclaimed. "He regretted that he and her uncle could not be here, but urged me to go on with the surprise. As for her aunt, she has never approved of me, which is one reason I planned this—to save Olivia the unpleasantness she would face day after day until we could be wed. Tell them, Olivia."

"Th-that's right. I got a message from Jason this morning. And Aunt Lavinia was quite livid when she saw Corbright."

Edmund's eyes narrowed. "So that's it. You've threatened her brother, haven't you? Or he's challenged you. It is what she fears most."

"This is beyond insulting. Take care you don't push me too far, Edmund."

"I will give you satisfaction on the instant. Bower, will you stand my second?"

"Not just now." Corbright spoke hastily. "Have your seconds call on me after we return from the honeymoon. Now, I have some friends who will escort you away from here, as I am sure you do not wish to watch me marry Olivia. You remember the Swalen brothers, don't you, Edmund?"

Suddenly two men materialized behind Edmund, clearly intending to grasp him and drag him away.

Terror raced through Olivia. *They mustn't get Edmund in their clutches.* "You shan't ruin our wedding day with a brawl, Edmund Debham," she shouted in her sharpest tone. "Take yourself off instantly. And Franklin, love, do invite your friends to join us." She smiled sweetly up at him, but her eyes were as hard as Corbright's as they met.

"Provided Edmund leaves, I certainly shall."

"Go away, Edmund," came one voice.

"Yes, do. We are almost in church, after all," came another.

Suddenly Edmund sprang forward and slammed Corbright against the side of the building, his hand grasping his throat. His other hand came up and thrust a small pistol into his adversary's rib cage.

"Understand me, Franklin," he said. "I will see you dead 'ere I let you rush Olivia into wedding you this day. Once I see her brother safe, and her family around her, if she still insists it is you she wants, I will disappear from your life— and hers—forever. But it won't be today. Give it up, face me like a gentleman, or die like a dog, I don't care which."

"Don't do this, Eddy. You'll hang for it," Heslington shouted.

"That should suit you well, dear brother. I will hang, and gladly, before seeing Olivia made miserable." He looked over at her. "Leave now, Livvy, while you can."

Olivia's heart was in her throat. The ferocious look on his face was the same he had worn when he told her how he fought out of anger at the sight of those he cared about falling around him in battle. He *would* kill Corbright, and then be hanged for it. She had to stop him.

"No, indeed. This isn't necessary or right. I n-never expected you to be such a bad loser, Edmund. I blame myself somewhat, for not having the courage to face you and tell you myself. But you must accept the inevitable." Olivia had made her way to Corbright's side, and she slid her hand down to where it met the pistol Edmund held there. Corbright pulled in his stomach and suddenly her hand was between him and the gun. Edmund looked down, then up at her, his face ashen.

"For God's sake, Livvy."

"For all our sakes, Edmund, please go. Leave it. In fact, leave England. I wish never to see you again. I shall see that no one hires you here. I am sure Lord Marcoombe will not, once I tell him how badly you have behaved."

"If you wed him at any other time, I will do as you ask. But not today." Edmund maintained his grip on Corbright's throat and shifted the gun so it pointed at his temple.

"Edmund! Please don't cause the death of the man I love," Olivia cried desperately. Tears began to roll down her cheeks.

The agony in her voice gave Edmund pause. He pulled away, and instantly Olivia inserted herself between him and Corbright. He dropped his hand, the gun hanging loose. "Livvy," he whispered. "Oh, Livvy." *She must truly love him. How can I bear it?*

Corbright's henchmen grabbed him then, wresting the gun from him and starting to bundle him off.

"Swalen brothers," Lord Bower said to his wife.

"Stop them," Cynthia screamed.

"A moment, if you please." Lord Aversley stepped between them and their obvious destination, a seedy hackney cab. Lord Bower joined him.

"Get out of the way," Arthur Swalen snarled.

Cynthia Bower confronted Corbright. "Are the Swalen brothers not the men you purported to have run from the valley for insulting Olivia?"

Corbright's forehead beaded with perspiration. "You misunderstood. Not Olivia. Her aunt, Lavinia. They said some insulting things about her. True things, actually, for she is a homely woman, but she is my beloved's aunt, so I suggested they settle elsewhere."

"Then why are they here, acting as your agents?"

"I . . . I . . ." Corbright looked furtively around.

"How dare you?" Peter Barteau cried out. "I ought to call you out, Nephew. You have insulted the woman I mean to marry."

"You? Marry Lavinia?" Corbright's face turned livid. "You can't. I . . . she . . ."

"She would no longer control her land, then, would she, Corbright?" Edmund snarled, suddenly energized by his obvious discomfiture. "You could no longer force her to do as you wish, to protect her niece. That *is* your plan, isn't it?"

Aversley held up his hand. "Enough. Release Lord Edmund. I do not believe there is to be a wedding today."

The Swalen brothers looked to Corbright for instructions. He stood frozen.

"By the way, they are *not* gentlemen," Edmund said. "They are deserters. Wanted by the military courts for murdering, raping, and pillaging. And those crimes were committed against our Portuguese allies. These are the ruffians Lord Corbright has invited to his wedding—for the express purpose of seeing that no one interfered with it."

At this, Arthur Swalen screamed, "You lying bastard." He tightened his choke hold on Edmund, who struggled furiously.

The murmurs of the crowd increased, and the comments were negative. "Smoky business," one said. "I for one will not be a party to it," another said.

Aversley glared at Heslington, who stood some feet from Corbright, frowning darkly. "Do you mean to see your brother taken away by such as these? Come, give me some assistance." He and Bower began to try to pull the trio apart. With an oath, Heslington joined them. The Swalen brothers gave up the struggle and released Edmund.

All eyes now turned to Olivia and Corbright. There was no mistaking the hostility on the men's faces, the concern for Olivia on the women's.

Corbright took Olivia's hands in his. "I am dreadfully sorry, my dear. I never meant for this to happen. Now you see the real Edmund Debham. A lying troublemaker, always has been, eh, Heslington?" Without waiting for a reply, he continued in a gentle, loving tone. "What say you, my love? Shall we go in and be married? I am sure we can find another witness to join with Heslington, and—"

"You will require more than one," Heslington said, "for, I, too, have decided not to participate. In fact, Miss Ormhill, you have but to say the word, and I will escort you from here, so that you will not be importuned further, at least today, by either of your suitors."

Olivia was startled by this turn of events, but her mind raced to see if anything had really changed, and she realized it hadn't. If she did not marry Corbright, he would destroy those she loved. Jason doubtless was being held somewhere by another of Corbright's men. Edmund would be assassinated. She looked at him, at his disheveled clothes and his furrowed brow, and felt such love that it made her dizzy.

"No, I thank you, Lord Heslington. What has happened here has only made me more determined to be wed today, before the forces that oppose us can gain strength. Lord Edmund has insinuated himself into my family's good graces, and put on quite a show for all of you, but he will not deflect me from my true wishes, which are to wed Lord Corbright. See, the other wedding party is leaving the chapel. Shall we go in?"

This last sentence she spoke loudly enough to be heard by all who stood nearby. But many turned away. Lord Bower looked deeply troubled.

"Will you not give me away, my lord?" she pleaded with him. "And allow Cynthia to stand up with me?"

"Not today, Miss Ormhill."

"Certainly not," Cynthia agreed. "Olivia, do give this up. Corbright, I advise you, for the sake of your reputation, to postpone this wedding."

"Come, dear Olivia, we don't need any of them. The vicar will doubtless have witnesses enough about the chapel somewhere." Corbright held out his arm, and when she took it, covered her hand with his.

"I would suggest that your henchmen disarm before entering the church," Heslington said.

"That's right. Bristling with arms like Turkish banditti,"

Aversley said. He and Bower moved to block the two from entering, so they disgorged several pistols and knives, placing them in the waiting carriage.

Barteau, the Bowers, Aversley, and Heslington stood with Edmund as Corbright and Olivia climbed the steps, accompanied by a few of the invited guests. The Swalens brought up the rear.

"You surprised me just now, Carl," Edmund said to his brother.

"I surprised myself. Are you content to let this happen?"

"Yes, what say you, Lord Edmund?" Aversley asked. "Except by force, I do not see how we can prevent this."

"It is my fight, gentlemen."

"No. No gentleman can stand by and see a woman forced to wed. But is she being forced?"

Edmund hesitated. "I . . . I am not sure."

"I can answer that!" They all turned at the sound of a strident female voice, to see Lavinia Ormhill exiting the Ormhill carriage, which had pulled up while their attention was on the wedding party. She hurried up to the knot of men. "You must stop this wedding. See this? After you left, I found it under the desk where Olivia had been writing."

She held out the bloodstained note. "It is Jason's handwriting," she said as the appalled group read it. "That is why she is here."

Edmund grabbed the paper and raced up the steps, closely followed by the others. Down the aisle of the church he ran, to where the wedding party stood. He arrived at the dais just as a stout vicar, leaning heavily on a cane, intoned, "if any man do allege and declare any impediment why they may not be coupled together in matrimony by God's law—"

"There could be no more unholy union than this, vicar." Edmund thrust the paper into the startled cleric's hands. "This note came to Miss Ormhill just before she agreed to wed Lord Corbright. She is doing it to free her brother."

"It . . . it asks for a ransom. That doesn't—"

"She is the ransom. She is being forced into this marriage."

"Father, please ignore him," Olivia begged the minister.

"He is mad with grief and rage that I am marrying another man." Olivia snatched the paper from Edmund's hand and tore it. "Please proceed."

"No, Livvy. Don't do this." Lavinia pushed between Corbright and Olivia. "I know you are protecting Jason, but you will be subjecting yourself to a lifetime of danger."

"I am free to choose—"

"And it won't end there. Will it, Corbright? It is not just her land you want. You won't stop until you have Jason's and mine, will you? Oh, Olivia, do you think any of us could ever be happy again or know a moment's peace with you in the hands of this monster? We, Milton and I, have already been through that torture once." Tears began to stream down Lavinia's face. "Don't do it to us again."

"You interfering old vixen, get out of here." Corbright grabbed her and shoved her aside. "Vicar, my fiancée wishes to continue in spite of her insane aunt's imaginings."

As Peter protested this treatment of his fiancée, Edmund picked up the discarded note. Piecing it together, he asked Corbright, "How do you explain that the two men named here as her brother's captors are present, under your orders? I speak of the Swalen brothers." He motioned to the glowering pair.

"Is this true?" When several people confirmed it, the vicar thumped his cane on the stone floor to silence the group. "I am sorry, but I cannot complete this marriage at this time. Miss Ormhill, I suggest you allow your friends to escort you from here."

"Damn you to hell, Edmund." Corbright's face contorted with fury. "You shall pay for this. George! Arthur!"

The two men left the pews and started for Edmund, only to be stopped by Bower and Aversley. A violent but brief struggle ensued, which Edmund, Heslington, and Peter joined. When they were subdued, Edmund said, "I think you two should go to the War Office, to answer to those charges against you."

"I'll see to them," Aversley said. "Bind their hands."

"Come, dear. Let us go home." Lavinia tugged on Olivia's hand and led her away.

"Olivia," Corbright called out. "We can still be wed. Come with me. I know a vicar who will wed us, not an hour's drive from here."

Olivia stopped and turned back. Edmund stood between them, fists clenched, the savage expression on his face again. *He'll kill Corbright before he'll let me marry him, even if it means he hangs for his crime.*

"No, Lord Corbright. My aunt is right. I can't live in fear, nor subject my family to such. If anything happens to my brother, sir, I shall see you hang. And the same goes for anyone else I love." She pulled herself from Lavinia's grasp and went to Edmund, who gathered her to him with a sob of joy. He led her from the church, followed by Lavinia and Peter.

Heslington sneered at Corbright. "If I were you, old boy, I'd take a repairing lease in Europe. You will find England a cold, lonely land from now on." He turned his back on his former friend and sauntered out of the chapel, followed by Bower and Aversley, who bent one last look of disgust on Corbright before turning away to escort their prisoners from the church.

Olivia blinked in the sunlight as they emerged. She clung to Edmund as they went down the steps, for her legs felt limp. "Oh, Edmund, we're got to find Jason," she wailed.

"We will find him, love." Edmund guided her to the pavement, then looked about him. "You and Lavinia go home. I'm going to haul Corbright before a magistrate, then see to the questioning of the Swalen brothers. Peter, one of us must stay with the women at all times. And send someone to Bow Street to get some men to assist us in our search." He cupped Olivia's chin in his hands. "Don't fret, my love. I doubt not the Swalens will tell where Jason is to save their necks."

"Don't count on it," Corbright snarled. He stood just behind them with the visibly upset vicar, who leaned heavily on his sturdy cane. "They're gallows bait and they know it. They hate you and all officers, Edmund. They'll keep silent and let Jason starve, for the pleasure of spiting you. Sleep well, my lovely Olivia."

"She may not sleep well, but I think you will be sleeping very poorly, in prison, for your part in this," Edmund said.

"You haven't the slightest proof that I was involved," Corbright snarled.

"I shall gladly be a witness for the prosecution," said a familiar voice, and Jason appeared around the rear of the Ormhill carriage, leading Storm. He was covered with bruises and cuts and his clothing was torn.

"Jason! Oh, Jason!" Olivia launched herself at him. He caught her up, laughing, and fell back against the horse, which reared, ears back.

"Take care with her around Storm," Edmund shouted. "He's dangerous." He jumped for the agitated animal's bridle.

"Sorry. When I got to the town house he was the only thing left in the stable." Jason jerked Olivia away from the horse, and Edmund clapped him on the shoulder. "So you got away from them, you young scamp!"

"The Swalens left some great lump to watch me. Talked him into freeing my hands to play cards. We shared a bottle of blue ruin." Jason winked at his sister. "When I'd cleaned him out he tried to tie me back up. He thought himself a boxer, but that dancing style you taught me, Edmund, completely flummoxed him, and then he proved to have a glass jaw. Oh, Livvy, tell me they were in time to prevent your marriage. I overheard Corbright telling the Swalens his plans."

"So that's how you found us. Oh, Jason! They were in time, but only just." She pulled him close, and Lavinia joined her. They both hugged the young man so hard that he groaned and pulled away.

"Careful, now. Think I've a broken rib or two; I—Edmund, look out!" At the same moment Cynthia Bower let out a high-pitched scream.

All eyes turned to where Edmund, his back to them, spoke soothingly to Storm. Corbright stood just behind him, in the act of slamming the vicar's stout cane down on his head.

Edmund moved just in time for the blow to miss hitting

him squarely on the head. Instead it sideswiped his face, then continued its downward path until it connected brutally with Storm's shoulder. The stallion shrieked in pain and reared, throwing the stunned Edmund to the ground. Storm spun around, keeping the others from going to Edmund's aid, and Corbright once again poised the cane for a deadly blow.

But it never fell. Storm reared and struck at Corbright. His flailing hooves hit the man in the chest and threw him against the Ormhill carriage. His head connected with the large rear wheel with a resounding clang. Not satisfied, Storm started for him again, but by this time Edmund was on his feet and grasped the horse's reins, pulling him back. Breathing heavily, blood streaming down his head, he warned Olivia, who wanted to run to him, to stay back.

"No, boy, no," he crooned to the excited animal. "The war's over, remember. No more battles for you."

Everyone's attention turned from the snorting, plunging horse to the figure of Lord Corbright, slumped against the carriage wheel. He wasn't moving.

Bower stepped over to him, bent down to feel his neck, then knelt and listened for a heartbeat. He looked up at Heslington. "Go ask my wife for a mirror, will you? She'll have one in her reticule."

A strange silence fell upon the group. Lavinia allowed herself to be drawn into Peter's arms. Jason held Olivia while Edmund tied Storm to the back of Peter's curricle. When Edmund joined them, she turned in to his chest, sobbing.

The sound of it tore at Edmund's very soul. Did she love Corbright, after all?

Jason knelt beside Corbright while Bower held the mirror to his nostrils. After minutes that seemed to stretch into hours, Bower nodded and stood. Jason stood, too, and turned to the others. "Dead."

Lavinia looked up at Peter. "Oh, my dear, I'm—"

"Sorry I had such a rotter for a nephew. So am I, my love. I hope you can overlook it?"

She smiled and held him even tighter.

Olivia had frozen in Edmund's arms at Jason's pronouncement. At last she lifted her head and her eyes sought Edmund's. "Dead?" she whispered.

He nodded.

"May God forgive me, but I am glad. We never would have known a moment's peace while he lived."

"Oh, Livvy, I was so terrified!"

Surprised at this admission, though he had every reason to be frightened of such a villainous man, Olivia hugged him. "I know. He looked like a fiend when he attacked you."

"That was not my meaning. Just now, when you were crying so, I wondered—"

"Edmund Debham. How could you suppose I wept for him?" She tried to pull out of his arms, glaring at him indignantly. "You do not know me very well if you think that! It was only the horror of the whole situation, the sight of you being attacked."

"Livvy, dear, I intend to know you very well indeed before our lives are over. We have a long, long time to become fully acquainted, do we not?"

The urge to fight left her at the warmth in those dear eyes. She melted against him, lifting her lips to be kissed. "We do, indeed."

Epilogue

O livia and Edmund pulled apart as the door to the blue salon opened. They moved apart just enough for propriety, though it would not have been the first time Buckman had found them snuggling since their marriage a week before. The butler carried a tray to Edmund, who read the card, then passed it to Olivia. "Show him in," he said.

"What does he want? He can't hurt us now, except to cause more scandal, and what care we for that?"

"You may not care about it, Lady Edmund, but I do," Lord Heslington said. He had entered on the heels of their butler.

He bowed, and Edmund stood slowly and returned the bow. "Olivia, perhaps this would be a good time for you to help Jason pack for his trip?" Edmund did not want his wife exposed to any more of his brother's rancor. Though Heslington had drawn back from Corbright at the wedding, Edmund did not flatter himself it was from any familial tenderness, but rather that he saw his friend losing the good opinion of the others in the wedding party, and did not wish to share in Corbright's well-deserved obloquy.

"I hope you will permit her to stay, Edmund. What I have to say is for her ears too, and I have reason to believe it will replace that angry glare with a smile."

"Does this mean you have decided not to sue to have my husband declared illegitimate, my lord?" Livvy remained standing, chin up, and good manners in abeyance as she confronted Edmund's spiteful brother.

"Yes, it does mean that. I apologize for making that threat."

"Yes," Edmund said. "After the scandal about Corbright's scheme, and your friendship with him, it would be something of an embarrassment for you, wouldn't it, Carl?"

Heslington's face flushed, and he nodded. "You might say that. But more to the point, I am embarrassed that I have not valued you as I ought as a brother, as a person."

Olivia gave an unladylike snort, but at Edmund's urging, sat down, indicating that her unwelcome guest should do the same.

Heslington leaned forward. "When I saw you put that gun in Corbright's ribs and threaten to kill him, saw that you were willing to hang for the woman you loved, I could but admire you." He turned to Olivia. "I doubt you will credit it, but I truly believed Corbright would persuade you to marry him willingly. I could not imagine a woman preferring my brother to a rich, titled man like Corbright, who professed to adore her."

Olivia again snorted in rude skepticism. Edmund, however, nodded his head. "I believe that. Your opinion of me made such a conclusion inescapable."

"Well, that opinion has changed."

"Is that what you came here to say, Lord Heslington? Olivia stood. "If so, I thank you. Edmund will see you out, for I have much to do."

"It is not all of my business here. I do not blame either of you for despising me, but please give me a few more moments."

Surprised at the tone in his brother's voice, the pleading in his eyes, Edmund pulled Olivia back down beside him.

"You see, I was always jealous of Edmund."

"Jealous?"

"Oh, yes. You were my father's darling, and born to the woman he loved."

"Wh-what?"

"Father loved Aunt Dorothea more than he ever loved my mother. And you, the child of that love, were his obvious favorite. I resented their happiness and envied you their love.

And the scandal of their irregular marriage embarrassed me horribly. When my father died, I had no wish to see you about me. I sent you away, knowing it would hurt your mother, and sincerely believing it was the right career for a boy of your intellect."

"Cannon fodder."

Heslington looked at his hands. "Just so. Oddly, it only increased my envy of you, for I always yearned to be a soldier. As the heir, I could not fulfill that dream. Your success, and your lack of gratitude to me for making it possible, infuriated me. I have not acted kindly to you, nor did I to your mother. I cannot make it up to her, but perhaps I can to you. Perhaps someday you can forgive me."

Edmund regarded his brother silently for a long time. Olivia felt his grip on her hand tighten so much that she almost cried out, then slowly relax.

"I can forgive you for myself. For the pain you caused my mother, you must look to heaven for forgiveness."

Years of Uncle Ormhill's preaching more than any desire to comfort Heslington made Olivia blurt out, "The Bible says if we truly seek it, we will find it."

"Thank you, Lady Edmund." Heslington looked at her, and to her amazement his eyes held a sheen of tears.

"And now, for the smiles I promised you. I will not sue to have your parents' marriage voided, but as you know, others might do so. Our brother James, unfortunately, drank deeply of the poison of my hatred for you. And then there are my sons. You will always be at the mercy of an ill-natured relative."

"I don't care for that, Carl. The title means nothing to me now. And her lawyers say the terms of the will have been fulfilled, so Livvy can't lose her land."

"Yes, but you see, when I saw her interpose herself between you and Corbright, and realized it was not for Franklin's sake, but yours, I knew such a gallant lady deserved a reward."

"And I got it in Edmund."

Heslington smiled. "I see I can offer you nothing, then. But I am of the same opinion as your father, Lady Edmund.

He thought you deserved to be called 'my lady,' and so do I. So I have taken steps to be sure that you always will be."

Both stared at him, totally perplexed.

"I have spoken to the Prince Regent, as well as government officials too numerous to mention. Even enlisted Wellington in the cause. I have succeeded in having an extinct title in our mothers' line revived, Edmund. It will be conferred on you soon. You are to be Baron Capsdale. And the Crown will make a grant of land with it, equivalent to the estate you should have inherited."

A surge of feeling swept through Edmund, so strong it astounded him. The thought of a title and land of his own filled him with pride, with joy. But even sweeter than these was the knowledge that his brother had done this for him.

"I remember Mother speaking of her great grandfather. He died a very, very old man."

"Yes," Heslington said. "My mother spoke of him, too, and of his sorrow that the title would die with him. It is a family title, Edmund."

"A family title," Edmund repeated. As they looked across the room at one another, the brothers shared a moment such as they had never known before. Then Edmund looked down at Livvy, who held her breath, awaiting his reaction. Suddenly he remembered their first meeting. He threw back his head and began to laugh. "I can't wait to tell Jason," he crowed, hugging Olivia to him. "When he brought me home to you, he really did find you a lord!"

She began to laugh, too, and Heslington smiled, though crookedly. He stood. "I will leave you now. Congratulations to you, brother, on an excellent wife, and Lady Edmund, on a courageous husband. I wish you all the happiness that life can bring."

Husband and wife stood, too. "Olivia, my dear, I think you ought to invite my brother to dine with us."

Olivia looked from Edmund to Heslington and back again. She saw how much reconciliation meant to them both, and surrendered her animosity. Her eyes dancing with mischief, she curtsied deferentially to her husband. "Yes, my lord," she said.

Signet Regency Romances from Allison Lane

"A FORMIDABLE TALENT... MS. LANE NEVER FAILS TO DELIVER THE GOODS."
—*ROMANTIC TIMES*

THE RAKE AND THE WALLFLOWER
0-451-20440-9

Young, awkward Mary Seabrook is delighted when handsome Lord Grayson enters her life. But she soon discovers that danger follows him at every turn-and that his many mishaps may be more than mere coincidence...

BIRDS OF A FEATHER
0-451-19825-5

When a plain, bespectacled young woman keeps meeting the handsome Lord Wylie, she feels she is not up to his caliber. A great arbiter of fashion for London society, Lord Wylie was reputed to be more interseted in the cut of his clothes than the feelings of others, as the young woman bore witness to. Degraded by him in public, she could nevertheless forget his dashing demeanor. It will take a public scandal, and a private passion, to bring them together...

To order call: 1-800-788-6262